Hail to the Chief

JOHN LESLIE & CAREY WINFREY

For Marguerite and for Jane.

PART ONE

-- 1 --

Barley Thompson died yesterday.

The *Times* obit said "from undisclosed causes," which, as we know, can mean anything. But with his history, I'd guess it was his heart. He was only 52. My God, what a life. What a shame! He and I had lost touch, and considering how close we once were, I suppose some people would find that surprising. But I know we both wanted to put it all behind us.

That's what makes Barley's death so distressing: all the memories it stirs up.

There were five of us in the know, more or less: his wife, Amanda; Margaret ("Maggie") Mathews, the first woman elected President of the United States; her husband Walter, the once and future secretary of state; and Barry Jagoda, the young newspaper reporter who got most, but not all, of the story. And then there was me, Maggie's campaign manager, Barley's *consiglieri* and...well, witness to history. (And "First Manipulator," as Walter took to calling me.)

I'd promised Barley I wouldn't write about him or what we went through together as long as he lived. And I've kept that promise. But now he's gone, and with his death the time has come, the *duty* really, for me to set down what transpired in those tumultuous last days of the presidential campaign and its awful aftermath. I'm willing enough. More than willing. And not just to make sure that history doesn't repeat itself—there's a cliché for you—because we all know it does, for good and ill. It's also personal; I played a role, a *critical* role, in those events, and I have a reputation to clear. History may or may not deserve the truth, something it seldom gets, but I deserve my own truth-and-reconciliation commission.

There were rumors, of course, and enough speculation to float a stock market, some of which came pretty close to the mark. But I'm getting ahead of myself. Where to start?

That election was hardly my first rodeo. I'd licked envelopes for Al Gore when I was scarcely 20, back in 2000. Four years later, I ran a Jefferson County (Birmingham), Alabama office for George W. Bush against John Kerry, helped Barack Obama beat John McCain in Connecticut in '08 and then, in 2012, headed Romney's entire Midwest operation. A hired gun? Guilty as charged, but I was never ashamed of that. A man—a person, I should say—has to make a living. At least I did. And for all my love of the game—particularly presidential—I was more idealist than ideologue. To this day I've never voted. In my line of work, a vote could come back to bite you. You didn't want to have to lie, two or four years later when you were pitching your services to his or her opponent.

But I digress. No matter how many rodeos, the ropes I thought I knew turned out to be poor quality thread on a cheap suit. Nothing prepared me for the bull ride that followed after Maggie asked me to pick up the pieces of her faltering campaign. By then she trailed Senator Blaine Ward by a dozen points in the polls. Which didn't matter to me. Of course I accepted.

The eight months I ran the show leading up to November were the most exhilarating of my life. Not that there weren't disappointments, setbacks and frustrations. I'll say. But what a finish! Two weeks before Election Day we were still eight points behind Blaine, and most of us on Maggie's staff— me included—had begun polishing our resumes. Then, with just five days to go, the third and final debate changed everything. Or I should say Ward's colossal stumble did. My jaw dropped when he said the first thing he would do as president would be to authorize the immediate deportation of fifteen million illegal"—not "undocumented"—immigrants.

For a moment moderator George Stephanopoulos struggled to speak. "Excuse me Senator," he finally managed. "But surely you remember that Donald Trump tried that in 2016. And we all know what happened to him."

"Trump was a joke," Ward responded. "Joe Biden nailed it when he said Trump didn't have a clue. But I'm a serious person and I have a plan, a well-thought-out plan."

And when moderator George Stephanopoulis asked him "with all due respect" to share that plan, Blaine grinned the goofiest grin I'd ever seen and said, "You leave that to me, George." Then he giggled. *Giggled.*

New York Times columnist Gail Collins called it "Gigglegate," and *Washington Post* columnist George Will dubbed it "the giggle heard round the world." Peggy Noonan said it was "cringeworthy." And Charles Krautheimer wrote that "not since the third Carter-Reagan debate of 1980, when Jimmy Carter said his 13-year-old daughter Amy told him the most important issue was the control of nuclear weapons, has a gaffe so changed an election dynamic."

In the days that followed, Ward's numbers plummeted. By Election Day our Maggie, as most of us still called her, had pulled even in the polls. Then our get-out-the-vote effort, in which I take no small measure of pride, carried the day; less than 20 minutes after the polls closed on the West Coast, America had elected its first female president.

It was a victory as stunning as it was improbable. Maggie Mathews had served only two terms in the House of Representatives and one term as Pennsylvania's governor before she called the Electoral College an "outmoded, outdated, outlandish anachronism" in a speech at the University of Pennsylvania. The *Times*—and most of the establishment press—put Maggie and her speech on the front page, and she was soon on CNN, Fox and MSNBC. By the time coverage had moved on to a school shooting in Winston-Salem North Carolina, Maggie had raised her profile by several notches.

Over the course of the next few months, her repeated

call—eloquent, resonant and commonsensical—to replace the electoral college with a popular election somehow caught fire. First the pundits and then more and more people started talking about a Maggie Mathews presidential run.

As the only female candidate in a series of eight debates with a lackluster Democratic field that one wag likened to Snow White and the Seven Dwarfs and another called "a three-legged horse race in Dustbowl, Oklahoma," Maggie transformed herself from an intriguing one-issue curiosity into a formidable national figure. As she articulated her positions—raising the minimum wage lifted all boats, increasing quotas for *legal* immigrants made the United States more prosperous, streamlining the Defense Department strengthened national defense, even that Social Security could be saved "in one fell swoop" by doing away with the annual limit on taxable wages—her poll numbers began to creep upwards. Even those who disagreed with, or even hated, her positions found her clearheaded, unthreatening manner refreshing.

Her main rivals for the nomination, Barley Thompson, a middle-of-the-road junior senator from Ohio who was running, the cynics said, only to raise his speaker fees, and Michael Wayland, the popular two-term governor of New York with a roving eye, split the centrist vote in the primaries, and Maggie was able to scoop up most of the delegates to their left. Her husband Walter, with an eye toward Ohio, persuaded her to put Barley on the ticket.

Though she knew him only from the debates, she was okay with Barley. After all, he had netted the next greatest number of delegates, had been vetted by the press in the months leading up to the nomination (and later by our team), but most importantly, he had assured her he could deliver Ohio's 18 electoral votes to, yes, the most outspoken opponent of electoral voting—an irony lost on no one in her inner circle, not to mention the more astute members of the press corps. As it turned out, Barley was good to his word, and Ohio put Maggie across the finish line. Then, to the great relief of the transition staff, and, I suspect to Maggie herself, Barley had the good grace to make himself scarce by going fishing in Montana.

Looking back, what I most remember about those first, adrenalin-filled, post-election days was the pace. Everything seemed speeded up. Meetings started before dawn, and we stayed at it 'til midnight, or even later, many a dark hour.

My title was transition facilitator, which meant I handled anything Maggie asked me to, as well as trouble-shooting whatever I came across. One of my first big assignments was contacting prospective cabinet members and feeling them out about joining the administration. If they expressed interest, and most did, Madam president-elect, as we had taken to calling her—at least in the presence of outsiders—would get on the horn and invite them to Robin's Nest, her Pennsylvania home.

I would take it from there and, with a staff of three, begin the vetting process. The one I remember best, for reasons that I think will become clear, was Morgan Walker, who we tapped to be secretary of defense. Though Morgan could be tough as nails when needed, he didn't look the part; with his wispy hair and horned rim glasses, you'd take him for an academic or an accountant. I liked his self-effacing manner, and I also liked that he didn't take himself too seriously. I've never met a man with more quiet confidence, which, as things turned out, was just what was needed.

No less memorable, or admirable in my view (though she had her critics) was Angela Mercado, the first female, and I must add, beautiful, Hispanic Attorney General, who accepted the job with a promise to reform the country's law enforcement establishment from bottom (the police) to top, her own agency.

By the time we were done, we had put together the most diverse cabinet in history, with five women and three African-Americans. (Deborah Rogers counted in both categories.) Despite the predictable quibbles from the predictable quarters, the media largely approved of our choices. Until right after Thanksgiving, that is, when the president-elect's bombshell announcement that she'd asked her husband, Walter, to take another turn as secretary of state threw the chattering classes into a frenzy. And, she'd added, he'd accepted.

"NEPOTIST IN CHIEF," read one of the milder headlines, in the *Wall Street Journal*, which was still publishing a paper edition. Writing in *The Washington Post*, also still on paper (though not for long), columnist Eugene Robinson said "the president-elect should have done a better job of *husbanding* her resources." (My italics.) Most of the other papers chimed in, and cable television, particularly MSNBC (pro Walter) and Fox (anti) went at it day after 24-hour-day. (In an effort at impartiality, CNN tried to straddle the two views.) Of the major papers, only the *New York Times* voiced grudging approval, reminding readers that John F. Kennedy's appointment of his brother Robert as attorney general in 1960 had worked out well enough, despite similarly dire predictions. And, the *Times* editorial went on, "it's not as if Walter Mathews was a croupier in a casino. He was, after all, Secretary of State in the Sutton administration. And he handled the job with nuance and dexterity if without a major achievement."

Not surprisingly, Blaine Ward, his giggle under wraps, called Walter's appointment "a travesty of incalculable proportions."

"The hubbub will die down," Maggie assured Charley Millbank, her spokesperson, and me. (She had made a few phone calls and counted votes in the Senate for her husband's confirmation.) "And when it does, I'll have someone at State I trust absolutely and who has my back." As we left the office, Charley whispered to me, "That's not the presidential body part Walter feels the most proprietary about." Striving for an expression I thought appropriate to an aspiring chief of staff, I suppressed a smile and gave him a stern look.

But before rumors of Walter's own personal failings came to light, the world, as I knew it, exploded.

-- 2 --

Tuesday, January 10. My appointment with the Capitol police to talk about security at the inauguration, just ten days away, was at 9:00 a.m. My cell phone rang as I drove south on Connecticut Avenue at 8:35. Walter Mathews.

"Skeeter?"

In his voice I heard all the anguish that I could bear to hear in that one word—my nickname.

"What is it, Walter?"

"Maggie. I'm at Sibley. Get over here now. Not a word to anyone."

"I'm on my way."

I turned off Connecticut and drove to Massachusetts Avenue heading west, then onto Nebraska, en route to Sibley Memorial, part of the Johns Hopkins medical establishment. I made a call to cancel my police appointment at the Capitol.

Maggie. Sibley. *Not a word to anyone.*

The phrase couldn't have been more ominous or disturbing. In the pit of my stomach, where all my anxieties first make their appearance, I felt the burning grip of panic. But while my stomach felt on fire and my mind was racing, as soon as I turned onto leafy Loughboro Road, I kept below the posted 35-mile-per hour limit. In the last year, I'd gotten two photographs of my Subaru Forester taken by the traffic control cameras at a speed trap there. Each photo came with a citation. Fifty bucks. Funny the way old patterns hold. My worry about a $50 speeding ticket was trumping a crisis that I suspected might have historic implications. Once past the DMV's photo op, I gunned the Subaru back up above 50.

As accustomed as I was to crisis, it never failed to cue the adrenalin. In the political world there was always an emergency, some fire to be put out, but nine times out of ten I'd found that it was more smoke than a five-alarm blaze. Critical as it might be to the individuals who'd first rung the bell, the situation was usually controllable. Smother the smoke and you avoided the flame. I was a known smotherer, and it was that dexterity I'd counted on to get me on the team as Maggie Mathew's top aide.

However, this had all the markings of a major meltdown, that one-out-of-ten occasion. Driving into the hospital's parking lot I did my best to calm myself, at least the exterior self. But just in case, I also checked to make sure I had my antianxiety drug.

‽ ‽ ‽

From the parking lot I called Walter to let him know I'd arrived. As soon as the doors to the hospital opened, two men were beside me, firmly escorting me to the bank of elevators. I recognized one of the Secret Service agents who had been assigned to Maggie as soon as she'd gotten the nomination. Neither spoke; they didn't have to. On the second floor they ushered me to a private room where Walter was waiting. The agents opened the door and closed it behind me once I was inside and alone with Walter.

"Waiting" hardly described Walter Mathews. Pacing and jiggling the coins in his pocket, the wild look in his eyes suggested more Secretary of Psychosis than State. He had on a V-necked sweater over a T-shirt, jeans, and a pair of mocs on sockless feet. Since it was still before 9:00 and I'd never seen him attired in anything other than a suit and tie, I assumed he'd dressed in a hurry, probably before sunrise. His rumpled hair added to his uncharacteristic appearance. He needed calming, which I assumed was the main reason I'd been called.

A parka lay in a heap on a chair. Newspapers were scattered around the room. A table held an urn of coffee, a tray of cups and glasses, cream and sugar and bottled water. A box of three sad looking muffins, a single bite taken from one of them, rested on the arm of a sofa.

"Talk to me, Walter."

"Christ." He dropped onto the couch and the box of muffins fell to the floor.

"What's happened?"

"The doctors haven't told me anything yet."

"How long have you been here?" Walter looked at his watch. "Not sure. Three hours, maybe more."

"And Maggie?"

"Bad. Bad headache. Worst ever. Couldn't talk. Couldn't walk. White as a ghost. By the time we got here, she was out cold. The Secret Service guys had to help carry her to the emergency room. I'd never seen her like that."

"You're going to have to walk me through this, Walter. We're ten days away from the inauguration. We've got to put out a statement. What appointments did Maggie have today?"

"Breakfast with the president and first lady at eight."

"Less than an hour ago. Who canceled?"

"I did. I called the White House and told them Maggie had the flu."

"This afternoon?"

"Separate meetings with the heads of NSA, CIA and Defense. One hour with each, starting at two o'clock."

"You canceled those?"

"No."

"Good. Let's not raise alarms until we have to. Walk me through last night."

"Maggie had dinner with Barley, just the two of them."

"Where?"

"Our townhouse.

"You weren't there?"

"I had dinner with the secretary of state. It was cut short when the president called and asked him to come to the White House." More smoke, no doubt.

"What time did you get home?"

"A little after nine."

"You saw Maggie?"

"She was still with Barley. She came to bed around ten-thirty."

"How was she?"

"Complaining of a headache and..." Talking seemed to have settled Walter somewhat. But now he dropped his head, and for a moment I thought he'd fallen asleep.

"And what?" I prodded.

"Upset."

"About?"

"Some tension with Barley. She wouldn't talk about it. Said she wanted to sleep on it. She took a couple of aspirin and something to relax her."

"What?"

"Ativan." For antianxiety. The very pill I had in my pocket and felt like taking myself right now.

"When did you decide to come here?"

"About four. The headache had gotten worse. Then she vomited. I thought maybe something she'd eaten, but she was also having balance trouble, so I called her doctor. Woke him up. He said to get her to the hospital. I alerted the Secret Service, and they brought us. By the time we got here, Maggie was completely out. I was terrified."

As I was about to suggest a course of action, a knock on the door interrupted me. Two doctors came in and introduced themselves. One was Maggie's personal physician; the other a neurosurgeon. One look said we were in trouble.

"Ruptured aneurysm," the neurosurgeon said. Walter hid his face in his hands. Finally he looked up.

"What does that mean?" he asked.

"Best case: two weeks in intensive care."

There went the inauguration. Nobody mentioned worst case.

"Based on the CTA scan," the neurosurgeon went on, "I'm recommending an endovascular procedure that will require a general anesthesia. I'll put a catheter into an artery in her groin, and pass it through the blood vessels to the aneurysm, which will then be packed with platinum coils to prevent further blood flow into that area. The next 24 hours are critical—touch and go. She may recover, but it could take months or longer to regain full function. Impossible to predict what deficit damage there may be. For now we'll do everything medically we can, then it's a waiting game."

Deficit damage? As cold as it might sound, "deficit damage" meant that Barley Thompson would be running the country for the foreseeable future in place of the candidate I'd worked for all these months, Maggie Mathews.

∾ ∾ ∾

"I want you as point man," Walter said to me when the doctors had gone. "Call a press conference and make the announcement. Be as vague as you can. Get the neurosurgeon there to provide medical information, but there's no need to go out on a limb at this point. I need to see Maggie and then get home. I'll be out of touch till tonight. Make it tomorrow morning. First let me get a sense of how this plays."

"What about Barley?"

"Call him."

"Are we clear on transfer of powers and, if it comes to..." I hesitated, "succession?"

"You're point man. Find out."

∾ ∾ ∾

I called the White House and spoke with Dennis McCloud, President Dubois's chief of staff, bringing him up to speed on the situation. Of course I knew I couldn't count on any further confidentiality—if it hadn't been leaked by now, it was just a matter of hours, if not minutes, before the rumors went viral. After putting me on hold, testing my patience, McCloud finally returned and said the White House would handle the press conference. It would be held in the press briefing room and press secretary Ron Peters would make the announcement, but I should be there to answer questions. "Two o'clock," pronounced the man whose job I'd hoped to have. "Get here by one, you can pick up your pass from the guard at the Southwest

Appointment Gate on West Executive Avenue."

Following the Oklahoma City bombing in 1995, Pennsylvania Avenue had been closed to vehicular traffic for security reasons, but 17th Street, which ran between the White House and the Old Executive Office Building (EOB), would get me close enough. And since I'd be driving, there was parking close to the gate.

The second call went to Barley Thompson's secure number.

"Yeah, I'm hearing things," Barley said. "You confirming?"

"We know nothing for sure, but it doesn't look good. Ruptured aneurysm. Should know more later today. You might want to lie low for a few hours."

"Hard to do with Treasury guys swarming."

"No statements from you yet. Wait 'til after the briefing at two."

"I just had dinner with her last night. Is she dying?"

"I heard about the dinner, and no, they don't think she's dying. Save an hour for me after the briefing, okay?"

"Can't you fill me in a bit more now?"

"You know as much as I do at this point, Barley. Later."

I wondered about the protocol of calling him Barley, but vice-president-elect seemed too cumbersome for the occasion. Besides, we were both Ohio boys. I figured he would understand.

Next I reached out to Angela Mercado, a member of New York's States Attorney's office, an official part of Maggie's legal team, and the woman she'd tapped for attorney general. I'd vetted her of course, so had spent some time with her. Quality time. I liked her no nonsense approach. A quarter-century earlier and just out of Albany law school, Angela had clerked for Supreme Court Justice Ruth Bader Ginzburg.

"I'm looking for a constitutional scholar," I told her.

"Yes, I've heard rumors."

I looked at my watch. Less than twenty minutes since my call to the White House; the laundry line was buzzing. Across the media, anonymous sources would be providing quotes, some of them accurate, most not. The press conference would take place not a moment too soon.

"Can you recommend someone?" I asked Angela.

"Me. Constitutional law was my first love. And it's lasted longer than some others."

That left open an interesting personal conversation for another time. "Can we meet?" I asked.

"Just tell me where and when."

I was sitting in my car in the hospital parking lot. It seemed the most hush-hush place to make calls. "How about The Palm in half an hour?"

"I'll be there."

The Palm, in Dupont Circle, was retro Washington. While it attracted plenty of tourists looking for a good steak, it was off the beaten track for politicos. And although the conservative columnist Charles Krauthammer had his office in the same building, most of the press steered clear of the place, a bar and grill with booths that offered a fair amount of privacy. The announcement of the press conference came over the car radio. NPR's Lakshmi Singh said rumors about Maggie's health were swirling. I got to The Palm ten minutes ahead of Angela.

≪ઙ ≪ઙ ≪ઙ

Carrying her coat and stylishly dressed in a dark blue suit jacket with wide lapels, matching trousers and a white blouse, Angela joined me at my booth. At forty-five, she was six years older than me, but despite the age difference, I found her most attractive. More than attractive. Angela made my blood pump faster.

As in my professional career, I'd bounced around in a wide-ranging run of romantic relationships. Except for a lack of commitment, nothing seemed to tie any of them together. Six months, a year, and I was ready to move on. Perhaps it was my childhood. When you're out of excuses, that's the fallback, childhood. At the age of two, with my parents killed in a car crash on Route 71, I'd been put up for adoption and lived with one foster family in Akron for three years before being handed off to another in Cincinnati, where I had to compete for attention with three biological children, all older. Let's just say I learned how to stay afloat; and how to manage entanglements or, if they were more than I could handle, where to hide. All good training for a political hack.

"We meet again," Angela said.

I stood. "Yes," I replied. "I wish the circumstances were different."

"Me too," she said, taking a seat. "But sadly they aren't. So let's get to it."

Sitting across from her, I told Angela as much about Maggie's condition as I thought would come out at the press conference. When the waiter appeared, we both ordered coffee.

"It's never happened before." Angela said. "If the president-elect dies, then the twentieth amendment kicks in. By law, the vice president-elect would act as president. One thing to keep in mind, someone will have to write a letter to the Senate president pro tem Thorne and to the speaker of the House, telling them that Mrs. Mathews will be unable to discharge the powers and duties of her office, as stipulated in the 25th amendment.

"Would Thompson be sworn in as president or vice-president?"

"In my view, he would take the vice president's oath of office to 'faithfully execute...,' etcetera, etcetera, but then would immediately be granted presidential powers by the Chief Justice."

"We're sure to get questions about succession, probably a fire-storm of them from the cable news outlets."

"If the vice president-elect is 'unqualified' to fulfill his duties, then Congress would get involved. That shouldn't be an issue, not at this point anyway."

"Congress determines who is qualified?"

"Since the Electoral College has cast its votes, qualification has been established."

"What if Congress doesn't agree?"

"I think I see where you're going with this."

"Where I hope we're not going is down some dark path toward mischief. We've got a president- and vice president-elect from one party, and a Congress none too happy with the election results, from another."

Angela smiled. "Yes, and because of the lack of precedent you can bet we're going to see all kinds of legal squabbles."

"I agree, no matter what happens, there'll be a political battle, possibly even calls for a new election."

"What if we swore Maggie in now?" I asked. "Then she could turn over the presidency to Barley under the 25th Amendment."

"Well we've got a president. I don't think Dubois is going to resign to accommodate us." Angela said. "Even if he did, if Maggie's not one hundred per cent mentally competent, I think it would seem ghoulish, not to mention opportunistic. I don't think it would pass the political smell test."

I had to agree. Just then the waiter brought more coffee and poured refills. Did we want lunch? he asked. The last thing I could think about was food, but I deferred to Angela. Thankfully, she shook her head.

When the waiter had left, I said, "Ten days before an inauguration, and we've got a president-elect who's incapacitated but alive."

"What would you *like* to see happen?" Angela asked me.

"For the sake of the country and continuity, Barley Thompson should, *must,* be sworn in on schedule." I said. "I would think the courts would rule in our favor on that. But after?"

Angela shrugged. "If she survives, it will all depend on her condition."

"Any advice?" I asked.

"I don't know Barley well, but he needs to take charge. And there is precedent. In 1963, when Kennedy was assassinated, Lyndon Johnson acted decisively. In the midst of a national tragedy, with all the mourning and uncertainty, he managed to keep a lid on things by taking charge and acting presidential. If I were Barley, I'd read up on that transition. And, like Johnson, I'd keep as many members of the Mathews team—her staff and cabinet picks—as will agree to stay on."

"You're one of them." I said. "Will you stay?"

"Of course. I regard it as my duty. I think most will. Probably everybody."

Over what was left of our coffee we made small talk, each of us sharing our hope that we would get through the inauguration without having to put up with the snow that had been forecast. From her resume I knew that Angela was divorced, with a teenage daughter at a boarding school in Connecticut. I asked if she would attend the swearing-in. Angela responded uncertainly, then made excuses for having to get to another meeting. We both stood up, a little awkwardly I thought, but I held out my hand and told her how much I appreciated her time and said I looked forward to working with her.

"If it's in the cards," I added. I was due at the White House in less than forty-five minutes.

-- 3 --

Though the press had never been my primary responsibility, I'd been dealing with our friends in the fourth estate for the better part of a decade, helping one and another reporter hopefully "improve" a story about a candidate I was managing, or, often as not, *not* managing. I'd also been to the White House on a couple of occasions. The first was to put my fanny in an East Room seat at a design award ceremony hosted by Laura Bush after one of the recipients had come down with a case of too-much-celebration-the-night-before. Then late in 2011, an Obama aide who'd probably only skimmed my resume, called me in for an interview I'd just as soon forget, after he offered a laughably low salary for my vaunted political skills (which is how I came to work for Romney).

On both visits, walking the corridors largely unescorted, I felt the full weight of the building's august history, most palpably the second time, when I stood alone for at least a minute before the familiar oil portrait of JFK, his arms folded, eyes cast down, his very countenance seeming to bear the burdens of high office. Or maybe just the dull pain of his sore back.

Even though Kennedy had been assassinated before I was born, and his unbridled sexual appetites had sullied his reputation, also in the distant past, I admired both the man and his presidency—his personal grace as well as the steely resolve that led to a successful resolution of the Cuban missile crisis. I particularly loved the way he handled himself at press conferences, defusing even the snarkiest questions with humor—the first president to allow these curious cat-and-mouse exchanges to be broadcast live on television. While other visitors to New York City raced to the Empire State Building, the Statue of Liberty or the art museums, on my visits to the Big Apple it was to the Museum of Broadcasting that I was inevitably drawn. I would order up one or more of the JFK press conferences and watch them, happy as a clam: invariably entertaining and, for someone in my line of work, always instructive. Of course, as a news junkie of long standing, I'd rarely missed a more recent televised presidential press conference, whether carried by the networks, which happened routinely when I was younger, or, lately on MSNBC, CNN or C-Span.

But as I walked into the West Wing briefing room that morning to, literally, meet the press, my legs turned to rubber and I wished I'd taken my Ativan. Too late now. The briefing room—once the site of FDR's swimming pool—was packed with pencil pushers, as my father used to describe reporters in the days before the ascendance of television. The room had never looked this crushed on TV, not even when a president came personally to the podium. (Could this be the most crowded it had ever been?) Not only were all 49 of the credited White House correspondents' seats filled, but Washington's supersized rumor mill had insured that every square inch of floor space was also occupied, standing-room only, by the ladies and gentlemen of the press (a term I've always preferred to "media").

Half a dozen klieg lights cast the room in an eerie, oversaturated glare. As if all that weren't enough, the buzz of the assembled reporters— more than a hundred I guessed— approached cacophony, which barely modulated when White House press secretary Ron Peters walked to the podium, gazed out at the sea of faces, shook his head in what I took to be wonderment and unfolded a single sheet of white paper.

"Ladies and gentlemen..." he began.

The room gradually quieted. "Before we take questions, I have a brief statement: At 4:20 a.m. this morning, President-elect Margaret Mathews was admitted to Sibley Hospital here in Washington complaining of a severe headache and dizziness. Under the care of her personal physician, Dr. Roswell

McInerny, and Sibley neurosurgeon Dr. Carlton Dawson, she underwent an MRI and a CAT scan, the results of which confirmed their suspicion of a ruptured aneurysm in the brain. At 9:20 a.m., the President-elect was taken upstairs to an operating room, where Dr. Dawson and his team performed microsurgery to alleviate the problem and stabilize her condition.

"The procedure went according to plan, though it is still too soon to assess its success. The president-elect is currently in recovery and, assuming all continues to go as anticipated, will be moved to the ICU sometime later today. Dr. Dawson is here..." Peters nodded toward a balding man of medium height standing to his immediate left, "to take your questions."

Peters then turned to his right and nodded toward me.

"Bruce Jamison, the president-elect's campaign manager, who many of you know as 'Skeeter,'"—slight smile— "is also prepared to take questions." This wasn't the time or place to debate Peters' use of the word "prepared." Suffice to say it wasn't the adjective I'd have chosen to describe my state of mind at that moment.

A hundred hands shot into the air. Peters called on Eleanor Booth of the Associated Press.

"Dr. Dawson. Can you tell us the president-elect's prognosis?"

Dawson bent toward the podium.

"At this point, we can't say with certainty," he answered, his eyes blinking in the harsh light. He looked as if he might have more to say, then his adam's apple bobbed and he stepped away from the podium.

The forest of hands again reached for the ceiling. Peters pointed to Molly Ames, the "Meet the Press" moderator.

"Where is the vice-president elect? And what has he been told?"

Peters turned to me again, indicating it was my turn to look like a deer caught in headlights.

"Mr. Thompson was notified of Mag...uh, Mrs. Mathew's condition this morning in a telephone call from her husband, Secretary Walter Mathews," I said. "It's my understanding that

Mr. Thompson will be releasing a statement later today, once we know more." As I had improvised that last part, I made a mental note to tell Barley I'd committed him to releasing a statement. Then I saw the cameras pan; Barley was surely watching, he wouldn't need reminding.

"What was he told?" Ames repeated.

"He was informed, as you've just been, that the president-elect suffered a ruptured brain aneurysm and was undergoing surgery."

Somebody I couldn't see shouted, "Is Thompson ready to assume the presidency?" The question came from a nicotine-scorched female voice toward the back of the room. I tried to locate it, without success. But I did lock eyes briefly with a young man with close-cropped dark hair. He looked familiar, though I couldn't place him. Ron Peters ignored the nicotine-inflected question and instead recognized Linda Watson of *The Wall Street Journal*.

"What causes an aneurysm?" Watson asked. Mercifully, it was another one for Dawson. The neurosurgeon said that high blood pressure, family history and smoking were all contributing factors and that women were somewhat more likely than men to develop the condition. He added that in cases like this, the first few days are critical; he and his colleagues wouldn't know anything conclusive until "next week at the soonest and more likely not until the week after."

More questions of a medical nature followed, which Dawson fielded with growing assurance. No, he could not give the odds for Maggie's survival. No, it was impossible "at this point to predict whether the president-elect would suffer any cognitive deficit." As Dawson grew more sure-footed, my mind returned to the unanswered question about Barley's readiness to assume the highest office in the land.

I realized with some contrition I'd never given much thought to his qualifications to be president. In fact, I hadn't thought much about Barley at all beyond the election and those 18 electoral votes. I had no idea if he was ready or able, or, for that matter, *willing*. I didn't even know Barley-the-man all that well. What kind of person was he? What motivated him? What were his beliefs? His values? I didn't know.

The few times I'd spoken privately to him, he'd seemed pleasant enough, in a bland, corn-fed sort of way. His performances on the stump had produced no major hiccups beyond his confusing the president of Iraq with the president of Afghanistan. (I'm not sure I'd have done any better). But I had the impression that Barley's adequate performances in town halls and press conferences reflected the many briefings given him by the experts we'd called in after Maggie had tapped him as her running mate, more than any deeply held beliefs. His policy positions were all middle-of-the-road conventional, as if he'd memorized the Democratic platform. In a way, I guess he had.

But there was something gnawing at the back my mind, in the place that acts like a petri dish for concern. When I thought about Barley now, what came to mind was Gertrude Stein's remark about Oakland, California, where she grew up: there didn't seem to be any there, there. Maybe it was just my general tendency to worry, compounded by the anxiety of the moment, but I felt a vague, free-floating discomfort that the man we saw—handsome, well-versed (well-rehearsed?), capable—might not be the man we'd get if he ever became president.

After graduating from Ohio State, where he majored in economics, Barley had married his college sweetheart, Amanda Whyte, an arts major, a couple years after he'd begun teaching economics and social studies at a high school in Columbus, where he had grown up the son of a hardware store owner and his homemaker wife. (His father died of cancer when Barley was twelve). In short order, Barley and Amanda had produced two freckle-faced daughters, Blake and Rebecca, both of whom later graduated from respectable colleges and were now gainfully employed in service industries: computers and consulting. Neither as yet was married.

After serving on the school board for three plus years, Barley ran for the Columbus city council in the early '90s, and as the *Cleveland Plain Dealer* put in a profile, "surprised just about everyone, possibly including himself, by winning a council seat by a hair's breadth margin." Three years later, he threw his hat in the ring for the Columbus mayoralty, putting together a campaign based on what the *Plain Dealer* profile called "bonhomie and boosterism." Defying the pundits' predictions again, he squeaked out a victory. His two terms as mayor were marked by fiscal responsibility—he balanced the city's budget—and enough ribbon-cuttings to earn him the nickname, "Scissorhands." Shortly before his mother died, in 2008, Barley took on a long-serving, born-again Republican congressman from Ohio's 15th congressional district, which includes downtown Columbus. This time few were surprised when he was elected. Two terms and four years later he rode Obama's coattails into the Senate.

In the campaign as Maggie's running mate, Barley supported marriage equality but admitted he still winced when he heard a man refer to his "husband" or a woman to her "wife."

He favored easing penalties for undocumented immigrants only if paired with an increase in border security.

He supported troop withdrawals from Iraq and Afghanistan but said the U.S. "must maintain a presence in the Middle East." (Well, yeah.)

And when pressed by a reporter about climate change, he said he thought it was real.

"Do you think it's manmade?" the reporter asked. "Caused by the burning of fossil fuels?"

"Could be," Barley replied affably, then added: "But I'm no scientist." Then he looked at his watch, said he was late for a meeting and beat a hasty retreat. Whenever he was asked about it in the future, he would say: "I've made my position clear on that."

Now he proclaimed himself "an ardent friend of Israel" but opposed the building of new settlements on the West Bank.

All predictable positions for a centrist Democrat. All expressed with something less than conviction.

"He's a hard man to pin down," Walter had said to me one night over drinks at the Jefferson Hotel. "I don't know what he stands for, other than Barley Thompson and apple pie." At the time, I thought maybe Walter was just being Walter, who never had much good to say about anyone. Now I wasn't so sure.

On the other hand, except for Walter, I've never met anyone who had a bad word to say about Barley. But I've never heard anybody get too excited about him either.

Now Ron Peters called on a TV correspondent I didn't recognize. My reverie was over. Her question was for me.

"Skeeter, what can you tell us about the inauguration?" she asked. "Will it go ahead on schedule?"

"I don't..." I began, then caught myself. "You have to understand that we are still gathering facts at this point," I continued lamely. "Since this happened, we haven't talked to the Capitol police—I had to cancel a meeting I was supposed to have with them this morning—nor to the Inaugural Committee, nor to the Democratic National Committee. But I'm hopeful the inauguration will go ahead as planned on January 20th, and I'm doing everything I can to make that happen."

A chorus of voices cranked the room's decibel level back to where it had been before the press conference began. Amid the cacophony I heard shouts of "Who, who?" I heard "Which one?" I heard "Mathews?" I heard "Thompson?"

In the front row, Fox News' Alan Adelson raised his voice. "Is there any question about the matter of succession if Mrs. Mathews should not survive?" he asked.

"Alan," Peters said, "Let's wait a bit before we have that discussion."

"I think it's valid," Adelson persisted, "since we're only ten days away."

Peters held up his hands like a minister blessing a congregation. "Thank you ladies and gentlemen. We'll let you know when we have more information."

The press conference was over. The TV correspondents grabbed their microphones and began rehearsing their stand-ups to camera.

As reporters milled about and others rushed out to file their stories, the dark-haired young man I couldn't place came up to me.

"Mr. Jamison?" he said.

"It's Skeeter," I said.

"Skeeter, then," he continued. "I'm Barry Jagoda. I wanted to talk to you. I have a question about Barley Thompson, and I knew Ron wouldn't call on me."

"How come?"

"Regulars-only on a news day like today," he said. "I'm not Washington. He held up his credential, clearly stamped DAY PASS. I'm with the *Plain Dealer*," he said, adding: "I'm a Buckeye." He smiled shyly. "Like you."

Of course. During the campaign, Jagoda had covered Barley for the once-proud Cleveland newspaper that had just gone through a succession of buyouts and layoffs. In fact, I now remembered, it was Jagoda who had written the profile that said that Barley was probably as surprised as anyone when he won that city council seat all those years ago. I returned his smile.

"Yes, I remember you, Barry" I said. "Nice to see you again. What can I do for you?"

Jagoda drew a breath. "Will Barley Thompson be the next President of the United States?" he asked.

I took my time answering. "First of all," I said, "At this point I have no more idea than you do. And even if I did, you know I can't answer that."

I turned to walk away.

Behind me came Jagoda's voice.

"Off the record," he said.

I stopped and turned back to him. What I saw was a tall, thin man in his late 20s with neat, dark hair parted and combed to the side. He wore a blue blazer over a blue button-down shirt that probably came from Brooks Brothers and a rep tie. His pale blue eyes made him look older than his years. I thought of photographs of Hugh Sloan, the Richard Nixon aide who became a major source for Woodward and Bernstein in their unraveling of Watergate. I guess he also reminded me of a younger version of myself. In any case, I made a decision I hoped I wouldn't come to regret.

"Off the record," I said. "And attributable only to a

source close to the president-elect."

"Fair enough," he said.

"If you burn me on this," I added, "you'll never get another thing from me as long as you live."

"I understand," Jagoda said.

I swallowed hard. "President-elect Mathews will not be taking the oath of office on January 20th or anytime soon," I said. Then I turned and headed for the exit. When I looked back, Jagoda was writing in his notebook.

I grabbed a quick lunch en route to the nondescript Dupont Circle building that housed the transition staff above a Bon Marche restaurant. As soon as I walked through the door, one of the volunteers I knew only as Julie raced up to me.

"Dr. Dawson has been trying to reach you," she said, handing me a piece of paper bearing his name and what I recognized, from its area code, as a cellphone number. "He's called three or four times. Says it's urgent. Wants you to call him as soon as you got back. He made me promise to watch for you."

"Thanks. I'll take care of it." I walked quickly to my desk and punched the number into my phone.

"Dawson." He answered on the second ring.

"This is Skeeter."

"Skeeter. Where've you been? We need to talk."

"What is it?"

"I'd rather not say over the phone."

"Is it Maggie?"

"No, she's still in recovery. Will be for another hour. She's stable for now. No other news on that front."

"What about Walter? He's still there, at Sibley, isn't he? Did you talk to him?"

"I've called him, but he doesn't answer. One of the staff nurses said he'd left the hospital but didn't say where he was going."

"Can you give me some idea what this is about?"

"All I can say is that it's important, a political rather than a medical matter."

"It can't wait for Walter?"

"The information is sensitive and I think you should hear it. I'll leave it to you to discuss with Mr. Mathews."

"Where are you?"

"I'm in my car, on Nebraska, just passing American University, heading toward Tenleytown. But I can come to you."

I gave him the address of the transition office, hung up and slumped in my chair. What next? I thought. Piled in front of me on my desk were at least 30 telephone messages. Most were from friends or acquaintances, some whom I hadn't seen in years, who because of the press conference, wanted to re-establish contact. I had no idea how they might have gotten my number. Two of the calls required immediate responses, but most could wait. No sooner had I gotten off the phone with a woman in the press office at the DNC—I told her I didn't know anything more than what I'd said at the news conference— than it began to ring. It was our receptionist.

"There's a Dr. Dawson here to see you," she said.

"I'll be right out."

We shook hands and I nodded toward the elevator.

"Let's get some coffee," I said. "There's a Starbucks across the street."

Minutes later we were seated at a small table in back nursing grande lattes.

"So," I said in a low tone. "What's all the uproar?"

Dawson took off his glasses and pinched his nose between thumb and forefinger. Then he sighed and gave me a look I hadn't seen before: a mix, I thought, of worry and weariness.

"Before I could get back to the hospital," he began, his eyes looking around to see if anyone might be listening, "I had to check in on the president-elect and another post-op patient. Couldn't have taken more than half an hour, 40 minutes at the most. I was with the second patient, almost finished, when I heard my name being paged. It was a phone call from a Dr. Randolph Tice."

He took no notice of my blank look.

"I hadn't seen or spoken to Tice in 20 years or more,"

Dawson continued, "but I recognized the name—you don't forget a name like Randolph Tice." A quick smile. "We were in med school together. At Penn State. We went our separate ways after graduation, and I lost track of him."

I wondered if he'd ever get to the point.

"Randolph said he'd seen the press conference. At first I thought he was calling for professional reasons. But that wasn't it. He told me his takeaway was that Maggie Mathews would not be sworn in as president, at least not any time soon. I was vague; I said I couldn't be sure at this point. He asked if I knew he'd become a shrink. I said I thought I remembered reading it in the alumni magazine.

"He said he was a clinical psychiatrist, the head of psychiatry at the Cleveland Clinic. I congratulated him. But that wasn't why he was calling. He told me that soon after setting up practice in Columbus fifteen years ago, he'd begun seeing a patient, a young high school teacher by the name of Barley Thompson.' "

"Did he say why?"

"No, he wouldn't do that. Doctor-patient privilege. But after treating him for several months he knew things about him, things that could be disastrous for the country if they came out. He said Barley Thompson should never become president. 'No way in hell.'"

-- 4 --

No way in hell. Why, I wondered, had Tice waited two months to come forward. The old saw about "one-heartbeat-away" was as relevant the day after the election in November as it was now, ten days before the inauguration. The only explanation I could come up with is that Tice could accept his former patient as veep—an office FDR's vice president, John Nance Garner, so famously described as "not worth a pitcher of warm piss" (usually cleaned to "warm *spit*")—but not as Commander in Chief.

But why? What did he know about Barley? And another question: Where the hell was Walter Mathews?

Of the string of calls I had waiting, none was from Walter. Shortly after the press conference, I'd left a message on his cell, then called again after meeting with Dawson, only to get the same voice message. Four hours had passed without a response. I'd last seen him when I left the hospital in the morning. In two more hours I would be having dinner with Barley, an encounter I wasn't looking forward to—*no way in hell*—without some backup. I needed help. I needed it hours ago.

I googled Randolph Tice. Nothing much there that I hadn't learned from Dawson. Head of psychiatry at Cleveland Clinic. The Internet wasn't going to tell me why Tice had treated Barley or what he knew about him that had prompted his call.

As a student of politics, I was well aware of the chicanery every administration had to control, or try to control, all of it bad news—particularly the sort that might lead to someone's ruin. Watergate had brought down a president, but it had also provided lingo for every corroded "gate" to creak open in the scandals that followed—from Billygate, when it came out that Jimmy Carter's brother, Billy, had represented the Libyan government as a foreign agent; to Irangate, when the Reagan Administration sold weapons to Iran and passed the proceeds on to the Contra rebels in Nicaragua; to Nannygate, when two successive nominees for U.S. Attorney General—Carol Bird and Sandra Woods—had to withdraw after in Bird's case, admitting having hired an undocumented immigrant as a nanny and failing to pay her social security taxes and, in Woods', to hiring an undocumented immigrant as a nanny, though it was legal at the time she did so; Woods, at least, had paid the immigrant's social security taxes. And who can forget "Deflategate," when, back in 2015, Bill Belichick's New England Patriots were called out for using underinflated footballs to win the AFC Championship and get into the Superbowl?

Why those scandals should have jumped into my mind at that moment was as worrisome as it was obvious: unless we got out in front of whatever Tice knew, we could well be on our way to a "Barleygate." Given the evening ahead of me, I couldn't be sure if I'd go down in history as another Daniel Ellsberg, who famously leaked the Pentagon papers to *New York Times* reporter Neil Sheehan, or one of the White House "plumbers," the crooks hired by Nixon aide John Erlichman to break into Ellsberg's psychiatrist's office in an effort to discredit him and later broke into the Watergate Complex, where Barley was now ensconced.

Thinking maybe a bit of both, I fished Barry Jagoda's business card from my shirt pocket, where it lay among other scraps of paper that would eventually have to be filtered. As I dialed his number, I remembered what he'd said to me: "Buckeye. Like you." Didn't that, on top of his burning desire to burnish his journalistic credentials, provide me with sufficient motive to call?

"Where are you?" I asked when he answered.

"Having a drink with a few guys at the Daily Grill—in

Georgetown," he said, referring to one of the more popular Washington watering spots.

I could've guessed. The Grill was casual and not too pricey. Good burgers. Bloody Marys with plenty of horseradish and not too much celery. A lot of reporters went there. Tourists did too, but there was no escaping tourists anywhere in D.C.

"If you can meet me, I might have something interesting," I said. "But not a word to your confederates."

Barry laughed. I hoped he was finding me humorous rather than someone to humor. He asked where and when.

"I'll pick you up at the corner of Wisconsin and Dumbarton in half an hour. I'm driving a Subaru Forester."

I liked doing business from my car. It felt safe and bug free. Presumably we'd be out of ear- and eyeshot of anyone wanting to keep tabs. In Washington, very little goes unnoticed—at least by those who have a reason to be on the lookout. Having an affair, or in some circumstances even a drink, could easily find its way into *Washington Post's* snarky "Reliable Source" gossip column the following day. I'm an introvert. During the campaign, I'd laid low, letting my deputy do most of the TV interviews. Prior to the White House press conference, I wouldn't have rated an eighth of an inch of "Source" column space. But that briefing changed things and made me wary.

Ten minutes early, I sat at the curb watching for Jagoda and listening to NPR's analysis of the day's events on "All Things Considered." I was mildly miffed to hear Angela Mercado being interviewed by Melissa Block. When we were together earlier, Angela hadn't mentioned anything about an NPR interview. Although there was no reason for her to call my attention to it, it meant I wasn't in the loop, which right now seemed the safest place to be, especially since I well knew that loops can easily become a noose around the neck. What else was waiting to catch me off guard?

As I watched Barry cross Wisconsin, Angela was saying there was always the possibility of someone attempting to pull a fast one in politics "and this is just the type of situation—one without precedent—where you might see some mischief, or attempted mischief."

"You aren't suggesting a coup?" Melissa asked.

Angela laughed. "No, nothing that dire, I hope. Cable TV is filled with talk of succession right now, even though the Constitution is relatively clear on the matter. I say relatively because again this election has given us an unprecedented circumstance. And politics will always manage to get in the way whenever there's a hiccup in the process. These days ideology seems to trump unity. I hope that won't happen here."

I turned off the radio and honked as Barry reached the curb. He waved and made his way to the car.

"What a surprise," he said as he was strapping on his seatbelt.

"As if the day hasn't been full of them," I put the Forester in gear and headed north on Wisconsin, past the "social" Safeway, so-called for the young Washingtonians who frequented it as much to meet kindred spirits as to buy groceries (and not to be confused with the "secret" Safeway on 20th street, so called because it was hidden away and difficult to find). "What're you hearing from inside the Beltway echo chamber?"

Jagoda chuckled. "Enquiring minds want to know where you got your nickname."

"Track," I said, my smile feeling foreign on my face after the day's events. "I once ran a 4:10 mile in high school, but I was best at sprints and hurdles."

"Where'd you go?"

"West Cincinnati. You?"

"East Sandusky."

"Very pretty," I said, having been there for a track meet. "But close enough to Cleveland to get you some big city vibes. You live there now, right?"

"Since college."

"Where was that?"

"Ohio State."

"Journalism?"

He nodded.

"And from OSU to the *Plain Dealer*. You must have

something going for you to get to D.C. so young."

"It's where I want to be."

"The next Woodstein?" I asked, as Woodward and Bernstein were collectively known.

He gave me a long look. "Skeeter, are you playing me?"

"It's that obvious?"

"You could have got most of my bio online without going around the same block three times."

"But as you know, it's better to establish a human connection when you're working a source."

"I thought you were *my* source."

"Looks more like a two-way street."

"All right, all right. So where do we go from here?"

"Ever heard of Randolph Tice?"

Jagoda scratched the back of his left hand for a few seconds. "Randy Randolph? Head of Cleveland Clinic's psychiatric department. Also on the hospital's board of directors. Not to mention a major fund raiser."

"That's the one."

"Covering the hospital was part of my first beat at the paper."

"A racy post?"

"You'd be surprised. Along with the Mayo Clinic, the Cleveland is a world-class medical center, as you must know. Hospitals and police stations make great training grounds for newbie newshounds. But what about Tice?"

"You know him personally?"

"Personally, no. I've seen him around, attended a press conference or two that he was part of, and once asked him a few questions for a story about a new facility once upon a time. It would be on the record if you want to check it."

I cut to the chase. "It's possible Tice may have once treated Barley Thompson."

"And you want me to find out when, where, why and how—to hell with doctor-patient privilege. You also want to know it before it goes public. That's why I'm sitting here and taking a tour of one of Washington's more picturesque neighborhoods."

"That's about the size of it."

"Okay high school hurdler, I get it. But you haven't said what's in it for me."

"Some exclusive stories. Inside stuff. Play this right and it could take you to an office next to Jeff Bezos' at the *Washington Post*."

"Bezos' office is in Seattle."

"Ok wise guy, but you get the picture."

We were back at the corner where I'd picked him up half an hour earlier. Now Barry opened the car door and started to get out, then turned back to me, one foot holding the door ajar, letting in the wintry air.

"I'll see you around," he said.

"I'm sure you will. But just in case you don't, make sure you keep me informed."

"I'll do my best, but don't expect miracles. Shrinks can be shrewd."

"So can journalists. Remember Deep Throat? Keep your eyes and ears open. Someone always knows something."

It was dark and cold, with snow flurries beginning to slash across the Forester's windshield as I drove to my rented, Victorian-era walk-up in a row of them just off North Carolina, a couple of blocks from the Capitol. As I approached it on leafy East Capitol Street, I could just make out the construction being erected for that celebratory ritual known as a presidential inauguration. The star-spangled banner o'er the land of the free, as Francis Scott Key had captured it over two centuries before, billowed showily in a breeze at the top of the illuminated cupola. Normally it would have lifted my spirits. But not tonight.

Once home, the hot shower I'd been so looking forward to did little to revive me. I'd been running on adrenaline, but the surge was ebbing, and I had to face Barley Thompson for dinner in less than an hour. The messages on my cell phone had compounded since I'd turned it on after Barry Jagoda's departure, but there was still no word from Barley or Walter. Everyone else could wait 'til tomorrow.

Thirty minutes after getting home, I was back in the Forester, headed west. Wearing the same worn overcoat, I'd changed into a navy blazer with a fresh blue and white pinstriped shirt, a solid dark tie and charcoal slacks. Following Angela's suggestion, I was carrying my copy of Robert Caro's fourth volume about the presidency of Lyndon Johnson: *The Passage of Power,* detailing his ascent to the White House. Driving to the newly anointed vice president-elect, I was not at all sure what I'd say to him. But I'd copied a passage I wanted him to hear:

"Recalling for his memoirs how he felt after being told that [Kennedy] was gone, [Johnson] said, *'I was a man in trouble, in a world that is never more than minutes away from catastrophe; I realized that ready or not, new and immeasurable duties had been thrust upon me. There were tasks to perform that only I had the authority to perform...I knew that not only the nation but the whole world would be anxiously following every move I made—watching, judging, weighing and balancing.*

"'I was catapulted without preparation into the most difficult job any mortal man could hold. My duties would not wait a week, or a day, or even an hour.'"

I was going to give the book to a man I wasn't sure was fit to take the oath for the second highest office in the land.

❧   ❧   ❧

Trailed by a Secret Service agent, a former president was in a long corridor of the Watergate complex. That was on Barley's floor, the sixth.

Jim Sutton flashed his infectious grin as he stopped me. His long fingers reaching out, he clasped my hand, small by comparison, and wrapped his left arm around my shoulders, "You ran a heck of a campaign, Skeeter." He said in his raspy Louisiana accent. "I wish Hope had had you on our team." All I could manage to spit out was "Thank you, Mr. President."

"Now look, you've got your work cut out for you. I've

been in there with Barley for about an hour and he's got cold feet. Walt's in there too. Have yourselves a good dinner with a nice wine, but when you leave, be damned sure Barley Thompson will stand on the podium ten days from now and take whatever oath of office he's called upon to take." He released me from his grip. "I'm in town for a couple of days, staying at the Hay-Adams. I'm up late, so call me after dinner if you need me."

"I'll do my best, Mr. President."

He strode off, talking a mile a minute to the agent who trailed him by a step. Before I could ring Barley's buzzer, Walter Mathews, looking as poorly as I'd ever seen him, opened the door.

-- 5 --

Walter stepped into the hallway, checked to make sure the lock to Barley's apartment was off, and quietly pulled the door closed behind him. Although I'd already been cleared by a Secret Service agent before I got on the lobby elevator, another agent eyed me warily from several yards down the corridor. Walter gave him a nod then Walter cocked his head toward me. "He's ok," he said. The agent's return nod said he was satisfied.

"Maggie?" I asked.

Walter shook his head and said he'd left her only an hour before. "They'd taken her up to the ICU and let me see her there, but she was still sedated. Dawson had left for the day, but the intern on duty told me her vital signs were "consistent," whatever that means. They don't expect her to regain consciousness until tomorrow at the earliest. When she does, they may want to induce a coma, depending on her vitals."

He wiped his forehead with a white cotton handkerchief from the breast pocket of his pinstriped navy blue suit. Despite being back in the attire I was accustomed to seeing him in, he still looked drawn and tense. "What a mess," he said.

Opening the door to Barley's apartment, he led me inside. Several impressionist prints hung on a foyer wall, including a Van Gogh I recognized in a plain gold frame. Then a spacious living room, one entire wall of which was glass, offered a dizzying view of the Potomac River six floors below. A large Persian rug covered its floor. The department-store modern furniture had a faded, been-around-awhile look. Next to a large, off-white sofa in the center of the room—I'd seen one just like it at the Spring Valley Crate-and-Barrel store on

Massachusetts Avenue—a Lucite coffee table held back issues of *Architectural Digest* and *Town and Country*, hardly fare I'd have expected Barley to favor.

We shook hands and, as if reading my mind, he said the apartment was a sublet maintained for VIP's by the DNC. "Not exactly my taste, but comfortable enough. And how about this view?"

"Spectacular. A realtor's dream."

He nodded as we stood at the window taking it in, where Walter joined us. Below, headlights of tiny cars sped in both directions along Rock Creek Parkway. A yacht festooned with lights was plying its leisurely way north on the river, and we could hear a faint tinkle of music from somewhere below.

Dressed in khaki trousers and a shawl-collared sweater over a button-down shirt, Barley turned to me, now smiling.

"Did Walter tell you? Jim Sutton was here. Just dropped by and stayed almost an hour. I've met him before, but this was the first time we chewed the fat, man to man, me and the president. I'm telling you, that guy's really something. When he talks to you, he makes you feel you could do just about anything you wanted to do."

"Or anything *he* wanted you to do," I said.

"If I remember correctly," Walter said, "Marsha Lewis lived right here at the Watergate."

"She did? How could she afford it?" Barley's wide eyes were bloodshot as if he'd been up late, been drinking or both.

"I think it was her parents' apartment. She holed up here after the scandal broke."

At the mention of "scandal," Barley's demeanor changed. "Marsha Lewis," he pronounced. "What a fiasco." Then he looked at me. "But enough of that. What can I get you to drink?"

I said I'd have a beer if he had any, and Walter chose to stick with white wine. He'd loosened his tie, which, except for this morning at Sibley, was about as close to casual as I'd ever seen him.

As Barley headed toward the kitchen for the drinks, I thought I saw some movement there.

"Is Amanda here?" I asked.

"She's in Columbus." He looked back at me as if expecting a reaction. When it didn't come, he said, "She's got her hands full." I wasn't sure how to interpret that but let it go.

Taking a closer look around the living room, I was struck by its absence of books. With no photographs either, it felt more like a hotel suite than someone's home. No sooner had I sat down in a wing chair facing the sofa than a slight woman with Asian features brought out a silver tray with three glasses and set it on the coffee table. In addition to a Stella for me and Walter's wine, a highball glass was filled with what looked like neat whiskey. Barley picked up the glass, took a healthy swallow and screwed his face into a grimace.

"This is Olive," he said, waving toward the woman, who looked about 50. "She's from Manila. She and her husband—he drives a taxi—came here 20 years ago. Now they have two kids in college, one a senior." Olive blushed, then gave us a bright smile and returned to the kitchen.

When she was gone, Barley added that Olive came with the apartment, five days a week. "A nice perk. Tonight she's making dinner. Hope you're both ok with salmon and broccoli."

"Forty-one's least favorite vegetable," Walter said, referring to George H.W. Bush.

"Hated the stuff," I chimed in. "Once he was president, he refused to eat it. Broccoli went into decline, at least among Bush supporters."

I wondered whether the odd expression Barley now wore was from weighing the culinary advantages of the nation's highest office. Or maybe he was thinking about something else entirely.

Taking a seat on the sofa, opposite Barley, Walter said he hadn't eaten all day. Not normally a beer drinker, I poured the Stella into my glass, which in my Ohio days would have marked me as a wuss; real men drank beer out of bottles. But I had to admit the trace of bitterness from the carbonated hops tasted very good on an almost empty stomach.

We sat holding our glasses until Walter turned to me, breaking an awkward silence. "Just before Sutton left, we were talking about the inauguration. Pete Dexter's been working on a draft of Maggie's address. I've asked him to stick with it, just in case." Dexter was Maggie's chief speechwriter.

Walter raised his glass to his mouth, then lowered it. "What do you think about Barley giving the speech if..." He left unsaid what now seemed obvious.

"I'm all for it," I said. "Dexter's good, I'm sure he'll do a fine job. With maybe a little editing..."

Having knocked back half the contents in his glass, Barley interrupted. "It's too soon. I can't think about giving an effing speech."

I could see Walter's jaw tighten as he stared into his glass of wine. A moment later, he said, "Barley, we have to be prepared for different eventualities."

Barley shook his head and took another drink. "Too soon," he repeated with a slight slur.

Walter shot me an exasperated look. Under a lot of stress already, he hardly needed the present situation. But who among us did?

"What about Sally Bingham?" I asked Barley, referring to his own speechwriter. "Has she been working on anything for you?"

It was hard to tell whether Barley's frown was from disparagement of Sally or more disdain for the idea of giving an address at the inauguration.

"Did you see the press conference this afternoon?" I asked.

"You handled yourself well," Walter said. "Deft the way you reminded Barley to put out a statement."

"Did you see it, Barley?"

"Yeah." Barley swallowed another drink. "The usual presser. Don't know any more than I did before it came on."

"Maybe," I said. "But it isn't just about Maggie. It's also about the country moving forward. You're going to have to make a statement to that effect soon."

"Rah, rah. Rally round the flag, boys."

Barley had obviously had enough to drink. He was clearly half in the bag, a state I'd never seen him in before. As for Walter, his exasperation was turning to anger. He stood up and carried his empty glass to the kitchen.

"Want another beer?" Barley asked.

"I'm fine for now, thanks."

Returning from the kitchen with a full glass and a glum expression, Walter announced, "Olive says dinner's ready."

I wondered how much the two of them had had to drink before I arrived. Barley took baby steps as we moved to a dining area at the end of the living room closest to the kitchen, but that didn't stop him from uncorking a bottle of Sancerre. He poured glasses for himself and me, while Walter brought his own to the circular dining table set with three places.

"To Maggie and a speedy recovery," I said, raising my glass.

"For all our sakes," Barley added.

The beer had gone straight to my head, and I hadn't realized how hungry I was. The salmon hit the spot, and the broccoli, new potatoes and a green salad were nice additions, to say nothing about the cold, crisp Sancerre. With all of that, I didn't notice that Barley barely touched his food. At some point another tumbler of whiskey had appeared before him. In spite of everything, however, I felt myself start to relax. The last sixteen hours or so had been among the most urgent and enervating of my life.

"Barley, I'm going to say something," Walter said, then stopped. I had a sense that he'd rehearsed whatever he was about to say, at least in his head. "No one's going to think the slightest bit less of you," he continued, "for having concerns about filling in for Maggie on such short notice, if it comes to that. I'd worry about anybody who didn't have qualms at a time like this. It had to have been a terrific shock, and it was only a few hours ago."

Believing it was the right thing to say, I looked at Barley and thought I could detect the slightest ease of tension. He nodded toward Walter.

"I think you should give it some time," Walter went on, "Let it sink in a bit. Let's see how Maggie is doing tomorrow or the day after. Even if she isn't back on her feet in time for the inauguration, in a month or two..." he let the sentence hang in the air, together with all its ambiguity.

"I hear you," Barley said. "And I 'preciate it. Thank you."

He pulled himself up in his chair, and looking at both of us seemed to try to sober up. "But, let's face it, we don't know what's going to happen. I'm sorry to have to say this Walter, but Maggie may never be a hundred percent. And if she isn't... I'm not sure it's just qualms I'm feeling. I'm not sure I'm up to this. The economy, sure, but foreign policy...I don't know much more than what I learned in those campaign briefings. I wasn't on the intelligence committee or foreign relations or even armed services. We—I mean the country—might be better off with somebody else. I dunno."

"It's too soon to make those kinds of decisions," Walter said. "Besides, they may get made for us. Things have to play out a bit, but the first order of business is to at least be prepared for the worst."

"The worst," Barley replied. "You know what the worst is?"

"I think I do, Barley. My wife may not survive."

"And I, along with a lot of other folks in the country would be damned sorry. It would be a loss on many levels. But let me tell you the worst. The worst would be if I had to replace her as the head of this government."

Olive came in with dessert, Ben and Jerry's rocky road. Rocky road indeed. I started to say something but thought better of it and held my tongue. Nobody took any ice cream, and Barley told Olive she could go home once she'd cleared up.

"Speaking of going," Walter said, "I'm sorry to eat and run but I've got to be at Sibley first thing in the morning, and I've got another appointment tonight. Would you mind walking me to the door, Skeeter."

In the hallway, he gave my shoulder a squeeze, as if for luck. "He's all yours," he said, sounding defeated. "I did my best. This is what you get paid for so see if you can straighten him out."

"Sure," I said, feeling utterly skeptical about my chances.

When I returned, Barley was sitting on the sofa, a bottle

of Maker's Mark on the Lucite table in front of him.

"There's something I want to read to you," I said, pulling the quote I'd copied from Robert Caro's book on LBJ out of my pocket. "'I was a man in trouble,'" I began.

I'd hoped the words might give him comfort but Barley's attention seemed elsewhere. Even as I tried to remind him that so large and confident a figure as Johnson had also been humbled by the prospect of the presidency, Barley didn't take it in, if he listened at all. But when I got to the description of the White House as a "world that is never more than minutes away from catastrophe," he cringed.

After Olive came in to say goodnight and left, I tried another tack: reminding Barley of FDR's death in April 1945. "When Eleanor called Truman to the White House to tell him her husband had just died," I said, "Truman asked if there was anything he could do for her. She replied: 'Is there anything we can do for *you*? For you are the one in trouble now.' " As with the LBJ reference, I had wanted to remind Barley that Truman, a humble Midwesterner like himself, had risen to the occasion and was now widely regarded as one of our most successful presidents.

"You keep repeating something I already know," Barley mumbled.

"Stop it," I said. "You're standing at the brink of the greatest opportunity any man or woman can ever have."

Again he acted as if he hadn't heard me.

I had one more quote, one from memory. It was President Obama speaking to his staff after his 2012 re-election. "We're in charge of the largest organization on earth, and our capacity to do some good, both domestically and around the world, is unsurpassed.' "

"I'm not Obama," Barley said.

"But you're a decent, successful Senator from the great state of Ohio. And who knows what you're capable of."

He took another drink and I switched gears.

"Do you remember a conversation we had right before Maggie asked you to be her running mate? Just the two of us. I asked you if you wanted this. Do you remember your answer?

"I said yes. Which I had no business saying."

"So what changed?"

He stammered something I couldn't hear, and I felt my anger rising.

"Look at me, Barley. Talk to me. This is a conversation you're going to have with someone sooner or later. Maybe even on TV. You'd better start your rehearsal now."

"I never thought it would come to this," he said at last.

"Jesus Christ, man. Anything can happen in politics. You know that. And vice president? What did Nelson Rockefeller call it? Stand-by equipment. The very definition of the job is to be ready to take over if something should happen to the president."

Barley was shaking his head. "Maggie was so far back in the polls. I never thought we'd pull this off, and we almost didn't. Blaine Ward and his stupid giggle."

"So you were content to go down in history as an also-ran, meaning a loser."

"Not a loser. A national figure."

"A national figure?" I barked, not quite believing what I'd heard. "What's that supposed to mean?"

Barley hung his head and muttered. "You know. Job security. Lobbying. Invitations. Maybe a TV gig. Speaker fees."

So the cynics were right!

I suppressed an urge to jump across the coffee table and strangle him. A lobbyist! What a poor excuse for a human being. For a long time I sat and stared at him—a man I'd obviously never known and now hardly recognized.

No way in hell, Randolph Tice had said. I still didn't know what Tice knew, but at that point it didn't seem to matter. Barley was a mess, a miserable mess. And I was charged with resurrecting him. What could I do?

"I want to ask you," I said, trying to control myself while he looked up at me with suspicion. "Last night, when you met with Maggie, you two argued. What about?"

"Nothing,"

"I know it wasn't 'nothing'. What was it?"

"It's personal."

"Maggie is out of the picture at the moment Barley, and you and I are beyond secrets. I *must* know what you two argued about."

He sat for a minute, disheveled and with all vitality drained. Finally, he lifted his glass, and I readied myself to knock it out of his hand.

"This," he said. "She was worried about the booze."
I didn't believe him. If he were a sot, his vetting certainly would have exposed it. I told him so.

"Skeeter," he repeated my name as though he'd never heard it before. "You're good."

"Come clean," I said, gently. "Now's the time."

He hesitated. Finally he whispered that Amanda left him. "I thought you knew when you came in tonight."

"First I've heard about it."

"Before Maggie even asked me to run, Amanda told me she wanted a new life, before it was too late. Then she agreed to stay through the election. And then, when we won, I persuaded her to hang in for a while longer. But that's it. We haven't told our daughters or anyone else. Maggie was the first person I told. That's why we argued."

I suspected there was more, there had to be—Randolph Tice, for one thing. But I decided that now wasn't the time to ask further questions. Barley was already spooked about January 20th. He'd never take the oath if he thought something from his past was about to come back and bite him. Plus he was drunk. Eyes empty, he lifted his head and we looked at each other like two boxers in opposite corners of a ring, seeing who would blink first. Finally, yawning, he leaned forward and held his head in both hands.

"It's late, Skeeter," he said. "And I'm beat. Done in."
"You're right."

Using everything he had, he drew himself up and said he was going to bed. Then he wobbled, steadied himself, and moved off. "Sorry if I don't see you out, but you know where the door is."

"Sure," I said. "Goodnight."
He didn't reply. God help us, I thought.

Dead tired, I wanted nothing more than to go home, get into bed, sleep and wake up the next morning to find that this day and night had just been a nightmare. Walking to the foyer, I stopped to study the Van Gogh print. Unlike my reaction to it when I'd arrived, the emptiness and solitude of the tortured artist's nighttime café now sent a chill through me that felt like a warning. Then I hesitated at the door. I had no idea how much Barley had drunk or if he'd continue drinking. But I'd seen his eyes and felt his distress—and he was still my charge.

Taking a deep breath, I walked back into the living room, where his bourbon glass was still on the table, together with the now half-empty Maker's Mark bottle. From the dimly lit kitchen, which was spotless, evidently as Olive had left it, I followed a runner carpeting a darkened hallway that led to three doors. The first one opened onto a small bathroom, the second to a den or office. It had a desk between two curtained windows and a small couch along one wall. Beyond a closed door there, I heard Barley snoring.

Returning down the hall, I used the bathroom, then went back to the den/office. The couch was small but would have to do. After removing my blazer and shoes and loosening my tie, I settled down as best I could to try to get some sleep. Barley continued to snore.

My reputation as the great smotherer of flames would probably be put to its hardest test so far. I certainly knew I was in the center of a firestorm but that concern apparently lasted no more than a minute before I fell deep into sleep.

++

PRESIDENT-ELECT MATHEWS IN COMA

by Barry Jagoda
Cleveland Plain-Dealer

WASHINGTON, D.C., — President-Elect Margaret ("Maggie") Mathews remained in a post-operative coma today, more than 24 hours after being hospitalized for a ruptured aneurysm in the brain. As concern mounted that she would not recover in time to take the presidential oath of office by inauguration day, January 20, Congressional leaders, pundits, scholars and concerned citizens turned to the U.S. Constitution to parse the 20th and 25th amendments, which address questions pertaining to a president or president-elect unable to perform their official duties.

The 20th amendment, ratified in 1933, states that "if the President elect shall have failed to qualify, then the Vice President elect shall act as President until a President shall have qualified." Samuel R. Seaton, a federal judge and constitutional scholar, said in a telephone interview that "in today's world, qualification for election as president"— natural born citizenship, at least 35 years of age and permanent residency in the U.S. for 14 years—"has usually been established well before election day. As a result, in recent decades qualification has been interpreted to refer to the actions taken by Congress on January 6, the date the votes of the 536 presidential electors are counted and a winner declared."

Judge Seaton said that because Margaret Mathews had been thus qualified by the electors before she was taken ill early yesterday morning, the application of the 20th amendment might be challenged in this case. But regarding the succession of the Chief Justice of the Supreme Court, at least one court has ruled that "qualify" may also refer to the taking of the oath to support the Constitution of the United States, which President-elect Mathews has yet to do. "Additionally," Judge Seaton said, "some people may—probably will—argue that a life-threatening illness or other severe incapacitation also constitutes a 'failure to qualify.' At the very least," he added, "I would expect some robust debate in Congress, and possibly at the Supreme Court" on the issue.

The 25th amendment, ratified in 1967, states that when the vice president and other high-ranking officers in the executive branch "transmit to the president pro tempore of the Senate and the Speaker of the House of Representatives their written declaration that the President is unable to discharge the powers and duties of his office, the Vice President shall immediately assume the powers and duties...as Acting President."

Judge Seaton said, "in this case, the amendment language refers to a sitting president and vice president, not the president-elect nor vice president-elect. So again, there's a basis to dispute the amendment's application to the current circumstances. That said," he added, "one would hope that common sense would prevail and the 25th [amendment] would apply."

Bruce ("Skeeter") Jamison, who was

President-elect Mathews' campaign manager and is an aide in her transition office, said in a telephone interview that "in the spirit of the 25th Amendment," Vice President-elect Barley Thompson had sent a letter to Senator Mavis Branch, president pro-tempore of the Senate, and to House Speaker Jacob ("Jake") Claymore, informing them that President-elect Mathews was currently unable to discharge the presidential duties due to reasons of health. Jamison said the letter was also signed on his wife's behalf by Walter Mathews, husband of the president-elect and her designated secretary of state, and by Angela Mercado, the attorney general designate.

Senator Branch's office confirmed receipt of the letter and said the Senator "was studying the matter." An aide to Speaker Claymore said only that the letter had been received.

-- 6 --

When I first came to in the middle of the night, I had no idea where I was. Half awake and trying to get my bearings, I sat up in the unfamiliar space. A trace of streetlight seeped through a slit in the curtain closed against one of the room's two windows. Looking at my watch, I saw it was a quarter past two in the morning. Then it all came back to me: The Watergate apartment, beer, dinner with Walter and Barley—accompanied by two bottles of wine. When the vice president-elect, who'd been drinking tumblers of bourbon, stumbled to his bedroom, I'd elected to spend the night. Just in case.

Wide-awake now, with adrenaline pumping again, I found the night too quiet. I turned on the light beside the couch in Barley's office, where I'd fallen asleep less than three hours before. My blazer and tie were on a chair, a throw I'd used for a blanket in a twist on the floor. Barley was no longer snoring. Standing up I stretched and ambled down the hall.

Barley's door was open and I peeked in. The bedding was rumpled, but Barley wasn't part of it. Along the bedroom's far wall, I could see a trace of light leaking from the threshold of the closed door, which I guessed led to the master bathroom.

Running my hand along the wall nearest me, I found a switch, and turned on an overhead light.

"Barley. You all right?"

No answer. Crossing to the closed door, I knocked. "Barley."

Nothing. I turned the handle. The door was not locked and it gave a little, but something blocked it. Something heavy. I pushed, and it moved. Putting my shoulder to the door I opened it enough to wedge myself in.

Barley was the "something". I was surprised he'd managed to get out of his clothes and into a pair of striped pajamas, but there he was, face up on the tiled floor. I knelt beside him. His breathing was shallow, his pulse weak. A prescription vial was next to him on the floor, part of its contents spilled. I picked it up and read "Xanax." Sleeping pills.

I grabbed the telephone attached to the wall beside the toilet and started to dial 911, but pushed the disconnect button before hitting the last digit.

The President-elect of the United States was unconscious in Sibley, with an aneurysm that would prevent her from being sworn in now nine days before the inauguration. And there was the vice president-elect, also unconscious, on his bathroom floor in the Watergate. I had no idea how much Xanax he'd taken and no clue if he'd taken it, or intended to, deliberately. Was I dealing with a potential suicide or just an inebriated pol who couldn't get back to sleep after waking in the middle of the night? Either way, the repercussions could be lethal—beyond even Barley's survival. Beyond his political if not his actual survival.

Call if you need me, the former president had said. *I'm up late.*

Would he consider two-thirty late?

With everything to lose, I took a chance, called the Hay-Adams and asked to speak to President Sutton in the presidential suite. An emergency, I said. Vice President-elect Thompson was on hold. More than a justifiable white lie, I thought.

Sitting on the closed toilet lid, staring down at Barley's motionless body, I heard the line go dead and assumed I'd been disconnected—another crank call. But before I could hang up, Jim Sutton's chipper voice came on as if it were two-thirty in the afternoon. "I wouldn't have taken you for a night owl, Barley."

"It's Skeeter, sir. We've got a problem."

"Tell."

When I'd finished, he said he'd send his personal doctor over pronto. "If I came myself at this time of night it might raise questions, but I'll swing by in the morning. Give me your cell number, I'll have Bill Macy call you right away."

"Thanks." The line went dead before I could add "Mister President."

Turning on my cell phone, I returned to my perch in the bathroom and waited for Dr. Macy's call. Barley was ashen but breathing.

Ten minutes later I gave Macy the same information I'd given the former president on the phone. He asked a few questions before telling me what I should do until he arrived "in less than a half hour."

I called the downstairs desk and gave Macy's name to the doorman on duty, then went to inform the duty Secret Service agent in the hall.

I'd led the team that vetted Barley Thompson. How had we missed the markers; a man with a drinking problem who was about to be divorced, a possible suicide?

An embarrassing, not to say colossal, failure, and I'd have to shoulder much of the responsibility for it. It had been a short-staffed, dark-horse campaign that was never given a shot until the home stretch, but that was no excuse—and anyway that didn't matter now. Should anything happen to the poor sod on the bathroom floor, and the lapse became public fodder, I'd never work in Washington again.

Apart from keeping Barley alive, the challenge ahead was to turn this around in very little time. The odds seemed insurmountable, especially because I'd probably have to do it alone if we were to avoid any more damage than we'd already sustained; but I had to try. That meant getting to the press first.

Barry Jagoda had tipped me off that the *Washington Post's* lead story that morning would take up the question: Where is the VP-Elect? It was too late to change the overall thrust, but I might be able to influence the last edition, plus the online story and the next day's lead. And reaching out to CNN and the networks with new information might blunt the impact.

Still in the bathroom with Barley, I called Paula Wertheimer's personal number. One of the *Post*'s political writers, she was also my contact at the paper.

Paula's "This better be good at three in the morning" was none too polite.

"Off the record," I told her. That got her attention.

"Ok."

"Barley's got a severe stomach virus. He's being treated for it, and the hope is it's only a twenty-four hour bug."

"Who's the doctor?" Paula asked.

"No further details," I said. "But once Thompson's recovered, you'll be the first reporter I get in touch with."

"Deal," Paula said.

That was always the deal. Everyone in this town wanted scoops. It was a tight rope to walk, but I hadn't fallen off it so far.

When Macy showed up carrying the conventional black bag, I let him in and led him straight to Barley. While beseeching science to afford us another chance, and with no interest in watching the doctor perform his medical magic, I left him to it. Besides, I had stuff to do. I told Macy I'd be in the next room if he needed me. Then I went back to the task at hand: attempting to hijack the day's news.

☙ ☙ ☙

It was almost four, forty-five minutes after he arrived, when Macy summoned me into the room where Barley now lay on his bed, asleep but breathing. When I asked if he was going to make it, Macy held up the Xanax vial.

"The prescription, filled a week ago, was for ten capsules. I found seven on the floor, so the most he could have taken would be three. Given his condition, and the amount he'd had to drink, I'd guess less than that. In any event, it was good that you got to him when you did. I induced vomiting, and whatever wasn't already absorbed is hopefully out of his system. With rest, he should be ok."

Rest seemed unlikely at the moment, but I didn't argue.

"I'd like to get a nurse in here, at least for the next few hours," Macy said.

"You understand the spot we're in," I said. "Not only are there security issues, but right now negative publicity could be disastrous."

"Of course. I can recommend a private nurse who's worked with me in similar situations."

Much as I'd have liked the details of those similar situations, I wasn't about to ask.

"Officially, the vice president-elect has a stomach virus," I said.

Macy nodded.

"I haven't given your name to the press, so you shouldn't get any questions."

"It's privileged anyway, and I wouldn't discuss it with anybody unless I had the authorization to do so."

"Thank you, Doctor. And I'd like a nurse only until Barley's responsive and able to get around on his own."

"That's reasonable."

"I'll make arrangements for her to be cleared."

"Him," he said.

"Beg pardon?"

"He's a male nurse," Macy said.

"Fine."

Taking a business card from his wallet and a pen from his pocket, the doctor wrote something on the back of the card and handed it to me. "My private number. You can reach me anytime. And the nurse's name is on the back. Meanwhile, I suggest you remain with Mr. Thompson until he gets here."

"In all likelihood I'm right where I'll be for the next several days."

I worked the phone while Barley slept. Waking up several disgruntled members of our team, I told them the cover story—a 24 hour bug. No one, not even Walter, had to know what had really happened overnight. Nobody's business but my own, Jim Sutton's and Barley's. And the doctor's, of course.

I had my integrity and thought I could trust the ex-president, but Barley would have to earn his.

At the reasonable hour of 7:30, I got Pete Dexter on the line and asked if he could adapt Maggie's speech for Barley by tomorrow afternoon. He asked a few questions, then said he thought he could have something for me in 24 hours.

With the TV on, I was clicking back and forth between CNN and Fox, when the doorbell rang. I opened it to find President James Kennedy Sutton with copies of the *Post* and the *New York Times*. The *Post* had indeed managed to get the stomach virus into the last edition, and it was also playing well on cable. Doctors, both spin and medical, were juggling the usual inane questions. I turned down the sound.

"What's the prognosis?" Sutton asked.

"Full recovery," I replied with more enthusiasm than it deserved.

"Great, Skeeter. Another fine save. Shall I look in on him?"

"If you like. He's sleeping. A nurse is coming in at nine. And I've promised Paula Wertheimer an interview as soon as Barley's up for it."

"You don't miss a beat."

"Let's hope not," I answered. "Now there's just the matter of Barley's resurrection."

Whether or not he got my irony, Sutton laughed. "If you want a job when this is all over, come see me."

"Thanks, but when this is all over what I'll want is some time off."

᷈ᔆ ᷈ᔆ ᷈ᔆ

At six foot four and two hundred pounds, Robert Bork, an African-American, looked more body-builder than nurse. Nevertheless, his geniality managed to complement his straightforward approach. Carrying a portable IV contraption, he set it by the bed and hooked Barley up to a slow drip of fluids.

I introduced myself and, taking the opportunity for a respite, told Bork I'd be back in a couple of hours. Then I drove home, showered again, and changed into a pair of jeans and a sweatshirt—comfort clothes for the job ahead. I also packed a bag with a few other personal items, including my Dover edition of *History's Greatest Speeches*.

Despite the raw cold wind that whipped the previous day's snow across a black-and-white canvas, the sun brightened everything, including my spirits, when it peeked through the clouds. Exhausted as I felt driving to a diner in a nearby shopping center, I also felt uplifted, with a sense of purpose that had been muzzled just twenty-four hours ago. After a breakfast of eggs-over-easy, link sausage and home fries, washed down by several cups of coffee, I walked the frozen food aisle of a nearby supermarket to stock up on provisions for the weeklong winter retreat I anticipated.

Back at the Watergate just before noon, Bork met me at the door.

"Any changes?" I asked.

"He's awake."

"In what sort of condition?"

"Weak."

"How do we make him strong?"

"Get him into rehab when he's up to it."

"When might that be?"

"Hard to say, a day or two."

"Have you worked with rehab patients?"

"I have. I *do*."

"Then let's say we start tomorrow. An hour at two o'clock and go from there."

"Sure, Mr. Jamison. Whatever I can do."

"Skeeter," I said.

"What?"

"Call me Skeeter, that's my name. And by the way, you're not any relation to the other Bork are you, the one who didn't make it onto the Supreme Court?"

He laughed. "I get that all the time. All I say is, I don't think so, but you never know, the woodpile runs deep."

We both laughed and I told him I was glad he had a good sense of humor. "Of course you understand that everything that goes on in this place is confidential," I added.

He nodded. "I do. I signed a form about that."

"Good. Now I'm going to take a look at the patient."

Entering Barley's bedroom and closing the door behind me, I found him looking hung-over but watchful.

"What happened?" he asked in a small voice.

"Too much sauce and not enough sense."

A look of hurt spread across his face, perhaps amplified by his hangover. I didn't care. For the next few days, I was on a mission of tough love. If it worked, fine. If not, I'd be calling President Sutton to take him up on his job offer. With my luck I'd probably get posted to Tennessee working for a candidate for the Chattanooga city council.

Meanwhile, Barley and I were about to be the odd couple, or perhaps a better movie reference might have been *My Fair Lady* with me in the role of Henry Higgins. At the end of the sojourn, I expected to elicit a sober, polished, confident and eloquent inaugural address from my Eliza, Barley Thompson, Vice President of the United States of America.

Little did I know. What Barry Jagoda came up with after the inauguration would have doomed us at any time prior to it. Fortunately, other things got in the way. By the time he actually held office, Barley Thompson—with more than a little help from me—was his own man. Or a reasonable facsimile thereof.

-- 7 --

Inauguration Day dawned grey and gloomy—par for the course. It was the kind of weather I most despise and had never gotten used to even after so many years in and around Washington. Whenever a bout of Seasonal Affective Disorder loomed, I would try to fit the curative light of the Air & Space Museum into my schedule. But despite the cold and my doubt that the temperature would get above freezing by the noon swearing-in, what I most felt on this auspicious day was gratitude.

A week before, I doubted we'd get here. Maggie still lay in an induced coma, barely clinging to life and Congress was still wrangling over whether Barley should be inaugurated and, if so, in what capacity. Barely recovered from his "stomach virus," he was still protesting that he was not worthy, a judgment I had increasingly embraced.

After five days in the coma the Sibley doctors had induced, Maggie was returned to consciousness, but her prognosis remained cloudy. Walter insisted she recognized him and had spoken his name on one occasion. But he admitted she usually managed only single-word utterances that let him know she was thirsty or tired or had a headache. At his urging, I visited her the day after she regained consciousness. As he led me into her flower-filled room, I had to stifle a sneeze.

"Darling, it's Skeeter," Walter said. Maggie remained unresponsive.

After a few minutes that seemed like hours, we crept out and closed the door behind us, then stood in the corner of the hallway talking in low tones. Walter brought me up to date on the little he'd been told by Dawson and the other medicos. "They say it's still too soon to determine whether she suffered any cognitive damage," he said with a grimace. "However, I continue to be optimistic."

It was impossible to tell if he was putting the best face on things or in denial.

We moved on to politics. In the wake of Barley's "stomach virus," Walter suggested the best use of my time would be keeping Barley on the straight and narrow. Walter would take care of inauguration logistics, which I welcomed.

So I stayed with Barley at the Watergate for most of that week, sleeping on the sofa where I'd spent my first night and venturing to my Capitol Hill apartment every couple of days to shower, pick up mail—mostly bills, of course—and change clothes.

To my relief, Barley acted reasonably contrite and agreed to the ground rules I laid out: no leaving the apartment, no outside phone calls not cleared by me, one small bourbon a day and rehab with Robert Bork three times a week. While Barley-sitting, I was often on my cellphone deflecting questions from the press with what I judged to be increasingly artful ambiguity. I gave more or less the same patter to each caller: Barley was recuperating from his virus, following the Congressional succession debate on C-Span, working on his speech and praying for Maggie Mathews. I promised a photo op as soon as he was fully recovered. To my surprise, despite knowing the way those things worked, his popularity was rising in the polls. I assumed he'd inherited some of the public's sympathy for Maggie. The last poll I saw put his approval rating at 62%, not bad for a borderline alcoholic who hadn't been seen in public for almost two weeks.

The first full day I was with him, Barley rarely came out of his bedroom and only then in his pajamas, slippers and bathrobe. He would wander into the living room for one of Olive's tuna- or chicken-salad sandwiches or to stare glumly at C-Span or CNN. The latter kept looping excerpts of the White House press conference—still a primary source of the few known facts about Maggie's condition—which were followed by the usual gaggle of political and medical "experts" offering up speculations that ranged from her imminent demise to Lazarus-like recovery in time to be sworn in as president.

Having satisfied his appetite for such fare in a few minutes, Barley channel-surfed to Fox and MSNBC whose panelists saw the same known facts through predictably different eyes. On Fox, which had attacked Maggie relentlessly during the campaign, the invited "experts" derided Barley as a political hack unfit to carry the handbag of Woodrow Wilson's wife, who virtually ran the country after her husband was laid low by a stroke. On MSNBC, Barley was most often compared to Truman, although one enthusiast displayed his affinity for wretched excess by likening the moment, if not the man, to Teddy Roosevelt stepping in for the assassinated McKinley. At that one, Barley snorted, shook his head in wonder at what I took to be the strange turn his life had taken, and turned off the TV with a flick of the remote. Then he thanked Olive for her culinary offerings and, with a little wave to me, padded back to his darkened bedroom.

What lifted him out of his listlessness, at least temporarily, was his first working visit from Robert Bork. As soon as the Secret Service agent in the lobby called up to announce Bork's arrival, Barley changed into shorts, a T-shirt and sneakers. But the greater change was in his demeanor. When Bork entered the apartment, Barley came out of the bedroom with a noticeable bounce in his step and eyes brighter than I could remember ever seeing them.

Bork gave me a mock salute, then smiled at Barley. "You ready to work out?"

"You bet."

And for the next half hour, he did just that.

The trainer favored interval training, a regimen that combines short, high intensity bursts of exercise with slow recovery phases. After about five minutes of stretching, he started putting Barley through his paces, holding a stopwatch and crying, "Go." For the next 30 seconds, Barley did as many push-ups as he could—I counted six—until Bork commanded him to stop for 45 seconds of rest. They repeated the on/off cycle three times.

Over the course of the workout, Barley ran through a similar sequence of sit-ups, crunches, jogging in place and burpees, a combination push-up and jump-up I'd never seen before. Bork had even brought barbells and had his convalescent do three repetitions each of curls and lunges before wrapping up the workout with more stretches.

When they were done, Bork asked about his drinking.

"I'm fine," Barley said. Bork turned to me.

"One a day."

"I'd feel better if you went cold turkey," Bork told Barley.

"Let me be clear," Barley said, "the other night, that wasn't me. It was just that after all that happened..."

"Well, I suppose one drink, if that's all it is, won't kill you. But no cheating."

"No cheating," he affirmed.

"Good workout," Bork said, giving Barley a fist bump. He actually looked happy.

But once Bork closed the apartment door behind him, his shoulders slumped and he headed toward his bathroom and a shower without a word to me. I wouldn't see him again until shortly before 6:30, when he came out to watch Scott Pelley deliver the CBS Evening News. He liked Pelley, who had moderated the vice-presidential debate between him and his Republican counterpart, Oregon governor Alison McKutcheon, which the chattering class, as well as opinion polls, had called for Barley by a whisker. (It was less by scoring debating points than keeping his cool throughout. By contrast, McKutcheon's eyes fluttered and she stammered when asked if she advocated restricting social media to curb extremists recruitment of young Muslims).

Watching the news, Barley nursed his bourbon. Pelley aired an interview with Samuel Ramsey, in which the Senate Majority Leader reported having told his caucus that it was time to legislate. (Another snort from Barley.) After Pelley had signed off following a saccharin story about a 12-year-old farm boy giving a dozen eggs each day to a nursing home, Olive served a shrimp and veggie stir-fry dinner while I tried my best to cheer Barley up.

"That's good news about Ramsey," I said.

"I guess." Barley's funk finally got to me. His lack of enthusiasm sent mine ebbing too.

"Look," I said at a volume that brought Olive out of the kitchen to see what was going on. "For the sake of my sanity, if nothing else, would you please stop wallowing in self pity and just accept the fact that you're going to raise your right hand next Friday, swear your allegiance to the Constitution, and take the oath of whatever office Congress decides is appropriate?" (I was betting it would be vice president with the temporary powers of the presidency).

"Give it a few weeks," I continued more calmly. "You'll probably be handing the whole thing back over to Maggie. And if not, and you still feel the way you do now, you can choose your own vice president, resign, build a cabin in Montana and tease perch and trout with bits of string and feathers for the rest of your life. But first, you're going up on that stand in front of the Capitol, take the oath of office and deliver Pete Dexter's excellent speech."

I thought Barley's rising color threatened that he might throw something at me. But in seconds, the air seemed to drain out of him like a beach ball stuck with a pin. Looking at his plate, then up into my eyes, the prospective leader of the free world finally said "okay."

The next morning, he rose before seven, shaved, showered, dressed and doused himself with too much aftershave. Then he asked Olive for scrambled eggs and bacon, orange juice and an English muffin, if she wouldn't mind. Digging into his breakfast as though he hadn't eaten in days, he read the newspapers I'd ordered, whose editions he'd only glanced at the day before: The *New York Times*, *Washington Post* and *Wall Street Journal* and, of course, The *Cleveland Plain Dealer*.

It was after eleven by the time he finished reading. Getting up from the wing chair and stretching, he asked if I could get him some magazines. I made a list of those he wanted: *Time, National Journal, Road and Track* and, to my surprise, *GQ*, which I'd have thought a tad metrosexual for him.

Then he opened his laptop on his knees. Peaking at the screen, I saw the home page of *Politico*, the political paper that's a must read for anyone even remotely interested in the District's primary industry. The headline that caught my eye was "President-elect Still in Coma; Vice President-elect 'Indisposed'. Who's Minding the Store?" Who indeed, I wondered.

Once done with *Politico*, Barley asked if I'd call the transition office and ask them to send over the briefing books he hadn't looked at in months.

"If they can find them," I whispered.

Two hours later, a Secret Service agent called from the lobby to say a cardboard box full of binders had arrived by messenger. Should he send them up?

"Please," I answered.

Barley dived into them like a sophomore before finals, while I retreated to my room to return more phone calls.

An hour later, there was a knock at my door: Barley, asking if I thought it ok for him to go downstairs for a light workout in the Watergate gym. (Bork would not be coming that day.) I thought about it for half a second, then shook my head.

"Sorry, but I don't think that's the best place for you to make your public debut." Although encouraged by the new and improved Barley I'd encountered that morning, I couldn't take a chance on what he might say to his fellow gym rats.

But maybe the time had come for him to reach out to Paula Wertheimer, the *Post* reporter to whom I'd promised the first interview. I worried that Barley's absence from public view would soon generate rumors beyond the "stomach virus." Unlike nature, the conspiracy-minded elements of the public love a vacuum.

"So," I said, "You up to giving an interview?"

"Yeah, I guess. If you think I should"

I sat him down and together we went over the more likely questions he might be asked. When I was satisfied with his answers and Barley said he was ready, I called Paula.

She picked up on the second ring and I put the phone on speaker.

"It's Skeeter," I said. "The vp-elect is feeling better. I have him for you if now's a good time."

"Now is a great time."

"No policy questions. You ok with that?"

"How come?"

"This isn't the time. Dubois is still president. And Maggie is president-elect. And by the way, you're the only one he's talking to today."

"Ok, Skeeter. I accept."

After I handed the phone to Barley, I heard her say "I'm glad to hear you're feeling better, Mr. Vice President-elect."

"Thanks, Paula. Yes, much better."

"So how are you feeling about January 20th?"

"Well I'm hoping the president-elect can be sworn in."

"We all are, of course. But if she can't, are you ready to stand in for her? Do you feel prepared?"

"I'm certainly not ready to fill her shoes, if that's what you're asking. But I am ready, or I will be ready, to serve my country and fulfill my obligations under the Constitution."

It went on in that vein, with Paula probing respectfully and Barley giving variations of the answers we'd rehearsed. Finally Barley said he had to take another call, which wasn't true, as Paula undoubtedly knew. She said she had just one last question.

"Do you feel you're ready to occupy the White House?"

Barley looked at me and I nodded to him.

"Paula," he said after taking a breath. "I doubt anyone ever feels ready to be president, and I hope, fervently hope, that President-elect Mathews can be sworn in as soon as possible. Until that happy day, what I feel ready to do is my best for the American people in whatever capacity I'm asked to serve. Thank you, Paula."

"And you, Mr. Thompson. Good luck."

Barley turned off the phone and I gave him thumbs up.

"Very good, sir," I said, feeling pretty good myself. Paula

would tell the world that Barley was alive and well.

That night he asked Olive for a Coke instead of his usual Maker's Mark. And he practiced reading Dexter's speech aloud so many times that by the time he went to bed I felt I could deliver it myself.

-- 8 --

The moment Barley had anticipated with fear and a little loathing, was at last upon us. He and I had just finished our morning coffee. I was reading the *New York Times*, Barley the special inauguration edition of the *Washington Post*—"Barley Thompson to Take Oath as Acting President"—when the apartment intercom buzzed. A Secret Service agent in the lobby said an Amanda Thompson wanted to see Barley.

"Says she's Mr. Thompson's wife," he added.

That was the first I knew about Amanda coming to town; Barley hadn't said a word. "Forgot," he said to me with a sheepish look.

So much for clearing all calls. And why hadn't he told me? I had no problem with her being there. In fact, I'd never bothered to take her off the various invitation lists, a detail that had slipped through the cracks. I hoped there weren't any others.

"Send her up," I said.

After she and Barley embraced convincingly enough, she said she'd flown in from Cleveland the night before under a false name. Then she took a taxi to the Georgetown Four Seasons Hotel. "Very comfortable," she pronounced it.

Turning to Barley, she said, "What a day. Can you believe it?" He looked at me and raised his eyebrows, as if for an answer. Amanda was right. It was all a bit beyond belief, but I had to admit that in his navy blue suit, white shirt and red tie, with a shiny new American flag pin on his lapel, Barley Thompson looked more the part he was about to play than I'd ever seen him. Hats off to Robert Bork and Pete Dexter. Thanks to them—I didn't feel I'd earned any credit—he looked confident.

Ten minutes later we were seated in the black, bulletproof SUV sent to bring Barley to the White House, me in front with the driver, the Thompsons in back. Ours was the second of a three-car convoy. Although it was too early for inaugural crowds on the street, many pedestrians stared as we negotiated Washington's icy byways. Some pointed, others waved, as if to forge a connection as we sped by. Our windows were too dark for anyone to see inside, but Barley waved at his soon-to-be-constituents just the same. As I watched him, I thought to myself that this was the first time since Maggie's illness—no, the first time *ever*—I'd seen him looking...well, *presidential*. As we made the turn onto Pennsylvania Avenue, my irritation with him and all it had taken to get him to this juncture yielded to the occasion. I even felt a proverbial lump in my throat.

After being waved through the Northwest gate, we glided to a stop beneath the historic front portico, where uncountable foreign leaders and other dignitaries had arrived for more than two centuries for presidential meetings. Now the president and his wife stood there, both wearing big smiles. The first lady responded with a friendly wave.

The official schedule called for coffee and small talk, after which Barley and President Dubois would climb into "The Beast," the 10-ton armor-plated presidential limousine for the 12-minute drive to the Capitol...and into history. Amanda and Deborah Dubois would ride in a lighter, more conventional—but still bulletproof—model. I'd stay in the SUV we now occupied, which, along with the other two that had brought us there, would join the presidential convoy.

"I know you're going to be terrific, Barley," I said as a young Marine approached to open his door. "Knock 'em dead."

"Thanks, Skeeter. I owe you." As I savored the surroundings and my proximity to the President of the United States, Dubois grasped Barley's right hand in his and pulled him into an embrace with his left.

"Welcome to the White House," the president said,

flashing his thousand-watt grin. Out of deference to Maggie, Barley and Amanda would move into Blair House—not the White House or the vice president's residence on the grounds of the Naval Observatory—later in the day. The White House would be officially "unoccupied"—a misnomer considering that scores of staffers would continue living there—until Maggie recovered or Barley got a promotion. The Dubois furnishings would be packed and loaded into moving vans during the inauguration ceremony.

After the two couples disappeared into the White House and the massive front door closed behind them, I jumped out of the front seat and got in back. A Marine closed my door and we pulled away, then turned into a parking area behind the West Wing to wait until The Beast was ready to roll. When we came to a stop, I studied the inaugural seating chart, pleased that Walter had seated me reasonably close to the podium with a good view of the proceedings.

I thought about Barley's offer two days before to be his chief of staff, the position I had hoped to have in a Maggie Mathews administration. I'd told him I appreciated the offer and would think about it, but to myself I said, "Not on your life. No more hand-holding, cajoling or ego propping." Now, however, it occurred to me I might have acted a little hastily. Maybe I should give it a try, if only temporarily. I could tell Barley I'd help him out until things settled down. If it turned out to be as bad as I'd earlier feared, I could beat a hasty retreat. But if it turned into something better than that, something I actually *wanted* to do, I could say I'd decided to stay on. *Indefinitely.*

My cellphone vibrated. I pulled it from my pocket and read the screen: Barry Jagoda.

"Barry. Your timing is exquisite."

"I know. I'm sorry. I've been running around like crazy all morning. And waiting for a phone call."

"What's up?"

"Are you sitting down?"

The urge to impress him proved irresistible. "Well, yeah, as a matter of fact I'm in the back seat of a Secret Service SUV at the White House, about to be driven to the Capitol for Barley's swearing in. What's going on?"

"The man whose inauguration you're about to attend."

"I'm listening."

"A little background first. Back when Randolph Tice first hung out his shingle in Columbus, a few headshrinkers thought it was possible to 'cure' homosexuality, as everybody then called it. Turn gays straight. Now we refer to it as conversion therapy."

Here we go, I thought.

"Tice was one of them, or maybe he just figured cultivating a gay clientele was smart marketing. It doesn't matter. He soon became one of the two or three go-to shrinks for Columbus' gay men, especially those who wanted to go straight."

"Go on."

"Well, of course Tice didn't change anybody's sexual orientation. Conversion therapy has long since been discredited. But that's another story. This one is about Barley Thompson being one of Tice's patients."

Barley gay? I actually felt relief. No big deal: we can survive that. The country had come a long way in the last few years. It was ready.

"But that's not the story," Barry continued

"It's not? What is?"

"Thompson was a teacher back then."

"I know. It's in his bio."

"Well, it looks like he may have had a relationship with one of his students—one of his *male* students."

"Relationship?"

"Sex. Apparently the kid was a few months shy of his eighteenth birthday. It may have been consensual, but the parents found out about it somehow and went ballistic. They had known their son was gay and accepted it, but the idea of a teacher taking advantage—a teacher almost ten years older— freaked them out. They said they'd go to the police. Since the kid was underage, Barley was looking at a rape charge."

"Jesus! Where did you get this?"

"The usual way. A hell of a lot of phone calls. A bit of luck when a friend of a friend of a friend knew the kid's mother and put me in touch with her."

"She talked?"

"Just enough."

Holy shit, I thought, if this get's out...I started to tell Barry how he had to keep this under wraps when he interrupted.

"There's more, I'm afraid."

While the voice in my head was moaning, "What next?" I asked Barry to lay it on me.

"According to the mother—the father's dead by the way: heart attack some years back—Barley came to them, begged them not to press charges, and said he'd do whatever they asked. He wrote to them, called them, went at them for days. He promised he'd seek help, leave town if they wanted, never have any contact with their son again. They went back and forth. Finally he managed to persuade them their son would be better off if nothing about this ever saw the light of day. In the end, they agreed to let the matter drop if Barley would turn himself in, plead guilty to a lesser offence— exposing himself on school property is what they came up with—and get psychiatric help. No rape; no child molestation. The parents and Barley signed papers binding them to indefinite silence."

"This is unbelievable, Barry."

"Yeah but I believe it. The police report, like the rest of the case, has been sealed, but there should be a way to get it. "

I should have said I didn't believe it; that's what big-league political operatives are supposed to do. I wasn't above a bit of misinformation in a good cause. But I'd waited too long to speak up.

Barry finally broke the silence. "I hear you loud and clear," he said. "I'll confirm it on my own."

"You know you can't go with any of this, right?" I said.

"Not yet I can't."

"What's that supposed to mean?"

"The paper has a double source rule. I've got only one

source. So far."

"The mother?"

"The mother, but even she was off the record. It was Tice's phone call I was waiting for."

"And?"

"Nothing. He returned my call a couple hours ago but wouldn't say squat. Wouldn't confirm. Wouldn't even say he'd treated Barley. The doctor/patient confidentiality mumbo jumbo."

I thanked the Fates—or was it the Furies?—for small favors.

"And the kid?"

"I'm still trying to reach him. The "kid," as you call him, is 41. Rob Craig and his partner were in the first wave of same-sex couples to walk down the aisle out in San Francisco, in '08. I've left a dozen messages, so it's pretty clear he's ducking me. I'll have to go out there, once we get through the Maggie/Barley crisis, which the paper is still paying me to cover."

"Listen Barry, you can't write this. Can't write anything about it. You know that, don't you?"

"I know I haven't nailed it yet, but when I do..."

"No, not even then. It's too dangerous, much too dangerous. Listen, if Barley once had a gay experience, and it's news to me that he did, it's not that big a deal. But ducking a potential rape charge and covering it up? And with an underage kid!"

"*You* listen, Skeeter. I'm a reporter and this is a story. A hell of a story. Just as you once said, maybe the biggest I'll ever get. And anyway it's not my call; it'll be the editor's. I seriously doubt she's going to bury the paper's biggest political story since we endorsed Wendell Wilkie—not to mention the Pulitzer that might come with it."

"Have you told her?"

"Not yet. We're talking after the swearing in."

I didn't say anything more because I couldn't. My mind was racing too fast for me to put words together, much less come up with a plan. In less than an hour, Barley Thompson would be the first vice president ever to be inaugurated with the powers of the presidency. And if Jagoda was right, he'd also be our first rapist head of state. I was pretty sure the nation could handle its first openly gay president—ok, first openly gay *acting* president. But it sure as hell wasn't ready for a pedophile president, acting or otherwise.

"Look Barry," I finally managed, "if this is true, and as far as I'm concerned that's a big if at this point, bigger than either of us. For starters, it's a matter of national security. Lots of countries would react in lots of unpredictable ways, none of them good. You've got to promise me you won't say anything to your editor for at least 24 hours."

"Why would I do that?"

I lost my cool. "Because, goddammit, I gave you this story. You owe me. And because it could blow up in our faces...in *your* face. Cooler heads need to think this through and weigh the consequences—*all* of them. You can't rush something like this into print. You've got to be just a little patient. For the good of the country." Then I thought of another approach.

"Listen, in less than an hour Barley Thompson will be sworn in. That makes Jake Claymore next in the line of succession."

Barry surely knew that the notoriously right-wing Alabama Republican Jake Claymore had been elected speaker of the House of Representatives early in the year after what was left of the Tea Party joined forces with the many lawmakers Cal Manning had pissed off during his years in the post. After that ragtag coalition ousted the conservative Manning, the House replaced him with more conservative Claymore, a total dark horse. He'd apparently been calling in favors he'd been quietly accumulating over six contentious terms.

I was pretty sure Jagoda shared my view of the Speaker as a dangerously loose cannon.

I took a breath and continued. "In a few weeks or months, either Maggie or Barley will be president—no acting about it. If *she*'s president, Barley's next in line to succeed her.

If *he* is, he'll appoint his own vice president. In either case, Claymore will be out of the picture. Or at least once removed.

"I don't know..." Jagoda said haltingly.

"Twenty-four hours, Barry. You owe me that, at least. Give me 24 hours and I promise I'll give you enough White House access to get you your damn Pulitzer. "

The silence seemed to last for days.

"Ok, Skeeter, twenty-four hours," he said finally.

"One more thing."

"What?"

"You've also got to promise you'll give me a heads up before you publish a word of this."

More silence.

"Barry!"

"Ok," he said finally.

I swallowed, then slowly exhaled and said thanks just as the SUV was pulling up to the inaugural stand in front of the Capitol. "I've got to go," I said to Barry, "but we'll be in touch." I was pretty sure the thumping I could feel in my chest wasn't from inauguration excitement.

Fifty-two minutes later, Barley was vice president and acting president of these United States. The nation's leader, at least for the time being. He'd done well; no stumbling over the oath and a flawless delivery of Dexter's speech. Better than that, he made it sound powerful, very nearly historic. The line that would probably be most remembered recalled both JFK and Neil Armstrong: "When future generations look back upon this day, they'll remember not the small steps that led us to it but the giant strides we took away from it. Giant strides toward our destiny as a great and good people."

The applause in the stands finally subsided, and it seemed every hand was reaching out to shake the acting president's. Despite the swarm of well-wishers between us, I could see him clearly, no more than ten or twelve yards away. (I scanned the crowd for Walter but couldn't spot him.) I figured it would take a while to reach Barley, but I was prepared to be patient. Suddenly, I saw him look around as if trying to locate someone or something. To my surprise, his eyes fixed on mine, and he raised his right hand and waved. Although he was talking to a woman standing next to him, his gaze returned to mine before he began striding briskly toward me.

"Congratulations, Mr. Vice President," I said seconds later while shaking his hand and looking him squarely in the eye. "Or should I say Mr. Acting President?"

"To you, I'm Barley, Skeeter. Let's leave it that way."

"Yes sir."

"Skeeter, I've said it before and I'll say it again: I couldn't have done this without you." He lowered his voice and brought his mouth close to my right ear. "You...saved...my...ass," he whispered.

Thank you, sir," I said, stepping back and holding his eyes with mine. He must have read the look on my face.

"What is it, Skeeter? What's the matter?"

"Sir, we need to talk."

PART TWO

-- 9 --

After the ten torturous days and nights of Barleysitting at the Watergate, I finally got back to my apartment and into my own bed, having dropped in on all ten inaugural balls. By the time I got home it was closer to dawn than evening, and because I had to be in NBC's Tenleytown studio at six in the morning for an appearance on "Morning Joe," sleep was little more than an extended nap brought brutally to an end at 5:30 by an operatic aria blast from Pandora. Joyce DiDonato sounded as though she and the New York Met orchestra were crammed into my bedroom.

Even for an opera lover, which I'm not, it was jarring—but that was precisely why I'd turned the volume up before crashing for my precious few hours. I managed to turn the light on and Pandora off just as Joyce was hitting high C in "The Barber of Seville."

Having danced with the attorney general nominee as often as I could at each of the balls we'd both attended, I'd come home alone, fortunately or not, via a taxi. I'd had my fair share of Chenin Blanc de Blanc, the Loire Valley's equivalent of Champagne, without the Champagne price. That snub to California's own wine industry hadn't gone unnoticed by the press. You'd have thought a war had broken out between our vintners and their French counterparts. But Walter Mathews, who had taken charge of wine selections, was a Francophile who fancied himself an oenophile, and he didn't back down.

"It's time for the California wine industry to get real," he said in an interview. "When I can get a French wine for half what I'd pay for its California equivalent, I'll do it every time, and I don't have to worry about guests going home with a headache." Maybe that wasn't the most diplomatic response from a former secretary of state, but it was classic Walter. Not running for anything, he wasn't running away from anything either.

Although I could confirm that even very reasonable French wines rarely cause headaches, my mouth was dry as the Mojave and my eyes as bloodshot as a slaughterhouse floor. The smell of coffee wafted from the kitchen where I'd also had the good sense and barely sufficient sobriety to program the machine before going to bed. I showered, brushed my teeth and rinsed my mouth, the cold water providing some relief for the dryness. After flooding my eyes in an optical solution, I pulled on a pair of chinos, a button-down shirt and a gray sport coat, and padded into the kitchen in chukka boots to swig from the o.j. carton before filling my thermos with black coffee. With a bagel stuffed into an overcoat pocket, I headed out into the dark cold carrying the thermos and a briefcase containing the day's schedule. I was behind the wheel of my Forester less than twenty-five minutes after the mezzo-soprano snapped me awake.

Welcome to my life, Skeeter Jamison, chief of staff to Acting President Barley Thompson. Jesus!

ॐ ॐ ॐ

Seated around the table with "Morning Joe" hosts Joe Scarborough and Mika Brzezinski plus *Post* political columnist Eugene Robinson, I waited for what I hoped would be a few softball questions before my eight o'clock breakfast with Barley at the White House.

"I'm told that the president-elect was awake and able to watch the swearing in ceremony," Mika offered. "Is that right, Skeeter?"

"News to me. The last update I had, yesterday morning, she was still unconscious."

"We wish her a speedy recovery," Scarborough said. "But what about 'Chief of Staff' Skeeter? The title didn't even exist until 1953. Before that, it was 'assistant,' 'advisor,' 'political consultant,' or 'aide to the president'—you name it. How'd you get the job?"

"I bought it."

Scarborough laughed and an ever-so-slightly aghast Mika managed a forced smile.

Why not? I thought. Despite its political overlay, the show was pure entertainment, highly-rated. So why not entertain? Especially since I'd be on the hot seat soon enough.

"How much did it cost?" Joe asked.

I grinned. "More than I care to admit."

"You're young," Robinson interrupted. "But not the youngest man—it's always been a man—to hold the position. An LBJ appointee—I forget his name—had that distinction."

"James R. Jones," Joe answered in a flash. "My producer just whispered the name in my ear. And while he functioned as chief of staff, his actual title was appointments secretary."

"Seriously," Mika broke in.

"Seriously? I worked my tail off. Since the president-elect became ill, and by the way, we talked about the same position in a Mathew's administration—I've barely slept. And I've been with Vice President Thompson day and night for almost two weeks."

No exaggeration there.

"And has your role been defined beyond the title?" Robinson asked.

"At this point I'm a political advisor and jack-of-all trades, but I'm sure it will evolve."

"What's on the schedule today?" Joe asked.

"We'll be meeting with the White House staff and congressional leaders. Hopefully, we'll begin to take some action on cabinet appointees."

"It's been a turbulent period. How about hazarding a guess as to the president's chances for success?"

"Joe, you've been there. You know as well as I do that in politics events have a way of determining success or failure of an administration."

"What's tops on your agenda?" Mika asked.

"Building on Dubois's success. He left us with a pretty decent economy. The vice president is committed to investing in infrastructure: rebuilding roads, bridges, schools. Those critical areas get talked about but never seem to get fixed."

"How about we begin right here in D.C.?" Joe asked. "I just learned the Metro system has been shut down again. You'd think that in the nation's capital at least, we could have a world class transit system."

Sensing my time was up, I simply nodded.

"Good luck, Skeeter," Mika said. "Thank you *so* much for coming on."

❦   ❦   ❦

When I arrived ten minutes early at the White House, an intern led me into a small room off the Oval Office where a table had been set for two.

"The vice president will be with you in five minutes, Mr. Jamison," the intern said. "He's on the phone. He said you should help yourself to coffee."

"Thanks, I'm fine. What's your name?"

"Bridget."

"Good. I'm sure I'll see you again, and I'll try to remember your name."

"Not to worry. There are lots of new faces around."

"I'm good with faces, lousy at names."

Seconds after Bridget exited smiling, Barley entered through a connecting door. "Morning, Skeeter." He wore a white shirt and tie, and a pair of jazzy suspenders held up his trousers.

"Morning, Mr. Vice President."

"I guess I can't convince you to call me Barley. With everything you've seen in the last ten days, the only thing that's changed is an oath on the Capitol steps."

"A significant change."

"So you say. How'd you survive the festivities?"

"Too long a night and too much wine."

"You were tripping the light fantastic with Angela Mercado every time I saw you."

"She's a good dancer, sir."

Barley smiled. "Well, let's have breakfast. You said you needed to see me and made it sound urgent."

"Yes sir. It *is*."

"At least drop the sir and let's get on with it. Scrambled eggs ok?"

"Fine."

Barley pressed a button and asked that breakfast be served. "It'll be a while before I learn my way around this place. And by the way, Amanda has put the divorce on hold indefinitely. So you can keep all that to yourself, if you don't mind."

"That's good news." I meant it.

Barley said, "Talk to me Skeeter," when breakfast arrived and we were alone again. "What's so urgent?"

I took a deep breath. "You've heard of Barry Jagoda? A young journalist from Ohio who writes for the *Plain Dealer*?"

"I believe he profiled me some time back. He was fair."

"I think he tries to be, so let's hope so. He's working on a story about an incident back when you were teaching in Columbus. A police matter."

Barley lowered a forkful of eggs destined for his mouth. "Police?"

"Afraid so. And I'm told there's a police report."

Barley swiped at his mouth with a crisp, white napkin. His hand was trembling as he tried to lift his coffee cup and the spilled coffee left a dark stain on the tablecloth.

It wasn't fun, but I knew I had to persevere. "Rob Craig? Randolph Tice, head of psychiatry at Cleveland Clinic?"

He laid his napkin on the table. "I'm being blindsided here, Skeeter."

"Yes sir, you are. But let me tell you what's going to happen if we don't get out in front of this story."

"What story?"

"According to Jagoda, the story is that you seduced this

Rob Craig, one of your students, when you were teaching in Columbus some twenty-five years ago."

"Not true."

"What part isn't true?"

"I never seduced anybody."

"Jagoda has a source, Rob Craig's mother, who still lives in Columbus. If he finds a second source, the *Plain Dealer* will almost certainly publish. Could happen as soon as tomorrow."

To his credit, Barley seemed to be less fazed by the news than I'd expected, apart from the tremor. I pressed on.

"I'm told the police report is for indecent exposure. Craig's parents signed a document that prevents them from seeking damages and acknowledging anything beyond what's in the report."

"So the mother can't provide much information."

"Sir, the boy was underage."

"Just barely. What are you suggesting, that I resign?"

"Not at all. This is a hurdle, is all, and I'm good at hurdles. But before I can do anything, I have to know what happened. What *really* happened."

Barley stood up, turned his back to me, walked to a window and stared out onto the west lawn. He must have stood there for at least a minute. When he began talking, his voice was so low I could hardly make out his words.

"Rob was a student in a history course I taught. He was also on the tennis team, which I coached. He'd written a term paper, I can't remember what about, and made an appointment to see me during office hours to discuss it. Between our classes and tennis we got to know each other."

"Did you know he was gay?"

"Skeeter, I don't recall. He may have told me, I may have guessed, but I really don't remember." He remained at the window.

"You understand that when it comes to your story, the facts are important. I have to ask. Did you seduce him?"

"I didn't," he shot back. "It was something that happened, that's all. It just happened, the way things do sometimes."

"Sir, if you ever have to talk about this publicly, he's Mr. Craig, not Rob. Never call him Rob."

He nodded. "It happened once. Just once, and I vowed it would never happen again." He turned to face me. "It didn't."

"What about his parents?"

"The only way they could have found out was through Rob—Mr. Craig. The father called me: angry but civil. I was 26, 27 years old and scared to death it would end my career. I asked to meet with the parents. His mother agreed. She knew her son was gay; I'm not sure about the father. We met a few times. It took awhile, but we eventually came to an agreement."

"Does Amanda know?"

"What there is to know, she knows."

"That's good."

"What's good about it? I seem to step into one pile of manure after another."

"You're not the first and you won't be the last. Imagine what Bill Clinton must have felt when he had to fess up that he'd lied about having sex with Monica Lewinsky."

"Humiliated."

"I should say so. But still human, and except for a few Neanderthals in Congress and elsewhere, a condition most of us can identify with."

With just the hint of a smile, Barley sat back down and drank more coffee.

"Why did you leave Columbus?" I asked.

"The obvious reason. I moved to Cleveland to start over."

"Everybody deserves a second chance."

"I'd say it's hard to quantify what people deserve. But what's your plan, Skeeter?"

"Rob Craig lives in San Francisco. He and his partner were one of the first couples to get married when the state authorities declared same-sex marriage legal. I think I'd better go out there."

"What for?"

"To talk to him. I'm sure he's got a story. I want to hear it. The more I know, the better I can deal with...*this*."

"I'm not sure that's such a good idea."

I didn't say anything and Barley walked again to the window.

"Well," he said finally, "you're getting paid for your judgment, and so far you've earned your keep. So I guess you better do what you think best."

"Thank you. I hope that will continue."

"And what about the journalist?"

"Barry Jagoda."

"What do we do about him?"

"I think you'll have to talk to him sooner or later—better sooner. I asked for a two-day reprieve on the Craig matter. Barry's ambitious; that's what motivates him. If he interviews you in the White House, we stand a better chance of controlling the story. We can set it up so that Craig is off limits; if Jagoda doesn't agree, he doesn't get the exclusive."

"He'll go along with that?"

"I think so. So long as it's exclusive."

Sitting down at the table, Barley pushed his fork through the now cold eggs.

"Trust me," I said.

"You and Amanda, you two are *it* right now."

He stood up as if to leave, and I said I had one more question."

"Shoot."

"You can tell me this is none of my business."

"Damn it, Skeeter, everything's your business now. Ask your question."

"Are you gay?"

"No. I'd say so if I were because I have no problem with being gay. But I'm not. It was just the one time, that's all."

"I don't have a problem with it either. And if you are, we can deal with it. But I need to know."

"You heard me. I didn't inhale."

He got up, excused himself and walked slowly toward the door that would return him to the Oval Office. I went out the other door in search of Bridget in the corridor outside.

"How does a guy find his office around here?" I asked

her.

"Follow me, Mr. Jamison."

"On condition you call me Skeeter."

"Sorry, that's the protocol."

"But I'm giving you permission to break the rules once in awhile."

"Yes, Mr. Skeeter. Right this way."

My office was on the other side of the Oval and the little alcove where Barley and I had breakfasted, if you could call a bite of egg and a sip of coffee breakfast. It had a desk, a computer terminal, two phones, a small conference table and a couple of filing cabinets with empty shelves behind the desk.

"Do I get a secretary?" I asked Bridget.

"Just pick up the red phone."

"The hot line?"

Bridget smiled, shook her head, and exited..

I closed the door, sat down, and picked up a telephone, then changed my mind and put it down again, having no idea whether White House phone conversations were recorded. Reaching for my cell, I keyed Barry Jagoda, who answered as if he'd been waiting for my call.

"How'd you like an exclusive with the vice president?"

"Now?"

"In a couple of days."

"On the record?"

"Of course."

"Conditions?"

"Where are you on the Rob Craig story?"

"Waiting for a green light."

"Are you in touch with him?"

"I've left several messages at his home in Daly City and on his cell."

"Maybe he's away."

"I don't think so. I've also called his employer, and I'm pretty sure he's going to work. He's just not returning my calls."

"So sit at the yellow light a while longer. Patience. Can you do that, in exchange for an interview with the president?"

"I guess," he said without conviction. Then his tone changed. "Yes. Sure I can." His gratitude sounded genuine.

"Don't mention it."

Looking up flights to San Francisco, I found that the next one I could possibly take departed at one o'clock. It appeared to be fully booked, but I suspected the White House had some clout. "Good morning, Mr. Jamison," a pleasant voice said when I picked up the red phone. "This is Sarah Benson. How can I help?"

"If you can get me on a fully booked one p.m. flight to San Francisco and back on tonight's Redeye, you'll be a miracle worker."

"Let me see what I can do".

I used the computer to google Rob Craig while I waited.

Ten minutes later, Sarah called back to confirm my reservation and ask if I needed a car to take me to the airport."

"Thank you. Yes, please, I do."

I'd seen too many "West Wing" episodes to believe the perks of the job could offset the long hours of turmoil and stress. Still, there was something to be said for getting a flight at the last minute, not to mention a car and driver.

I found an array of daily newspapers, a copy of *The Economist* and for some reason, *People* in the back of the Lincoln Town Car that took me to Reagan airport. The driver had the radio tuned to WTOP, Washington's all-news station. I asked him to turn up the volume.

"A real mess, this Metro system," someone was saying, "Twelve years ago eight people killed in a crash. Every winter the tracks freeze. Fires in the tunnels. Broken escalators, constant delays, you name it. You'd think we were living in a third world country."

I opened my notebook and started a To Do list. *Fix Metro.*

-- 10 --

Daly City lay in the hills between the airport and San Francisco. Mountain View Drive hardly lived up to its name. Foothill View Drive would have been more accurate, or No View if the fog was in, which it was not. Sunset was approaching when my taxi pulled up to Rob Craig's apartment unit, housed in a tangle of condos. Having found his address and telephone number from my computer search in Washington, I'd called and left a message, giving him my name, rank and serial number, as it were, before boarding my five and a half hour flight at Reagan airport (which I still called National, along with many old-time politicos.) I'd also told Rob's voice mail that I was determined to talk to him and wouldn't return to Washington until I had— and that I was equally determined to keep the press at bay.

Maybe that was the key phrase, because as soon as I was able to check my cell phone at SFO, I heard a message from Rob saying he'd keep the evening open. I called from the terminal to say I was on my way.

My computer search had turned up a few other things. Rob was a writer for a Silicon Valley software outfit in San Jose that dealt in specialized chip technology for a new—not yet on the market—educational tool for those afflicted with Parkinson's disease, autism and attention-deficit-disorder.

There was more. Rob's husband, Gunther, was from Germany and taught physics at the City College of San Francisco. Intriguingly, I also learned that at 50, Gunther was ten-years older than Rob.

The man who answered the door did not look more than thirty-five. Maybe it was his shaved head or a wrinkle-free complexion that an ingénue might envy.

"Come in," he said in a thick German accent. "Rob's on the phone but won't be long. You have a good flight? Something to drink

"Yes thanks, some water, please."

Gunther smiled, his face ruddy with apparent pleasure. "Of course. One sec." Pointing toward the living room, he led me to a chair and gestured for me to sit in it.

The apartment was small but comfortable, with every totem of conventional domesticity; brightly colored contemporary paintings on the walls, an alcove with a computer terminal, shelves filled with books, an outmoded CD tower next to a Bose Wave radio. As I sank into a pillow-fluffed couch, I heard a man's voice through a closed door. The door opened as Gunther arrived with my water, and Rob, in jeans and a sweatshirt, appeared.

"This is the first time I've met someone who worked in the White House," Rob said as we shook hands. As Gunther retreated, I said I hadn't worked there long. Despite their age difference, Rob looked and acted like the older man. He also seemed more guarded. A look of worry was etched into his forty-year-old countenance. It occurred to me that we were about the same age.

He sat in a chair opposite mine.

"A journalist keeps calling and leaving messages," Rob began. "He's hassled my mother, and he says he wants to come out here."

"Barry Jagoda. And he's partially why I'm here. To keep him from bothering you."

"How can you do that?"

"It depends on our conversation."

Gunther returned, carrying a canvas tote. "Tae Kwando," he said to me in explanation.

"Don't hurt anyone," Rob joked.

"I'll try not to." Gunther's wide grin displayed perfect teeth. Once he'd left, I asked Rob about him.

"Grew up in East Berlin. He was eight when his father was killed by the Stasi, the East German secret police, in 1975.

He and his mother managed to get out of the country and made their way to Chicago, where they had distant relatives. Gunther grew up there."

"And now he teaches physics?"

"You've done your homework."

"I didn't know about his past."

"Is there a secret file on me?"

"No more secret than the Internet, as you must know."

He smiled. "You know where I work, what I do, all my habits?"

"Only where you work. And the project you're working on."

"Plus Columbus twenty-five years ago."

"A particular incident from that life."

"Which you'd like me to talk about?"

"I would. To help clear things up."

"You probably know about the confidentiality agreement we all had to sign back then."

"I do."

"Then why should I talk to you any more than I would to the newspaper guy?"

"Because I want *you* to control your story, not the press."

"You mean you want to protect the president."

"We've just come through a turbulent election. And yes, I'd rather not have the president brought down by a scandal."

"By scandal, you mean a sex act between two consenting adults."

"Hardly. I mean a sex act between a man and an underage boy."

"I was eighteen," Rob said, then added, "almost." He fixed his gaze on me. "When do you go back to Washington?"

"I'm booked on tonight's red-eye."

"You expect a lot in very little time."

"I don't expect anything. I was *hoping* to get your version of events. If I can't, then I go back empty handed and the chips will fall where they will."

Rob nodded. "It might help if I knew who I was talking

to. And I don't mean just your job. The man behind the title."

"Fair enough."

"But I'm beginning to find it a little claustrophobic in here." He stood up.

"I'm not putting pressure on you."

"Sure. The president's chief of staff flies all the way from Washington instead of sending an underling. You bet I'm feeling pressure."

"So is the president. And the reason it's me and not an underling is to keep a lid on this as long as we possibly can."

"Ok, but I'd still prefer to do this in neutral territory."

"Wherever you're comfortable suits me. The last time I was here was last summer, on a campaign swing with Mrs. Mathews."

"I remember. You didn't stay very long."

"It was a fund-raiser. San Francisco's Democratic vote is always reliable, at least nationally. And so is the cash. So about all I saw was the inside of a hotel ballroom."

"We supported her. It was a big loss when she...collapsed."

We walked outside and got into Rob's Corolla, parked in the driveway. I did most of the talking during the twenty-minute ride into the city. Telling him about my youth in Ohio, I mentioned the high school I'd attended in Columbus.

"Then we were crosstown rivals," Rob said.

"I was on the track team. You?"

"Tennis."

"I'm a couple of years younger, but our paths might have crossed."

"Maybe. You have any gay friends?"

"None that I was aware of. Some kids I thought might be, but nothing was confirmed."

"And today?"

"People of all stripes, although I don't have much time for a social life, unless you count politics. But I know plenty of gays. So, if you're asking whether I'm homophobic—no."

"I never imagined you were. Are you married?"

"Never."

"Know about San Francisco's Castro District?"

"I've heard of it."

"We're in it now."

The sidewalks were filled with people from another era—hippies maybe. Bohemians.

"A gay neighborhood?"

"Probably no more than any other city neighborhood these days, but at one time it was the center of the counter-culture. Harvey Milk started here."

After his election to San Francisco's Board of Supervisors, Milk was shot and killed by a homophobe on the steps of City Hall in 1978. I'd seen the film starring Sean Penn.

A damp cold wind was blowing off the Pacific when Rob found a parking place just off Market Street. I was about the only person on the street in a Burberry, let alone a suit.

"You're on a different clock," Rob said. "You want a drink or something to eat?"

"Anywhere out of the wind would be fine."

"Twin Peaks Tavern is right around the corner."

"Sounds good."

As it was early for a Friday evening, we had no trouble getting a table. Realizing I was indeed hungry, I ordered a pastrami sandwich with a bottle of Stone's India Pale Ale. Rob asked for coffee.

"Barley Thompson must have been about twenty-seven," Rob said, making me think I must have passed Rob's test.

"And you were ten years younger."

"A senior, but I looked older. Barley taught history and coached tennis."

"You were in his class?"

"And on the tennis team."

"And you knew you were gay?"

"I think I always knew it. I was attracted to boys from the time I was eight or nine."

"And sexually active?"

Rob laughed. "Not really, just fooling around, until I was about thirteen. How about you?"

"Later than that."

"Getting started may be easier for gays."

"Your parents knew about it?"

"By the time I was fifteen they did. At least my mother did, not sure about my dad. We never talked about it."

"And she was okay with it?"

"They were both pretty cool, especially my mom. I never hid anything from her."

"Not even Barley?"

Rob took a deep breath. "Ok," he said finally, "here's what happened."

Barley had told him he had real tennis talent and mentored him, going so far as to work with him after regular practice hours. Although Barley might have guessed his sexual orientation, they never discussed it. Their teacher-student relationship continued for a year-and-a-half, developing into a friendship that respected the usual boundaries. Until the season's last tournament, when it turned out that Rob Craig, not Barley, had been concealing a crush.

"Nothing unusual about that," he said. "Guys fall for their teachers—men and women—all the time. Maybe even you?"

"A couple of times," I had to admit, "in both cases with black women. One in the sixth grade and another in high school. Nothing ever came of those infatuations, but the preference for the exotic remained." Of course it wasn't lost on me that I could have been jailed or worse for dating a black woman if that had been in an earlier era and in certain parts of the country. And now, Angela Mercado was my latest crush.

"So you can understand."

"I can, but how often is the teacher-student attraction acted on?"

"Probably more than you think."

Instances abounded of abusive relationships between mentors and children. Rob mentioned Jerry Sandusky's repugnant behavior at Penn State a few years ago. Schoolteachers, male and female, had lost jobs, gone to jail, had their lives ruined for pursuing inappropriate sexual impulses.

"Physical obsessions, like addiction, are often hard to resist," Rob said. "Then there are the Lolitas and the Lotharios who work their seductive charms to their own advantage. I could show you places around here where fifteen- and sixteen-year old boys and girls are selling themselves for the price of a hot meal."

"That's prostitution, not what we're talking about," I said.

"True, but it's still a twisted form of desire. Does the schoolboy or girl who crushes, to use today's term, on his or her teacher fall in love, or are the motives more tangled? And the teacher who responds; is it out of a desire for the forbidden or something deeper? The ancient Greeks didn't have a problem with it; neither do a few other societies today. In some places, girls are married by the time they reach childbearing age, and since their virginity is so important to the marriage, men take pleasure with boys, all the while denying any homosexuality."

"But we have *laws* against sex, heterosexual or homosexual, with underage partners."

"Yes but eighteen is an arbitrary number, presumably enacted to protect children. However, individuals vary and who's to say when childhood ends?"

"That's what the law is for, to protect the innocent, even if the age of innocence is trending downward. Someday the law may be changed to reflect that, but right now eighteen is the number."

"I lied to Barley."

"About your age?"

He nodded. "I told him I was eighteen, and I seduced him. He could have said no, but he didn't. He was twenty-six, we were out of town, where I'd won the state championship. I attributed a lot of that to his coaching skill and encouragement. I suppose sex that night took him into the sort of forbidden world where excitement tends to hold sway. In any case, it was a spontaneous and highly charged moment."

"Did you see him again?"

"Not that way."

"Ever talk about it?"

"Never. I graduated a month later and never saw Barley Thompson after that. Not until he was tapped to run with Maggie Mathews, and then only on TV. Wow, that blew my mind. Of course I heard he left school at the end of that year."

"How did your parents find out about you and Barley?"

"We got into an argument. I can't even remember what it was about. But they said something like they knew what was best for me, and I said they didn't know me at all, they knew nothing about me. To prove it I told them about what being gay involved. That they knew, so then I told them I'd had sex with a teacher. What a mistake! It took them a while but eventually they pried Barley's name out of me. My father confronted Barley and the whole legal business started."

It was 7:45. I'd finished my sandwich, and I asked the waiter for the check.

"You've got plenty of time to make the red-eye," Rob said. "I'll take you to the airport."

"This has all been very interesting. But there's a coda you surely don't know."

"What?"

"A psychiatrist in Cleveland treated Barley. After the episode with you, Barley worried that he might be and wanted to nip it in the bud. He told the shrink about your encounter."

Rob rolled his eyes.

"So far he hasn't said anything: doctor client privilege."

"So why would he now? Times have changed. Even the DSM, the bible of mental problems, has removed homosexuality as a disorder." He paused. "You think he might talk?"

"I've no idea, but the story's there, and a reporter's chasing it."

"I've told you what happened, but I don't want to go into it with anybody else."

"Even if it could bring down the president?"

"I don't see how I could prevent that."

I thought about that and realized I agreed with him. No matter how much of the blame he took, no matter how old he looked, no matter that he lied to Barley, if it came out that as a teacher the acting president of the United States had had sex with an underage student, he'd be toast, with the gay angle the cherry on top.

I tried another tack. "Rob, who knows about you and Barley other than you and your mom?"

"Well, the shrink you just told me about. And this reporter, sounds like *he* knows."

"He thinks he does."

"By the way, you should know that all that my mother did was confirm what was in the police report. If the reporter says otherwise, he's lying."

"Are you and your mother still close?"

"Yes, very."

"In that case I don't think you have too much to worry about. Jagoda's paper needs two sources to confirm a sensitive story like this before it will print it. As long as you don't talk, I think we'll be ok."

"But there's nothing to prevent him from blogging about it."

I shrugged. "Most blogs don't have a lot of credibility."

We were pulling up to the departures entrance at the SFO terminal. As I got out of Rob's Corolla, I told him how much I appreciated his time and candor.

"I'll do what I can to protect your privacy," I said. He thanked me and we shook hands.

In the terminal, I turned on my phone to check my messages—a string of them. Standing below a TV monitor, I listened to Fox News' Chris Wallace reporting a major bridge collapse in Toledo, Ohio. Several cars had plunged into the Maumee River. At least a dozen people were feared dead.

I added *Repair infrastructure* to my to-do list.

-- 11 --

I returned to Washington at 8:30 in the morning, hoping to head straight home after three hours of fitful sleep on the plane. That prospect was dashed by a man at the arrivals gate holding up an iPad screen displaying "Skeeter."

"Mr. Mathews wants to see you immediately at the State Department," he said before leading me to a black Town Car waiting at the curb. Arriving at the C Street entrance twenty minutes later, I entered the stately building, picked up a security badge at the reception desk and hung it around my neck. Then I was ushered to an elevator and delivered to the glorified broom closet Walter was using while he awaited his confirmation.

He held up a finger and gestured to a seat in front of his desk while he finished a conversation on the phone.

"Yes, yes, Mr. President. I'll be there. Ten thirty with Skeeter." He hung up. "Good morning."

"Good morning, sir. We're meeting with Barley?"

"Yes, hope you don't mind. You look a bit sapped."

"Eight hours sleep since the inauguration, most of it on planes. What news from Sibley?"

"Guarded. Cautious. Optimistic. Take your pick."

"I'll take optimistic."

Walter's nod seemed tense, as if he was on edge. "Kind of a rushed trip, wasn't it? San Francisco?"

"Out and back."

"It had to do with the president?"

"Sort of."

"Why the mystery?"

"Sorry, but I can't discuss it."

"I see. Anyway, I have some news for you."

"Of course."

"I'm about to withdraw my nomination."

"I'm not surprised."

"Really? I thought you would be."

"Maggie, right?"

"She's certainly the uppermost reason. But there are others, one of which involves you."

"In what way?"

"I'm going to be blunt."

"Good."

"I know you had your heart set on it, but you'd never have been made chief of staff in a Mathews administration."

Since I *was* chief of staff, I felt less of the sting I might have felt if Maggie had assumed office. Still, I had to admit it caught me off guard. I guess my expression reflected that.

"Listen, Skeeter. You'd have been rewarded, believe me. You were invaluable to us and would have been going forward. Just not in that position."

"I'm sure you have your reasons."

"You don't have the legislative chops. I've seen other presidents make that mistake and wind up having to backtrack. I didn't want that to happen to Maggie—or to you."

"And you see a way around it."

"I do."

"Which is?"

"Me."

I smiled. "You want my job?"

"Hardly. More of a behind-the-scenes adviser, a sort of *eminence grise*, if you'll pardon my French."

"Your French is fine. And you're going to make this pitch to Barley?"

Walter looked at his watch. "In about half an hour. Are you on?"

"What have we got to lose."

How naïve, pardon *my* French, his thinking would turn out to be.

෨ ෨ ෨

The president met us in an upstairs office off the living room in the private quarters of the White House. (Although not living there, Barley made occasional use of the residence during working hours.) "All that formality below us makes me uncomfortable," Barley said. "Besides, you two know where the dirty laundry is."

"I'm sure you've got a pair of sweaty socks I haven't seen," Walter said.

Barley laughed but looked to me, as if for an explanation about why we were here. All I could provide was a shrug. The president, as we were now calling him, although he was still "acting," sat down in an easy chair in front of the fireplace. It held two gas burning logs that radiated heat. Walter and I sat opposite him on straight-backed chairs.

"There are rumors the Metro workers are going on strike," Barley asserted.

Walter asked who was it that said "Never let a crisis go to waste?" When I said I thought it was Rahm Emanuel, Obama's first chief of staff, he nodded. "Anyway, it's an opportunity. Let's get out in front of it."

"Suggestions?" Barley asked.

"Bring in Paul McNulty," I suggested. For labor secretary Maggie had made a brilliant choice of the former Republican congressman who'd headed the committee on Transportation and Infrastructure. He'd already been thoroughly vetted, and both parties had agreed that confirmation would be quick.

"Skeeter's right," Walter offered. "Why not also call the head of the Transport Workers Union and put whoever he is in a room with McNulty. Then play to their egos by putting them on TV. Quash it before we've got a full-blown strike."

"You've got political capital, right now," I added. "Use some of it, or a lot of it, on infrastructure. We've been talking about this for a decade or more. I've already put it on my To-do list. Let's get started."

Now Barley nodded. Looking up from a legal pad on

which he'd been jotting notes, he pushed his glasses above his brow. "Political capital I may have. Hard currency is in short supply with this Congress. They'll do everything they can to block *any* spending."

"Make your case," Walter said. "Sell it to the country. School's are crumbling, bridges collapsing, roads in disrepair and public transportation insufficient or overwhelmed."

Barley shook his head. "I don't know."

I said it was worth a try. "If you can sell it, Mr. President, a fifty cent tax on gasoline would go a long way to paying for an overhaul not seen since Eisenhower lived here."

"If I could sell a tax like that I'd be a magician." Barley looked at his watch and then at Walter. "Now what did you want to see me about?"

Walter told him that he was withdrawing his nomination.

"Please," Barley groaned. "I need you."

"So does Maggie. And you're not going to lose me. If you'll have me, I'd like to stay on as an informal adviser."

Barley nodded noncommittally.

"And the next secretary of state?" he asked. "You given any thought to who might fill that role?"

"As a matter of fact, I have. Ted Jorgenson."

"Really?" Barley looked uncertain.

"He was undersecretary in the Sutton era. He worked for me. He's sixty years old, moderate, no political baggage. Well respected."

Glancing over at me, Barley said that the job would make Jorgensen fourth in the line of presidential succession after himself, the speaker of the House and the president pro tem of the Senate. "Something to consider."

"But that probably won't be a factor," Walter replied. "In any case I don't think his ambition ever extended to the White House."

"Nor did mine, but here I am."

"Congress will probably want to deal with this issue soon." I glanced at Walter.

"Maggie?" Barley turned to Walter. "Any news?"

"Optimistic."

"Well that's something." Then looking Walter square in the eye, he asked:

"You sure you want to withdraw?"

"Absolutely."

"Then you should probably make an announcement from the White House. Sooner rather than later."

"Whenever you think appropriate, Mr. President." Walter stood. "I appreciate your understanding." Barley shook hands with Walter. "And of course I'd be glad to have you aboard as an unofficial adviser."

I stood as well.

"Would you mind staying for a minute?" Barley said to me. "We've got a couple more things to go over."

Walter gave me another look before departing.

"Is Walter pulling out just because of Maggie?" Barley asked.

"I don't know, sir." And I truly didn't.

"Do you have confidence in him?"

A good question. Walter had become an enigma to me. To say that I was disappointed to learn that I wouldn't be chief of staff in a Mathews' administration would be an understatement. Since he'd told me, I'd grown ever angrier. Since it was no longer on the table, why bring it up at all? Pointless and tactless—not befitting a secretary of state, even one withdrawing from service. I held my tongue and took a deep breath. Maybe I should cut Walter some slack. With Maggie's collapse he'd lost a lot, not least the first husband title he'd conjured for himself.

"I'll get back to you on that," I said.

"Fine," he said after a pause. "Now what happened in San Francisco? Where do we stand?"

"For the time being I think we're ok. Craig remembers it pretty much the way you do, says he was the aggressor. Jagoda doesn't have his confirmation. Neither Randolph Tice nor Rob Craig is talking, and neither is Craig's mother."

Putting his legal pad on a table, Barley dropped back into his chair. "Sit down, Skeeter. I should be relieved, but I'm not. It's all too humiliating."

"Twenty-five years ago."

"If it gets out, it might as well be yesterday."

"I'm doing what I can to prevent that from happening, sir. You've got other things to think about."

"Do you really think I could sell this Congress on a gas tax big enough to make a difference?"

"I can't say for sure. But oil prices are still down and, if explained properly, the public might come around."

Barley mused. "Walter has a friend in the oil industry he wants me to talk to. Maybe we should get his opinion."

"Who's that, Mr. President?"

"His name..." Barley rummaged through the table in search of a notebook that he then thumbed through. "Here it is. Klaus Hunt. He's in the master Rolodex."

"Shall I see if we can set up an appointment?"

"What have we got to lose?"

The same question I'd asked Walter a couple hours earlier. The answer, of course, was *everything*.

-- 12 --

I just don't know about Walter. Sometimes I think he's Mr. Public Service, with nothing but the good of the country on his mind. Other times I think that's how he wants to be seen, but there's something else going on. When Maggie was...before she collapsed...I tended to give Walter the benefit of the doubt. Now I'm not so sure. I mean, why tell me I was never going to be Maggie's chief of staff? Was he just trying to piss me off, or was he messing with me to some end that he alone knows? Or maybe it's all a game with him. And withdrawing his nomination? What's up with that? I simply can't believe it's only about Maggie. At least Barley agrees that he bears watching. But as far as I'm concerned, that's about all he bears at this point. Besides, there are too many other things to worry about.

The first order of business was to follow-up on the gas tax question. I asked the White House operator to place a call to Klaus Hunt. After a few minutes she called back to say his "assistant" said he was out, so she left a message for him to call back at his earliest convenience.

"You should be hearing from him shortly," the operator added.

"What do you mean?"

"You'll see," she said. "Calls from the White House tend to get returned quickly."

She was right. Not five minutes later, the phone rang. It was the same White House operator.

"I have Mr. Hunt for you."

Did I detect a slight smile in her voice?

"Good afternoon, Mr. Hunt, I'm Skeeter Jamison, President Thompson's chief of staff."

"Yes, I know who you are, Mr. Jamison. What can I do for you?"

I told him that Barley had asked me to meet with him.

"He said you could give me a short course on OPEC and the price of oil."

He laughed. "No such thing as a short course on OPEC. Or, for that matter, on oil pricing." Hunt paused. "I'm not sure when I'll next be in Washington."

"Of course the president would like to meet with you, as well. Have a chat. He said you might like to bring..." I looked at the Rolodex card that had been given to me by Linda, Barley's assistant..."Diane and..." another glance at the card, "...Michael and Charles and Joanie."

I thought the silence at the other end had a different timbre to it.

Finally Hunt spoke. "Well, I suppose there are a few people I should touch base with in D.C. Tomorrow soon enough?"

"Tomorrow would be fine. You and I could meet for half an hour or so, then I'll take you and your family to the president." I looked at my calendar and the president's schedule. "Say, 3:30?"

"Let me check." A moment later he confirmed the time, adding that he had his own plane so booking a flight shouldn't be too difficult.

Assuming he was looking for a laugh, I obliged. "Fine. Just come to the north gate. And bring a government ID, whatever you use to get through airport security."

"I'll do that."

❧ ❧ ❧

Barry Jagoda arrived early and after letting him cool his heels at reception for a few minutes, I had him brought to my office ten minutes before his appointed time with Barley.

We shook hands.

"Congratulations," he said. "Nice digs."

"Thanks. The walls are a bit bare. No time for decorating."

"So what should I know about the president?"

"He's settling in, finding his way around. He seems more comfortable every day. I think he likes it."

"Can I quote you?"

"No, this is just you and him. Keep me out of it."

"What's the latest on Maggie?"

"She's..." I stopped myself. "Same rules as before. Deep background only."

He nodded.

"Maggie is better," I said. "She's conscious. She recognizes people. She smiles and says a few words."

"But..."

"But she still has a long way to go. A *very* long way."

"She'll never be president."

"I didn't say that."

"No, but you *implied* it."

"You *inferred* it.

I didn't want to do semantics.

"Look Barry, I don't know about the future, what's possible medically. I'm no doctor and I'm not sure even the doctors know. All I know is that she's got a long road ahead of her, whether it's weeks, months or, possibly, years. I don't know if she'll ever be her old self. But I'm not ruling it out."

"I understand. I take it asking the president about Maggie is not off limits."

"No," I said, "but I wouldn't want you contradicting him in print with what I just told you."

He agreed. I stood. "It's time. I'll lead the way."

             ❧   ❧   ❧

Klaus Hunt was hardly what I'd expected. He looked more like a Wall Street hedge fund manager or an investment banker than the Texas oilman I'd envisioned. Of course, my idea of what a Texas oilman looked like was based on images of T.

Boone Pickens and George W. Bush. With Hunt was a blond-haired boy I guessed to be about 12 and who I assumed was Hunt's son. He was almost as tall as his dad. We shook hands.

"Skeeter, this is my son Charles. Both Michael and Joanie had things at school they couldn't tear themselves away from. And Diane is in real estate and has a closing today she couldn't postpone. But she asked me to thank the president for inviting her."

"Next time," I said. I told both Hunt and his son that I appreciated their coming all this way on such short notice. "And nice to meet you, too, Charles," I said. Then, turning to Hunt, I continued: "I'm a little surprised. I expected cowboy boots and a ten gallon hat." Charles smiled.

Klaus Hunt laughed—an open, friendly laugh. "You know what they say about hemorrhoids and cowboy boots."

"You got me there."

"Sooner or later every asshole gets 'em." Charles looked embarrassed, but his father laughed even louder. "As for the hat, I've got plenty of Stetsons at home but not enough chutzpah to wear them in Washington."

I liked him. He seemed open and easy to talk to. Then again, I had already noticed that being the president's chief of staff made talking—to *anyone*—so much easier. If I said something even remotely humorous, I'd get a laugh.

"Enough small talk," Hunt said. "What is it you want to know?"

I told him I needed to understand oil prices, what's driving them, how long they're likely to stay low, what OPEC is up to. Oh, and climate change and its relationship to oil..."

"Whoa there pardner. I'm on a plane back to Houston tomorrow night. We don't have enough time to solve *all* the planet's problems."

"I'll settle for Oil 101."

Hunt gave me an appraising look. After a while he took a deep breath.

"Ok. I'll give you an overview," he said. "For much of the past two decades, oil prices have been high, around a hundred bucks a barrel, due to rising consumption in China and diminished production in Iraq. As with any commodity, when production doesn't keep up with demand, prices rise."

I'd always been a chronic note-taker, a habit that had saved a lot of embarrassment, especially in the political arena, where people tended to deny things they'd said if the winds started blowing from a different direction. But listening to Hunt was like trying to keep up with a fast talking college professor.

Higher prices had made new kinds of drilling, fracking mainly, economically feasible, particularly in the US and Canada. With the 2008 worldwide recession, Europe and China cut back on consumption and prices began to fall. When OPEC met in November 2014, everybody expected them to cut production to get prices back up. But led by Saudi Arabia, which still calls most of the shots at OPEC, they *didn't* cut production. Most analysts think the Saudis hoped the lower prices would hurt the U.S. shale oil boom. So the price of oil plummeted. In the U.S., consumers enjoyed the cheapest gasoline prices in years. But oil producing countries like Russia, Venezuela and Iran were hurt bad."

"But oil's come back, hasn't it?" I asked.

"A bit, yes, but nowhere near where it was just a few years ago."

"Isn't that good for us? Cheap oil, cheap gasoline, cheap home heating oil."

"In the near term, yes, but global instability is no good for anybody, including the U.S."

"Will gas prices stay low?"

"Short answer: yes. But they've already risen somewhat and they're likely to rise more, if not right away, over the next few years."

"Ok, but with prices low, wouldn't this be a good time for a gasoline tax increase?"

"Why would you want to do that?"

"Our infrastructure—roads and bridges—is crumbling. Wouldn't such a tax be a good way to pay for their repair?"

"Maybe in an ideal world, but Barley would be pilloried for suggesting one. Political suicide. It'd take somewhere around fifty cents a gallon to make a real difference. He'd never get a fifty cent gas tax through Congress, not *this* Congress."

"Ok, I got it. So from your perspective what do we do about global warming?"

Hunt frowned. "Are you asking about alternative energy?"

"That's a start."

"Well, I hate to rain on your parade, but alternative energy is just a drop in the bucket. You can have all the solar and wind you want, even nuclear, which ain't gonna happen, and it won't change the fact that fossil fuels aren't going anywhere. Never mind China, with a million new cars on the road every year, but think about India, Afghanistan, Iraq, Iran, and the list goes on and on. Each of them is using more coal and oil every year than the year before."

"You're saying we're doomed?"

"Not necessarily. Those new sources can help, no question. So does reducing carbon emissions by improving efficiency and conserving usage. Also, encouraging plant growth, which traps atmospheric carbon. But the real answer is technology. Innovation. There're a lot of smart people at a lot of smart companies working on combatting global warming."

"Examples?"

"You want me to be specific?"

"Please."

"There's a company in California, Carbonaide I believe is the name. It's turning millions of tons of carbon into liquid that can be stored underground. That's one. There's another that's adding iron ore to oceans to promote algae growth. More algae means more underwater plants to absorb carbon. I don't remember the name of that one, but I can email it to you when I get back if you like."

"Yes," I said, "I would."

"There's another idea I've only read about," Hunt said. "Something about adding droplets of water to the atmosphere to increase cloud cover and reduce solar radiation. I forget just how that helps control climate, but apparently it does. I'll find out more and let you know."

"Thanks. I didn't know any of this."

"Well not many people do," Hunt said. "And there are no guarantees. But the more you and Barley can do to stimulate technological innovation, the sooner we're going to bring climate change under control."

"Makes sense," I said.

"If I can leave you with one thought," Hunt said, "it's this: fossil fuels are here to stay. We can manage them better, we can make our use of them more efficient, and we can learn to rely more on alternative energy sources. But we're not going to halt climate change by controlling fossil fuels alone. We have to find innovative, proactive, technological solutions."

I winced at his use of "proactive," which I think should be banned from the language. But I'd learned something, and I thanked him.

"Not a problem," he said. "Happy to be of service."

Turning to Charles I said, "Enough science for one afternoon. How 'bout we go see the president?"

Charles nodded, then looked at his dad.

With that I led the way to the Oval Office.

+++

ACTING PRESIDENT'S FIRST INTERVIEW

by Barry Jagoda
Cleveland Plain-Dealer

WASHINGTON, D.C. --- Acting President Barley Thompson is a man in a hurry with a lot on his mind. "I have many things I want to do," he said today in his first interview since taking the oath as vice and acting president of the United States. "And I'm anxious to do them."

In a wide-ranging conversation in the Oval office on his eighth day on the job, the vice president appeared eager to carry out the

106

duties of his new position—the first vice president to be designated acting president, unsubordinated to a serving vice president.

His running mate and the president elect, Margaret ("Maggie") Mathews, remains in "guarded" condition in Sibley Hospital in Washington, D.C. Because of her incapacitation, the result of a ruptured aneurysm she suffered on January 10, she was unable to attend her inauguration or to be sworn in as president. After Mr. Thompson was sworn in as vice president on January 20, Congress conveyed the powers of the presidency to him on a temporary basis.

"She's doing well," the vice president said of Mrs. Mathews, who he has visited twice since she was admitted to the hospital. "She's getting better every day, thank heaven. She's talking and even walking on her own. And we're all very hopeful that she will assume her rightful duties in the not very distant future."

Other sources have suggested that the president-elect's recovery is taking longer than her doctors first hoped and was not imminent.

"It's taken me awhile," the president said, gesturing toward the White House grounds beyond a window, "but I'm finding my way around this place and have begun settling in. I'm happy to say that Mrs. Thompson is also."

Turning to matters of state, Thompson said his first priority was "protecting the nation and its people." To that end, he said he "hoped Congress would see fit to give the Defense Department the 5% budget increase it has requested." When asked about his other priorities, he listed repairing the nation's infrastructure and introducing educational reforms "so that our schools are more about children learning and less about their ability to take tests.

"You might say that for however long I'm here [in the White House], my priorities are defense, roads, bridges and schools."

Unsure where the money for infrastructure would come from he and his advisors, including Secretary Designate of the Treasury Adrian Hawkings, were "exploring several options.

"At this point, I'm not ruling anything out. George H. W. Bush made that mistake, and I have no intention of repeating it. But neither do I have any plans to raise taxes at this time."

He said he thought that the radical Muslim terrorist groups Al Qaeda and ISIL (aka ISIS and the Islamic State) were "equally dangerous and equally worrisome, along with other less well-known terrorist groups. We have to be vigilant everywhere in the world. Where there is a lack of human rights, where there is poverty, where education is substandard—these are all breeding grounds for hostility, much of it focused on the United States.

"People look to the U.S., quite rightfully, as the most successful, freest, wealthiest nation on earth, with the most opportunities. And to some people, particularly those denied the freedoms and opportunities we enjoy, that spells resentment and anger. Even hatred. So we have to be vigilant 24/7."

Thompson said he was encouraged

that Russian President Vladimir Putin had not pursued territorial expansion beyond the Crimean area of Ukraine, but "We're not out of the woods yet. With oil revenues way below historical norms in Russia, President Putin has been focusing on economic problems at home. But that could change."

Asked how he would assess his new job after a bit more than a week, Thompson said, "You know, I approached this job with great sadness because of President-elect Mathews' hospitalization. And with real concern that I might not be up to filling her shoes. But before she was taken ill, she had picked a terrific team, and the longer I'm here, the more I feel that as a team, we can accomplish things. We can make our country better."

-- 13 --

In the White House media room, with its bank of TV's tuned to various networks, all were muted except CNN where Walter Mathews announced he was withdrawing his nomination for secretary of state. Walter being Walter had managed to create drama around this disclosure, making the announcement from Sibley, alongside Maggie's neurosurgeon, Carlton Dawson.

Walter had given his wife's recovery as his reason for rescinding—Maggie had to be his top priority, he said. He just wouldn't be able to provide the necessary level of energy to run the State Department, with all the travel it entailed. Having done the job before, he knew the rigors involved.

"Did the possibility of a difficult confirmation process influence your decision at all?" Anderson Cooper asked.

"Not in the least," Walter replied. "As a matter of fact, after talking with several on the committee, I was confident it would have gone smoothly."

"Have you and the vice president talked about anyone else for the position?"

"I've made a suggestion, but I'm unaware if he's acted on it."

"What about Maggie? How does she feel about your exit?"

"Why don't you ask her that question?"

"What!" I shouted at the TV. "What the hell are you doing?"

A couple of staff members who had stepped into the room looked at me quizzically. It was ten o'clock in the morning. From the president's printed schedule that was posted daily, I knew that Barley was now meeting with a congressional delegation in the East Room. I was pretty sure he knew nothing of the circus unfolding at Sibley.

Dr. Dawson smiled into the camera. After explaining that Maggie had been in and out of consciousness over the last week, and this was the first full twenty-four hour period when she'd been fully alert, he turned to Cooper and said, "I'm confident that she would be very happy to see you."

Now Dawson, followed by a beaming Walter, then Cooper, sauntered down the hospital corridor before stopping at Maggie's door.

Should I get Barley, or wait until this theater-of-the-absurd had played out? Why hadn't Walter, who no doubt was the ringmaster, let us know that he was going to pull this stunt? And why had he chosen now, the moment he was backing out of a cabinet post to do it? Why hadn't the White House been informed? (I would of course have advised against this charade.) Perhaps knowing I'd be opposed was reason enough for Walter to keep us in the dark. He grew more mystifying—make that maddening—by the day.

Still, political operatives seldom made public moves unless they had a very good reason. On a personal level, Walter was clearly sending a message. I suspected it was aimed at Barley and, by extension, me. Was he trying to warn us that it was just a question of time before Maggie would be back on her feet and looking to reclaim her rightful place on the throne?

"Five minutes only," Dawson said, as the door opened: long shot of Maggie, the head of her hospital bed raised so that we could see that her face had been made up. A French beret at a jaunty angle covered her head, which had been shaved for surgery. Wearing a blue silk robe, she actually seemed to smile into the camera. Was there that twinkle in her eyes I knew so well?

While seeing Maggie alive and alert gave me a jolt of jubilance, questions about the entire unscripted event left me more angry than perplexed. Couldn't they have waited another twenty-four hours?

Despite my disapproval I watched transfixed as the camera zoomed in on Maggie. Cooper stood at the foot of her bed, while the neurosurgeon and Walter took up positions on either side of her. Walter held his wife's left hand; Maggie turned her head slightly to look up at him. Without question it was obvious she'd been prepped for the event.

Word must have gotten out in the White House because the media room was now filled with staffers.

"Sorry to barge in like this, Mrs. Mathews," Cooper said.

Maggie's smile remained; Walter chuckled.

"But the entire country, the world, has been anxious for news of you," Anderson continued. "It's been quite an ordeal. How are you managing?"

I saw her mouth move, heard her voice, but without understanding what she said.

"What did she say?" I asked.

"I couldn't make it out," a staffer replied.

As if on cue, Walter provided her scripted answer, "Free at last."

The camera moved to Anderson, who wore a broad smile. "She's feeling free at last," he announced. "Well, Maggie Mathews' sense of humor seems to be intact."

Maggie lifted her hand away from Walter's and gave a twitch of a wave in Anderson's direction. It was impossible not to notice that her other hand, stretched out on the bedcovers along her right side, did not move at all.

"And how do you feel about your husband's decision to step away from politics?" Anderson asked.

Maggie returned her left hand to Walter's. Looking up at him, she said, for all to hear: "Free at last."

≈ ≈ ≈

The networks, major and minor, went into full Maggie mode. The parade of doctors slash consultants, especially those with some knowledge of aneurysms and strokes, marched back on the air. Each would be asked more or less the same question. What did this portend? And the answer, inevitably, was the same: Good news certainly for Maggie. Still hard to predict a long-term outcome. They analyzed her makeup, her expression, the color of her bathrobe—one noted that it matched the bedspread. The lack of movement in her right hand was also significant, as was her initial difficulty speaking. But that only heightened the triumph when she got it. Free at last, indeed.

Once the medicos had weighed in, the pundits had their frenzied say. What would this mean for the presidency?

"A game changer for sure."

"Not much at this point."

How would it affect the role of the acting president?

"Definitely weakened."

"Strengthened, no question."

"You'd think nobody had work to do around here," I said to the mob of staffers, all of us entranced by the spectacle. "Let's get to it. We've got a country to run."

Barley had fifteen minutes to spare between his time with the congressional delegation and before his twelve o'clock lunch with the forty-two governors who had committed to attending. Republicans still dominated the state offices. Knowing the importance of getting the states behind his programs, Barley had committed to working with them. It had been one of my first political directives: call in the governors.

"What's with Walter?" Barley asked when I opened the door to in his smaller private office just off the Oval.

"Oh, not much." I said, "He's only succeeded in shifting the national conversation from you back to Maggie and himself. In one highly coordinated maneuver."

"Deliberate?" Barley asked.

"Well, let's put it this way, he didn't bother filling us in on his intentions."

"How much harm done?"

"Hard to tell. But the discourse in this town changes as fast as the click of the remote."

"What do you suggest?"

"For public comment, we're delighted to see Maggie doing so well, we wish her Godspeed, etcetera, etcetera."

"And Walter? You still want him as an advisor?"

"I want him closer than ever," I replied. "Better inside the hen house where we can keep an eye on him than prowling the perimeter out of sight."

Barley clapped me on the shoulder. "Good man, Skeeter. I know your strong feelings for Maggie. So I'm particularly glad I've got you aboard. Don't forget we're meeting with the cabinet nominees at two thirty." Barley winked. "I believe Ms. Mercado will be with us."

I missed Maggie. I'm sorry she wasn't in the White House, but in politics, loyalty is fungible—emotions offered up only one form of commerce.

I ate lunch alone in my office. A ham and cheese sandwich on a baguette from Bon Marche. Once a week I cleared the nearest store's supply, also pocketing extra packages of mayo and mustard. At home, my freezer was stocked with them. Next month I'd switch to roast beef— assuming of course I still had a job that made a brown bag indispensable: in politics, one of the few things that was.

❧ ❧ ❧

Angela Mercado, in a slate gray pantsuit that fit her tall, lean figure perfectly, sat near one end of the oblong table in the room dedicated to cabinet meetings, as well as other official business where large attendance and photo ops were *de rigeur*. Twelve other cabinet nominees sat around the table. Walter Mathews was conspicuously absent.

Sitting along the back wall with a few other staffers, I'd positioned myself in a direct line of sight with Angela; occasionally our eyes met. We hadn't spoken since the inaugural dance marathon more than a week before.

Barley laid out his agenda for his first six months; most of the items he'd already made public to Barry Jagoda at their first interview. Now he sought comments from the prospective heads of the departments who might be implementing his plans.

Morgan Walker spoke up, impressive in his command of how the Pentagon would run under his leadership. Essentially leaner meant meaner. Underused or outmoded bases would be closed or combined with others whose strategic functions might overlap. He had every intention of keeping his budget proposal below previous administrations. (The first time I'd ever heard *that* from a secretary of defense.) He talked about the continuing war against ISIL, emphasizing that there could be no military solution to the conflict. It had to be political, and it had to come from joint efforts within the Middle East nations themselves. He advocated greater cooperation between the departments of state and defense working in tandem to sway public opinion, at home and abroad, away from a climate of war and into the social and political realms where true change might take place. While drones might be cost-efficient in their targeted use, he told them, they were of doubtful efficacy in changing hearts and minds in the countries they were deployed. On the contrary, they were undoubtedly radical Islam's most effective recruiting tool. Walker recommended stricter control and civilian oversight to gauge their overall effectiveness.

Hard to believe I was listening to a former Republican congressman from Wisconsin. More kudos for Maggie's instincts. I thought if anyone at defense could sell this ambitious and controversial blueprint to Congress, it would be Walker.

Barley called on Paul McNulty, the nominee for secretary of labor, for an update on efforts to coordinate with the unions to divert a mass transportation strike.

"It's in the works," McNulty said. "We're meeting tomorrow and we expect to make a joint statement afterwards. We've both been invited to appear on "Meet the Press" on Sunday."

"Excellent," Barley said. "Good work."

"Just keep the metro running for a few hours," Morgan said with a smile. "I've got to get home tonight."

ல் ல் ல்

I caught up with Angela as she walked out the East Wing door to an awaiting car. "You got a sec?" I asked.

She smiled, a steady gaze, as if she could see right through me. "Of course. I've got a question for you, too."

We walked across the East Lawn toward the Southeast gate and probably into the picture behind a TV reporter, bundled in an overcoat and scarf, who was doing a stand-up for one of the networks.

"The president didn't mention immigration," Angela said. "Was that deliberate?"

"It's a work in progress," I answered. "We're trying to work up initiatives we stand a chance of getting through Congress. At the moment, immigration doesn't have a prayer."

"As you know, it's an issue close to my heart. My parents left Cuba in 1960, just after the revolution and ten years before I was born in Miami."

"It's one of the things I want to talk to you about."

"And the other?"

"I was wondering if we might have a drink sometime?"

"And when were you thinking of, Skeeter?"

"How about this evening at the Hawk 'n' Dove?"

"You really think that's wise? You and I having a drink together in public. You know Washington."

"Do you have a better idea?"

"My daughter will be home from school this weekend. Why don't you come for dinner on Saturday? You can meet her."

"I'd love to."

"Seven thirty?"

"I'll be there."

Angela extracted a business card from her shoulder bag and handed it to me. "Here's the address."

"Thanks. I'll bring wine."

"And my daughter will chaperone." She winked. "I've been told of your reputation."

I smiled. Angela walked back to her waiting car.

I was still at my desk a little after seven p.m. when news broke of an explosion on the metro's Blue Line at the Arlington Cemetery stop. All I could think of was Morgan Walker's joke about keeping the train running until he got home.

-- 14 --

Minutes after the news of the explosion broke, my cellphone buzzed and displayed a one-word message: "A-Rod." Uh oh, I thought. A-Rod stood not for Alex Rodriguez, the controversial New York Yankees infielder, but for "All (direct) Reports on Deck." When we'd set up the acronym a few days earlier, we never thought—at least, I never did—we'd be employing it so soon.

On that day, "A-Rod" meant that Barley's chief of staff, press secretary and three special assistants should get their asses to the Oval Office pronto. There were other HOD ("Hands on Deck") codes for White House personnel and for cabinet members. From the looks of things, the HOD phone tree was working well enough—several "former A-students," as Washington's bureaucrats and other municipal worker bees were sometimes called, were already moving about purposefully, barking into telephones or punching computer keyboards in cubicles.

My office was less than a one-minute walk from the Oval, but by the time I got there, Barley, in khakis and a sport shirt sans tie, had arrived from Blair House. He was on the phone, pacing like a caged tiger. All three monitors on his console TV were showing Rosslyn Metro station shrouded in smoke and chaos. Barley had muted the sound, but from their dazed and disheveled looks, I saw what had to be surviving passengers talking into cellphones or standing stock still with glazed expressions on their faces. A TV crew's klieg lights illuminated one end of the station, where firemen in heavy yellow slickers, EMS personnel and police bustled about without discernable purpose. Now the feed cut to a reporter interviewing a passenger.

"No, we can wait," Barley said into the phone. "It'll take a while to know anything."

"Jeb Merriweather, Homeland Security," he said to me, after hanging up. "Coming in from Bethesda. ETA 20 minutes."

"Doug Black?" I asked. He was the FBI Director.

"On his way, and so is Patricia." Although I'd never met her, I knew Patricia Washington was the aptly named D.C. police chief.

"Who else?"

"Dick Alison. He called; on his way." Alison was Barley's choice for CIA, yet to be confirmed.

"What about Donner?" Dubois's CIA director had agreed to stay on until Alison got confirmed. Josh Donner.

"On his way also." Just what we needed: two CIA honchos.

Barley shrugged when I rolled my eyes.

"And the NSA?" I asked.

"Timothy O'Shea"—Dubois's director—"will be a little late and Bill Johnson"—Barley's unconfirmed director—"is out of town." Thanks for small mercies.

"Walter?"

Barley shook his head. "Need to know, only."

"Angela?"

Another headshake. "Sorry."

"So what do we know?"

"Not much yet. But from the TV, it looks bad. A bomb, probably in the first car, stopped the train cold and caused a lot of injuries. And deaths."

As if on cue, Patricia Washington appeared at the doorway. A tall, slender African-American woman who looked to be in her mid-40s, she conveyed both strength and competence in her tailored dark-blue uniform.

"Come in, chief," Barley said. "You know Skeeter?"

Washington gave me a tight smile as we shook hands.

Barley said her timing was excellent. "Skeeter just asked what we know."

"Before we get to that, let me tell you what's been done. We immediately contacted the Arlington police and asked them to request our assistance, which they did. We're now a combined task force, and we've closed both the Rosslyn and Arlington Cemetery stations. As you may know, the Blue Line between them runs deep—between 90 and 110 feet, in a tunnel blasted out of solid rock. That's why the explosion was contained—no surface damage—which is the only good news. The bad news is that because it's so contained, the wreckage—and casualties with it—is massive. Bodies hurled forward when the blast brought the train to a sudden stop. We're talking hours to evacuate the dead and wounded and months to repair the damage. Maybe longer."

"How many dead?" Barley asked.

"We're still working on that. But it looks like everybody in the first car. Twenty. Thirty. Maybe more."

"Terrorists?" he asked.

"Almost certainly, especially considering where the blast occurred."

"Meaning?"

"The next stop was Arlington National Cemetery. We think that's where whoever did this wanted it to happen. For maximum imagery, but they miscalculated."

I looked up to see FBI Director Black at the door and press secretary Charley Millbank just behind him. Black was in a grey suit and red tie. Charley wore a blazer over grey slacks and no tie.

"Director Black," said Barley, motioning them in. Although Black had agreed to stay on as director, Barley had only just met him. They hadn't had a single extended conversation.

"Mr. President," Black said as they shook hands.

Turning to Charley during the awkward silence that followed, I said, "The president will want to address the nation as soon as possible. Start thinking about what he should say."

"Somber and resolute," Barley added, "beginning with 'our hearts go out...' "

"Right," Charley replied.

"But don't go anywhere yet," I said. "We need to agree on what you can say..."

"... and what you *can't*," Black completed my sentence.

"Chief Washington was just saying it looks like terrorism," Barley said to him. "Do you agree?"

"Sure looks like it. Certainly a bomb. There's nothing on those trains or in the tunnels that could do this kind of damage. But I don't think you should use the word until we know more, get some idea who's behind it."

All heads turned in my direction, and I could feel my hands go clammy when I said I disagreed. "Anybody watching on TV will be thinking terrorism. If we don't at least mention it, we'll look out of it, or worse."

"I agree," Black said. "Okay to mention it but nothing specific. Say we're pursuing all leads, *including* terrorism."

"Where are we on who did it?" Barley asked.

"We're on it," Washington answered, noncommittally.

"It's Virginia," Black said, turning to her. "You don't have jurisdiction, so we're taking the lead. Our bomb squad's in place. Plus forensic and dogs."

Washington said nothing.

"Don't forget Homeland Security," Barley said, filling the silence. Looking around the room, he added. "Jason is on his way."

"I'm sure he'll be happy to leave the on-scene investigation to us," Black said. "Jason and his people will do what they do best: checking traffic and fine-tooth combing their watch list."

"Traffic?" Barley asked.

"Meaning chatter," Black said. "Communications, foreign and domestic. Josh Donner and Mike Rogers should do the same. And of course Josh will be working his sources and Mike will be looking for phone patterns."

"Did I hear my name?" Josh Donner spoke from the doorway.

Barley told him to come in. "We were just talking about who does what."

"And I just got off the phone with Langley. Nothing

from the field."

"Meaning what?" I asked.

"Meaning we've no indication from field agents of any international involvement, at least not yet. No claims, no signatures. Which doesn't mean the ISISs of the world aren't responsible. But so far, the patterns aren't there."

"Okay, I think it's time for you to get cracking," I said to Charley. "Like the president said, 'terrible tragedy, hearts go out, police, FBI, CIA and NSA, Homeland Security all pursuing leads.' And make it..."

"Forget the alphabet soup," Barley interrupted. "Just say all intelligence resources are being brought to bear, words to that effect. Pursuing leads is good. Whoever did this will pay. Make it personal. I will not rest until whoever did this is brought to justice, that's a pledge."

"Yes sir," Charley answered, getting up to leave.

"And Charley, " Barley added. "Not too flowery. Keep it short." Then, turning to me, he said, "I think you should go."

Which meant he was dismissing me? For a second, my heart sank.

"Go where?" Soon I'd recognize those two words as possibly the stupidest question ever posed in the Oval Office. To my relief, nobody seemed to notice.

"Get down to Rosslyn. Let them know you're my personal rep. Tell 'em I'll be there myself as soon as I'm done with TV. "

"You think that's wise?" Black asked.

"Wise or not, it's what I'm doing," Barley said.

"I'll alert Secret Service," I said.

"Good," Washington said. "And we'll handle Rosslyn station security."

"All right, you two better head out," Barley said.

As Chief Washington and I left the Oval Office, we bumped into an out-of-breath Jason Merriweather, head of Homeland Security. In jeans and a plaid shirt, he looked like he'd walked out of an L.L. Bean catalog. He and I had met at the inauguration, and Washington and Merriweather had worked together under Dubois, so introductions were unnecessary.

"I'll meet you at the portico in five," Washington said to me after greeting Merriweather with a quick hug. "I've got a couple of calls to make."

Once she was gone, Merriweather asked me what he'd missed.

"Not so much. Everybody agrees it looks like terrorism. Otherwise the meeting was mostly pissing over territory: who does what to whom. With the FBI claiming on-scene priority."

"What else is new?"

"I think there's plenty to go around. This is ugly."

"Where're you off to?"

"Rosslyn station. To show the flag and advance the president's visit." I took out my wallet and handed him a business card that had my cell number on it.

"Whatever you find out, no matter how insignificant, give me a call. I'll take it to the president."

"That may be sooner than you think."

"How so?"

"There's nothing firm yet, but there's a Muslim kid we've been watching, local guy, maybe 19, lives in Southeast. He's been sending some interesting emails, a lot of them in the last few hours."

"Interesting?"

"Meaning they don't make a lot of sense. It looks like bad code, probably improvised, and his emails have gone out to four or five people, all domestic. The replies are in the same gibberish. As I said, we've had an eye on this kid."

"Have you deciphered the emails?"

"Not yet. It wasn't a priority until a couple of hours ago. We're working on it."

Jerking a thumb toward the Oval Office, I asked if he was going to tell them about the kid.

"I'd rather hold off until we've nailed it down. But you can brief the president."

"I will. And don't forget to let me know the minute you learn anything."

"You got it." He took a deep breath before opening the door to the Oval Office.

After I'd briefed the Secret Service on Barley's plans, Washington was waiting for me at the portico. We walked through the visitor's gate to a Ford Escort police car parked just outside. Although she rated a driver, she got in behind the wheel and turned the ignition key.

"I came up the ranks," she explained, probably because she'd read my expression. "I always loved vehicular patrol, so I rarely miss an opportunity."

Turning on the siren, she made a left and headed south on 17th street, accelerating while neither of us spoke. Less than ten minutes after leaving the White House, we pulled up to Rosslyn station. The entrance was blocked by sawhorses and police tape marked "Do Not Cross." Five ambulances from five different hospitals idled nearby, their drivers waiting. Just inside the station, under an open-air roof, about twenty men and women, some holding cameras, were milling about. I spotted Barry Jagoda among them but avoided him. This wasn't the time.

Although the escalator was still working, Washington took the stairs, and I followed her. There must have been a couple hundred of them, so my legs had turned to rubber by the time we reached the southbound platform. A man with a badge pinned to his dirty raincoat came over to us, and I thought of the endless reruns of Columbo I'd seen over the years. (More than one girlfriend had pointed out that my taste in popular culture was oddly anachronistic.) My puzzling subconscious chose that moment to remind me that the TV detective was based on a gumshoe in Dostoevsky's *Notes from the Underground*. With so many more important things to think of, why in the world had I thought of that?

Anyway, "Columbo," as I now thought of him, brought me back to reality. "It's a mess, chief," he said to Washington. "The train's a couple hundred yards down the track. Getting survivors off has been our first priority, after securing the area, that is. But it's slow going."

"How many we talking about?" Washington asked.

"Well, maybe seventy made it off on their own, including a senator." He pulled a notebook from his pocket.

"Senator Morgan Walker."

"Ex- senator," I said. "He's up for secretary of defense."

Looking at me, then at "Columbo," she said, "Charlie, this is Skeeter Jamison, POTUS' chief of staff." Then, "Skeeter, Charlie Bruhn, my operations captain."

"Where's Walker now?" I asked as we shook hands.

Bruhn looked around. "I dunno. I asked him to stick nearby, but he may have left. It's been a bit busy here. As I was saying, about seventy—seventy-five—people walked off the train and made it through the tunnel to the station. Walker said another fifty or so were unable to walk. The medics are with them now. He also said he thought everybody in the first car was toast."

Washington closed her eyes and grimaced, but I wasn't sure whether from contemplating the many dead or Bruhn's use of "toast." "Where're the Feds?" she asked.

"Eight of them. All at or on the train, I think. Three with dogs. Three more from forensics plus two special agents."

"And the media?"

"Upstairs."

"Good. Keep 'em there, POTUS should be here within the hour. Set up a secure perimeter around the station—no one inside without credentials—plus another area within the perimeter. I don't want any media too near the president. He may want to come down here, although I'd advise against it."

"I'll tell him there's not much to see," I said.

Washington told Bruhn to alert the FBI, Virginia police and Fire departments together with the local EMS. "One rep from each to answer any questions the president may have. One pool print reporter, one TV crew and that's it."

When I said I'd like to speak to an agent, Washington asked Charlie if there were any Feds there now. After looking around the platform for a moment, Bruhn cocked his head toward a slender man in a brown suit talking on his cell. The three of us made our way to the FBI agent and introduced ourselves. Special Agent Kit Carson wore an expression that said no wisecracks.

I asked him what he knew "officially or otherwise."

"Not much."

"Look, I'm here on behalf of the president. You can tell me what you've learned."

Carson looked uncomfortable. Washington stared at him and Bruhn said nothing.

"Nothing official, but the first car is as bad as anything I've ever seen. Mostly blood and body parts of maybe thirty people. No survivors. Total carnage."

I asked what else he'd learned, and he said that was about it.

"What *else*?" I repeated.

Carson looked at Bruhn, then at Washington, and back at me. "This is very preliminary. From the splatter and what's left of the bodies, it looks like the explosion was almost dead center in the car. You don't leave a bomb dead center on a subway car, then walk away."

"A suicide bomber?" I asked

"It looks that way."

I shook my head, trying to take it in.

"That's everything." Carson added. "We should know more when forensics is done. But that'll be hours."

As I thanked him, my phone vibrated. Merriweather had timed it perfectly.

"Aashif Abaan," he said.

"What?"

"Aashif Abaan, the kid I told you about. One phrase turns up again and again in his emails: 'Arlington Cemetery.' At this point, that's all we've got except for one other thing."

"Which is?"

"He's gone missing."

"Listen, Jason."

"I am."

Telling him I was at Rosslyn station, I summarized what I'd just learned from Carson.

"Katy bar the door," he answered.

++

32 DEAD IN METRO EXPLOSION
by Barry Jagoda
Cleveland Plain-Dealer

WASHINGTON, D.C. --- An explosion police say was from a bomb detonated on a Blue Line Metro train at 6:56 p.m. this evening, leaving 32 people dead and 43 injured. The explosion prompted police and Homeland Security officials to mount a massive search for the perpetrator or perpetrators and sent the newly-inaugurated acting-President Barley Thompson rushing to the scene. The explosion halted all Blue Line trains and threw the Metro system into disarray, stranding thousands of commuters during the evening rush hour.

"We will find the cowardly scum who did this," the president said before television cameras at the White House just minutes after the explosion. "We will pursue them to the gates of Hell, and we will punish them to the fullest extent of the law, so help me God." The bombing marked Thompson's first crisis, only one week after his inauguration, following the incapacitation of President-elect Maggie Mathews, who remains hospitalized with a ruptured aneurysm at Sibley Hospital here in the nation's capital.

Immediately after his White House television appearance, the president departed by limousine for the Rosslyn (Va.) metro station nearest the explosion, arriving less than an hour after the disaster occurred. Speaking to reporters there, he called the explosion "an act of cold, calculating, unmitigated terrorism." Appearing both confident and forceful in his new role, the nation's chief executive remained at the station for more than an hour, personally thanking individual police, firemen and EMS workers.

Metro police said that the Blue Line train had been headed for the Arlington Cemetery station when, less than a minute after departing Rosslyn, a bomb detonated, halting the train and apparently killing all of the passengers in its first car. Names of the dead have yet to be released.

According to police, injuries to 43 other passengers in the train's other six cars were the result of impact within the train when it stopped abruptly following the explosion. A spokesperson for George Washington Hospital said 16 people, including a mother and her 3-year-old toddler, were admitted for treatment of injuries that included broken arms, a broken hip and several concussions. All 43 are expected to recover.

Washington police Chief Patricia Washington said police, in concert with investigators from the National Transportation Safety Board (NTSB), were pursuing several leads but had no suspects at the time she spoke, a little after noon. She said that while the damage bore the earmarks of a crude bomb, which might suggest a small number of perpetrators, "nothing has been ruled out. "

According to a Department of Homeland spokesman, there was no unusual "chatter" among known terrorist organizations before the explosion, unlike before 9/11 and other international terrorist attacks. He also noted that as of 7:00 p.m., no terrorist organization had claimed responsibility for today's attack.

Joseph McCullough, a NTSB spokesperson, said investigators would be on the scene for at least two weeks and the investigation itself could last six months to a year or even longer. "We want to assure the friends and loved ones of those who perished or were injured today that we will get to the bottom of this, no matter how long it takes." He added that initial examination of the first car led him to believe that TNT was the primary explosive. "But that's just a preliminary impression."

Among the train's passengers was Senator and Secretary of Defense designate Morgan Walker, who said he was on his way to the Pentagon for a meeting. Several passengers credited Walker, who was in the second car, with taking charge of the passengers and leading them to safety at Rosslyn station.

"He was terrific," said Robert Rowan, a director of communications for the Department of Agriculture and a passenger in the second car with Walker. "He calmed everybody down, got medical help to the injured and led us all out of that Hell-hole. I don't know what we would have done without him."

Madeline Jaynes, a civilian translator for the Pentagon, agreed. "I think he saved our lives," she said.

-- 15 --

After the Metro bombing, checkpoints were set up throughout the city, its airports, Federal buildings, Amtrak and all bridges crossing the Potomac. All traffic into and out of Virginia was halted, while a joint task force searched vehicles. A customary thirty-minute drive to McLean could now take an hour or even two, depending on the day and time.

During the first twenty-four hours after the bombing, the capital was as deserted as I'd ever seen it, but life began to return to a semblance of normal on the second day. A wet snowfall with temperatures in the mid-30s covered the city in slush.

By Saturday evening and my "date" with Angela, the gridlock had abated. Leaving early enough to accommodate delays, I was surprised to have only a twenty-minute wait at the Theodore Roosevelt Memorial bridge before showing my White House pass and driver's license to armed military personnel. They shined flashlights under and around the car and dangled a mirrored wand beneath the Forester's chassis before waving me through. Even so, I arrived in McLean more or less on time.

Angela had called on Friday to cancel our dinner, citing concern for my security. But she'd relented when I reminded her that the president had urged everyone to go about business as usual. I was looking forward to seeing her. Apart from any possible romantic notions of mine, I also had important questions to ask her.

My GPS made it easy to find Angela's two-story colonial house on a cul de sac among old growth trees. A stained-glass fanlight window above the door reflected the home's warm interior. I walked onto the porch bearing two bottles of Rioja. Before I could knock, the door opened and Angela stood in front of me wearing a pair of dark slacks and a cable knit sweater.

Despite her smile when she invited me in, I saw tension in her features, a look shared by just about everyone in Washington the past few days. People were grim-faced and anxious.

"What a scary time, Skeeter. It must be chaos in the White House."

I nodded. "You got that right," I said. Things were certainly out of sync there.

Angela took my coat, and hung it on a peg rack attached to the wall by the door. Following her down the hall, I passed a small family room that looked inviting. Two settees faced a fireplace and a crackling fire; a hook rug covered much of the wide-board flooring.

At the end of the hallway, a large kitchen branched off the back of the house, where the aroma of roasting meat wafted from a warm oven. I suddenly felt weak in the knees— from want of sleep and the lack of a decent meal in several days, or just the sense of peacefulness that arose in the midst of such disquiet. Putting the wine on the tiled island counter in the center of the kitchen, I sat in one of the ladder-backed bar chairs.

"You look a little pale, Skeeter."

"A glass of wine and some food should perk me up. It smells good in here."

"Roast pork." Angela examined one of the bottles of wine. "A Rioja. Perfect with pig," she said. She pulled the cork and poured two glasses. I wasn't sure the wine would revive me or put me to sleep, or which would be more welcome.

I asked about her daughter.

"With all the brouhaha, we decided it would be better if she stayed at school. All the delays would have meant we wouldn't have had much time together before she'd have to head back."

"So no chaperone. Hmm."

"You're an attractive and interesting man." Angela sipped her wine. "But I'd never get involved with someone I might have to work with."

"I learned a long time ago never to say never."

"You're a risk taker."

"That's my job. And the nature of politics."

We clinked glasses and drank. The wine hit my near empty stomach and went straight to my head.

"Do you know anything more than the newspapers about the bombing?" Angela asked. "Anything you can talk about?"

"To you, yes. We're not releasing it yet, but it was a suicide bombing. A local Muslim kid from a middle-class family. As it happened, Homeland has had an eye on him for a few weeks."

"Is Merriweather still in charge there?"

"Yeah, a good man, like a lot of Dubois' holdovers. But not having our own people in place is creating problems."

"I'm sure. Turf wars."

"On multiple fronts."

"What else do you know about the kid?"

"He's nineteen and his name's Aashif Abaan. His father teaches religious studies, of all things, at George Mason. They're Jordanian."

"How long have they been here?"

"Twenty years. Aashif was born in D.C."

"And radicalized?" Angela took the pork from the oven, its crisp top layer of fat sending up plumes of steamy fragrance.

"It looks that way. A couple days before the bombing, Homeland intercepted some strange messages, not exactly encrypted but in a crude sort of code, that he emailed to four people. One of them is here, two in New York and the fourth in New Jersey. All are being questioned by the agencies that pulled them in."

"And the kid's parents?"

"Totally distraught. They apparently had no clue."

"When do you plan to go public?"

"Only after we confirm that it's an isolated incident."

"My God, what a world."

Nodding, I helped myself to a second glass of wine. Befitting her professional status, Angela was drinking more judiciously.

"Do you think this is a religious war?" she asked. "Muslims against Christians."

"Don't you?"

"I'm not so sure. Some of those groups would like us to believe that, but there may be more to it. Or less. The kids are easy prey. No clear sense of where they belong, even if they're not alienated."

"There are swarms of them, all across the globe. But most losers and misfits don't put on suicide vests."

"True, it's extreme but the recruiters, the so-called jihadists, understand disaffection. They've turned it into an organizing principle."

"You've given this some thought," I said.

She nodded. "Imagine if a ragtag band of thugs, with no real political identity or philosophy other than a desire for power, had tried to exploit racial anger in the 1950s and '60s. However disruptive the turmoil and riots were then, they could have been much worse if there hadn't been a social and political structure to keep them in check. Also reasonable people who knew how to operate within that framework. Martin Luther King. The Southern Christian Leadership Conference. Even Malcolm X, in his later years. Plus people in government with the courage and the smarts to defuse things by making political reforms."

"What about ideology?"

"Exaggerated," she said. "The Arabs have been ruled mostly by despots. Until someone like a Ghandi or a Muslim Martin Luther King comes along, there's not a whole helluva lot we can do."

"Except contain them militarily."

"Containment by us is provocation to them. That's the problem. It's a great recruiting tool, as Morgan Walker pointed out the other morning."

"I found him impressive. And you?"

"Very." She took a sip of wine. "And the president?"

"Foreign policy isn't Barley's strong suit. He'll need to rely on Morgan and whoever winds up at State."

"Any ideas about who that will be?"

"Walter recommended Ted Jorgenson, a former under-secretary."

"I don't know him. But it will take someone strong, with good credentials and respect in the Middle East."

"Do you have a suggestion?"

"Maybe." Angela smiled. "But let's eat first."

"You'll get no argument from me. Bring on the pig."

"I've got photos my mother gave me from my grandparent's farm in Pinar del Rio. They kept a pig on the roof of one of their buildings. It must have weighed four hundred pounds."

"Why the roof?"

"If I was told, I don't remember."

"Did they eat it?"

"They were Cuban."

"Which is like asking if Italians eat pasta?"

"Exactly."

I watched Angela mound several thin layers of pork onto two plates, adding carrots and something that looked like a turnip.

"A tuber called yucca," she explained. "Marinated in lime juice, olive oil and garlic for twenty-four hours before cooking. Very Cuban."

"I'm sure it tastes better than its name sounds."

"I hope so. Do you mind eating in the kitchen?"

"I doubt I could get out of my chair to go anywhere else."

Angela took a baguette from the oven and cut it into rounds before laying them in a breadbasket and adding butter. Nothing beat buttered warm bread except maybe roast pork. Still, with all the mouth-watering pleasure of the moment, I felt some apprehension as Angela uncorked the second bottle.

☙   ☙   ☙

Across the island from each other, we ate, drank, and talked. The roast pork came from a recipe handed down from her mother, who was a great cook. "The gene didn't get passed along to me, but I can read directions and on occasion conjure one of my mother's favorite dishes."

"You certainly conjured this one. It's delicious."

"You were hungry."

"A steady diet of sandwiches for a week can have that effect."

"You live alone?"

"In a rental apartment a couple blocks from the Capitol. I've been there six months. It functions more like a motel than a home."

"Were you ever married?"

I shook my head. "Even though the hours suck, my work's enough. For now anyway. What about you?"

"I'm sure you know most of it from the vetting process."

"Some scraps here and there. You grew up in Miami, went to university there, then to Albany Law School. After that you worked for Janet Reno."

"Good memory."

"You married a lawyer who did legal work for CIA and divorced him a couple years ago."

"Three-and-a-half to be exact, and my ex is still at Langley. The house came with the settlement."

"Very nice. Are you happy here?"

"It's been home for seventeen years: a refuge from the Washington turmoil."

One bottle of wine was empty, and by my reckoning I'd drunk two-thirds of it. Angela's glass was still half full. I determined to make the glass I was pouring from the second bottle my last.

"Sticking with Cuba, I'm offering flan for dessert," she said.

"Great."

"I didn't make it."

135

"Then I won't feel obliged to eat it."

I lifted my glass, and we clinked again before I told her I liked her political wisdom. "Can I count on your advice now and then?"

"Of course."

"Starting now. I need your opinion."

"Legal?"

"And political. It's time we get Barley off the acting list and make him the outright head of the team."

"That may be difficult with Maggie Mathews doing so well. I saw her on TV."

"Regardless of Walter's stunt, it'll be months—at a *minimum*—before Maggie's sufficiently recovered. If then. We can't keep playing wait and see. We need Barley in command and with his own vice president. Besides, I think Barley's proven himself, well, *proving* himself. I wouldn't have said that three weeks ago, but he's getting better every day."

"Sometimes the least likely characters surprise you."

"I'm betting on this one," I said.

"But you know it will take an act of Congress. There's no precedent. With Barley's poll numbers up, I'd say now's the time to make the move. And I'd start with Claymore."

"I know a guy on Claymore's staff, a legislative assistant," I said. "I'll give him a call."

Angela nodded. "Claymore's the place to start," she repeated.

"He's also a Republican and next in the line of succession."

"You asked for my advice, so I'll give a bit more. I'd worry more about Walter than about Claymore. I was at Justice when Walter was secretary of state during the last years of the Sutton administration."

"And?"

"I've heard rumors."

"What kind?"

"Some other time. Not tonight."

Just as well. I felt a little fuzzy, with Angela out of focus. The bottle of wine was now half empty and my glass was half full—which meant I'd poured myself more despite my resolve not to.

"I think—" Leaning against the counter, I tried to stand up.

"Are you ok?"

"Not quite. Will you point me toward the bathroom?"

Angela took my arm and led me down the hall.

"I can take it from here," I said, pushing open the door to the powder room and wondering where that phrase came from. Take a powder?

After peeing, I leaned against the sink to steady my shaky legs and stared at my bloodshot eyes in the mirror. Splashing cold water on my face didn't help much.

"Sorry," I said to Angela, who was waiting in the hall.

"Nothing to be sorry about."

"Hardly knowing you, I come to dinner and drink more than I should."

"I expect it's more than that. From the sound of it, you've been pushing yourself hard. Barley's lucky to have you, but everyone needs some down time."

"It's hard to get when you're in the middle of the game. Speaking of which, have you ever thought about running for president? I'd run your campaign if you asked me."

She laughed. "You're drunk. Let me get to be attorney general first."

Angela was still out of focus. "Better call a car service, I should go home."

"Skeeter, I have two spare bedrooms. You're welcome to one of them. It will save you from coming back here tomorrow to get your car."

"What will the neighbors say?"

"That he's too young for her. And they'll be right."

"In that case, please lead me to the spare bedroom."

++

METRO EXPLOSION WORK OF SUICIDE BOMBER

by Barry Jagoda
Cleveland Plain-Dealer

WASHINGTON, D.C., — Intelligence officials said today that the terrorist explosion that derailed a Blue Line Metro train, leaving 32 dead, 44 injured and seven unaccounted for, was the work of a suicide bomber. Officials said they were awaiting DNA confirmation before releasing the suspect's name.

Carl Rogers, a spokesman for the Office of Homeland Security, said officials were focusing on a domestic copycat or so-called "lone wolf." "There's been no international claims of responsibility and no organizational signature or pattern." Rogers said.

Acting President Barley Thompson, who pledged in a television address "not to rest until the perpetrator of this outrage has been brought to justice," praised the work of Homeland Security, the FBI and both the District of Columbia and Arlington, Virginia police departments. At an impromptu press conference at Rosslyn Station, where Thompson appeared less than three hours after the explosion, he said the agencies "worked harmoniously together to identify this outrageous act as the work of a suicide bomber." He also praised former senator and secretary of defense designate Morgan Walker, who was on the train and who, according to other riders, led passengers to safety.

"He's a true hero," Thompson said.

According to Metro officials, the suicide bomb was detonated at 6:56 p.m. yesterday, killing all the passengers riding in the train's first car and causing those in the remaining six cars to be thrown forward when the train came to an abrupt halt in almost total darkness. According to passengers, several people were screaming or sobbing in the first moments after the explosion. It was then, they say, that Walker, riding in the second car, stood up and began speaking.

"We couldn't see him and we didn't know who he was," said Richard Albury, a statistician for the Federal Communications Commission who was also in the second car, "but we heard this soothing voice telling us to remain calm and asking if anybody had a flashlight."

Fortunately, Mr. Albury continued, an unidentified woman passenger produced a small, keychain flashlight from her purse.

"Senator Walker—we learned only later that's who it was—told passengers with cell phones to turn on their flashlight app if they had one."

Mr. Albury said there was no cellphone service but "the light from the flashlight and from the cellphones really helped settle people down."

According to passenger Megan Kagan, a National Parks Service employee at Arlington National Cemetery, the secretary-designate then asked if anyone had medical experience. Margaret Robinson, a nurse, and Edward Hartigan, a former Marine Corps medic, both came forward.

"Mr. Walker, the nurse and the medic slowly picked their way toward the front of the car, stepping around, and in some cases over, stunned and wounded passengers," Ms. Kagan said. "But when they got there, they couldn't open the door. "

According to Ms. Kagan, Walker then asked passengers to move to the rear of the car. He told those unable to walk to make themselves as comfortable as possible while they waited for assistance," Ms. Kagan said. Ms. Robinson and Mr. Hartigan stayed with the injured passengers, providing what comfort and assistance they could.

A group of about 20 passengers then moved with Mr. Walker to the third car, where he repeated his request for flashlights, cellphones and medical expertise. The Walker group grew by about 20 passengers per car as they continued to the seventh and last car. There the group, now numbering more than 100 passengers, exited through a door they forced open onto a dimly lighted walkway along the track.

No sooner had Mr. Walker and the other passengers begun walking toward Rosslyn station than they saw some dozen first responders approaching them.

The passenger group then continued some 200 yards to the Rosslyn station platform. When they got to within about 50 yards of the platform, Ms. Kagan said, cell phones started ringing. "It sounded like a public television pledge drive," she said.

By then, police, FBI, Metro workers, doctors, nurses and members of the press had begun to converge on the station, which had been closed to the public. Mr. Walker told D.C.

Police Operation Captain Charles Bruhn that he estimated there were more than forty people in need of medical attention still on the train. Walker told Bruhn that several passengers with medical training had stayed behind to assist the wounded.

Many of them had heard Mr. Walker tell Bruhn to "make sure you thank the ones who stayed behind to help. They probably deserve some sort of commendation."

-- 16 --

I woke up before dawn, dressed quickly and scribbled a note to Angela. *You have no idea how much I enjoyed last night. Pls blame my overindulgence on the delicious food and the company. I even liked the yucca. Hope to see you soon."*

My thoughts kept returning to her as I drove into Washington. Had she really meant what she said about never getting involved with anyone she worked with? And that she was too old for me? She was certainly right about one thing: I'd been pushing my limits of endurance and needed a timeout.

A good night's sleep in a quiet room in suburban Virginia had made a difference: despite the Rioja's lingering effects, I felt energized. But going home was out of the question. After crossing the Roosevelt Bridge and clearing the checkpoint in light traffic, I drove straight to the White House.

A scattering of lights were on when I arrived at seven a.m. I felt at home where people worked 24/7. After parking in my designated spot I walked through the West Wing entrance, into the portico and past a Marine guard. Grabbing a handful of Sunday papers, I headed to my office.

Although the editorialists of the *Post* and the *Times*, as well as the *Plain-Dealer* and the *Wall Street Journal*, wrung their ink-stained hands over the implications of the first "successful"—curious use of that word—suicide bombing on American soil, I was happy to see that they gave high marks to Barley for his hands-on response to the bombing. The *Plain-Dealer* carried a sidebar about Morgan Walker by Jagoda.

At Barley's urging, Walker had agreed to appear on all five Sunday morning interview shows: a "full Ginsburg," as it came to be known after William H. Ginsburg, Monica

Lewinsky's attorney, first performed the feat at the height of the Clinton intern scandal.

Walking down to the White House Mess, I bought two Danish and a ten-ounce coffee and returned to my desk to check email. Nothing from Angela. Why would there be before eight o'clock? I pictured her still asleep in the master bedroom, or tucked up with coffee and the papers. However, there *was* something from Klaus Hunt.

> *"Hi Skeeter, if I may call you that. It was a pleasure to meet you the other day. I enjoyed our little chat and Charles appreciated it too. Also enjoyed meeting the leader of the free world. Speaking of which, he thinks the world of you. Says you made him what he is today. Anyway, as promised, I looked into those three companies you asked about. The one liquefying carbon in Calif. is called 'Carbonaide.' The one dumping iron ore in oceans is 'And/Ore.' And the company salting the atmosphere with water droplets, or trying to, is 'Dew Drop Inc.' The names are bit too cute for my taste, but I'm told they're all on the up-and-up and run by grown-ups (even if the names sound sophomoric). Anyway, good luck and thanks again for letting Charles meet the Barleymeister."*

After adding "Brief Barley re Hunt" to my to-do list, I returned Klaus' email to thank him for the info and his "short course in bringing climate change under control." In retrospect, I suppose alarm bells should have gone off, but the fact is I hardly gave it any thought at all.

For the next hour or so I raced through at least a hundred messages, answering those I deemed urgent, saving others to deal with later and deleting the rest. What had people in this building done in decades past, I wondered, before email and social media had given everybody access to public figures—or in my case, semi-public. They probably got a lot more work done.

At ten o'clock, I caught Walker's "Meet the Press" appearance and envied his ease before the cameras. His self-deprecation was as refreshing as it was rare in such precincts. I also caught a bit of him on "Face the Nation" and "This Week with George Stephanopoulos," where he appeared no less modest and natural.

At eleven, as I was preparing to leave, Amanda Thompson appeared in my doorway. She'd kept a low profile since moving into Blair House. If she had any intention of creating a position for herself by focusing on some particular cause, she had yet to let any of us know about it. In fact, I'd seen her only a couple of times with the president.

Her face was drawn. She said Barley had had a bad night; she looked as if hers hadn't been so hot either.

"How bad?" I asked. The last thing we needed was for Barley to falter.

"He was having palpitations around midnight. I had to call the doctor."

"Was he hospitalized?"

"No. He gave Barley something for his blood pressure and to help him sleep."

My mind began racing. Maybe the tension of the last few days had gotten to Barley the way it had to all of us. But if it were anything really serious, the doc would have put him into Walter Reed Hospital.

"Is he awake? Shall I go over?"

"No, he's sleeping. The doctor will check back this afternoon."

"Good. It doesn't sound too serious, but keep me posted. You've got my number."

"I do and I will."

"And let's not make anything public out of this yet."

"Of course. I understand."

On the drive home, I tried to locate the line between my professional and personal interests, which had intertwined in a discomforting way I couldn't put my finger on. Now Barley was very much on that axis.

Once home, I hoped a brisk walk of several blocks would clear my head. My usual route to the Capitol to Union Station to the Supreme Court often settled me and lifted my spirits. But now it did neither, maybe because the sight of added security measures everywhere was hardly a tonic. Instead, I felt even more aware of my loner status and dependence on my professional life. Not to mention the very difficult times we were living through, as Angela had said.

Amanda called late in the afternoon to tell me Barley was better but had been advised to reduce his work schedule for a couple of days. He'd keep his morning appointments, work from Blair House in the afternoon. He'd wanted me to function as his liaison during the next two days.

Unlike most other working stiffs, I welcomed Monday mornings, even at 6:30 with my clock radio offering Anna Netrebko belting out arias from Tchaikovsky's "Eugene Onegin." The beginning of the week meant no time for questions about my shortcomings and lack of a personal life. Wool gathering, naval gazing or whatever you want to call it, didn't suit me.

While shaving, I thought about an affair that started to unravel several months before I'd signed on with Maggie Mathews. My soon-to-be ex had accused me of lacking an "inner life." While I'm sure she meant it as an insult, I took no offence and didn't even disagree with her. I'd always plunged myself into work, radio, TV, music, movies, and books in order to avoid an inner life. In any case, it was too late to change.

At seven-thirty, I looked out the window and saw a black, government-issue SUV idling at the curb. Although I'd have preferred to have shown solidarity with my fellow Washingtonians by riding the Metro, security was still very tight. It was still less than a week since the "Blue Line Bomber," as the media now called him, had committed his atrocity. More than that, schedules were too erratic to ensure getting to work on time.

Arriving at the West Wing a little after seven-thirty, I had plenty of time to read the Daily Briefing before the eight o'clock staff meeting. CIA Director Donner or his deputy briefed Barley every Monday morning at 7:45. I assumed today would be no exception.

After Jason Merriweather's release of Aashif Abaan's name the night before, every paper led with the suicide bomber and his four alleged conspirators.

≈ ≈ ≈

Attendance at staff meetings varied, depending on who was in town and what was on the agenda. As long as Barley remained in Washington, those sessions were held in the Oval. If he'd travel, which he had yet to do, we'd convene in the Old Executive Office Building, now officially re-designated the Eisenhower Executive Office Building, although I knew no one who called it that. Today the agenda was Aashif Abaan, and every seat was occupied.

Barley looked better than I'd expected. Sitting to his left was James Conover, Dubois's Director of National Intelligence, who'd agreed to stay on as long as Barley needed him. The DNI position had been created by George W. Bush in 2004 to bring the various intelligence agencies that competed with each other—and almost never shared information—under a single authority. Of course, like so many well-laid plans, it hadn't worked out as intended. Although there was marginally more sharing of information, the inter-agency rivalries had, if anything, intensified.

Barley turned the meeting over to Conover, who updated us on the four Abaan accomplices who had been identified from Abaan's laptop. The four were now in custody, charged with providing material support to a foreign terrorist organization. Like Abaan, all four had been born in America to Jordanian parents. Abaan and Abdul Jawad had gone to school together in Arlington. They'd apparently met the other three on the Internet. It was unclear from their emails whether all five had ever been together physically. The four now in custody were each employed in blue-collar jobs: Jawad worked in a pizza parlor, the kid from New Jersey was a dishwasher in a Vietnamese restaurant. Of the two New Yorkers, one was an apprentice mechanic in a garage; the other drove a delivery truck.

Conover said all except Abaan, who came from a middle class family, bore the hallmarks of the so-called "lone wolf" terrorist wannabe: poorly educated sons of first-generation immigrants. Almost invariably, they were disillusioned and disappointed with their lot in life. It was typical that Abaan and his pals had no girlfriends. The wannabes were obsessive, Conover added.

Such people, he continued, were highly susceptible to the slick videos and other propaganda that terrorist groups such as ISIS, Al-Shabab and Boko Haram distributed on the Internet.

"The message goes something like this," he said: "You're special but unappreciated. Join our noble cause and find redemption, glory and meaning in your lives. And if you can't come to us, wreak your vengeance on your homeland." According to Abaan's emails, which NSA had quickly managed to decipher, the train bombing was the first of four acts intended to bring the United States to its knees. The other three were a drone strike on the White House, a bomb at Union Station and the assassination of Barley Thompson.

Looking up from the legal pad on which he'd been taking notes, Barley let his eyes flit around the room. "Jim," he said to James Atkinson, his special assistant for domestic matters, "any ideas for legislation to better target these homegrown extremists?"

"We're working on it," Atkinson replied. "As you know, when somebody visits one of these sites, NSA captures their names and IPO addresses, which they pass on to the FBI. There may be a way to make the act of visiting certain Internet locations a crime, as it is with child pornography."

"Good. Sounds promising. Let's move quickly on it."

His presentation complete, Conover took a few

questions before leaving the meeting, which then wrapped up quickly. Charley Millbank reported that Barley's poll numbers were "in the stratosphere"—64% approval—and that Morgan Walker had wowed the blogosphere with his TV appearances the day before. I complimented Charley on managing to invoke two "spheres" in a single sentence.

Adding my approval of Walker, I called him very impressive. "No bombast. No braggadocio. He's a workhorse, not a show horse."

"Let's move on his confirmation," Barley said. "I think he was always a shoo-in, though you should never count your chickens with this bunch. But after his Blue Line heroics, I doubt anybody in either party will oppose."

"Talk to the majority leader," he said to Atkinson. "See if he won't fast-track this."

When I said I thought the majority leader would want something, Barley asked what we had. Then my suggestion of a state dinner got a laugh.

"Dream on, but work on him," Barley answered. "Maybe he won't stall a fellow Republican." Then he brought the assembly to a close and asked Charley and me to stay behind.

After everyone had filed out, he said he liked Atkinson's idea about criminalizing the viewing of terror recruiting sites but felt it didn't go far enough. "I've been briefed on the cyber terrorism threat.

"It scares the shit out of me," he continued. "A big enough attack, carried out anonymously, could ruin the economy. Hell, it could cripple the country. I know we're working on it but not fast enough."

He wanted me to set up a cyber terrorism task force and brief him on my recommendations of who should be on it. "The goal has to be measures to prevent Internet attacks, to apprehend and punish—I mean really *punish*—those cyber terrorists."

"What else you got?" Barley asked.

I gave him the gist of my conversation with Klaus Hunt: cutting back on fossil fuels won't do it, not with the developing world using more coal and oil—and burning more carbon—

every year.

"We've also got to do more to encourage private enterprise to come up with technological solutions," I said. "Start-up costs are usually high and revenues are often years in the future. But entrepreneurs are getting into it."

I told him about the three companies Hunt had mentioned. Then I took a printout of Hunt's email of the day before from my jacket pocket and handed it to him. I didn't know whether his chortle while reading it was from one or more of the company's cutesy names or Hunt's reference to him as "Barleymeister."

"Ask one of your people to look into the companies," he said, passing the email to Charley. "If they're legit, it might be worth a mention."

Turning back to me, he asked what I made of Hunt. I said he seemed to know his stuff and wasn't too full of himself. Barley asked if I thought he had an ulterior motive.

"I don't think so. He couldn't recall the names of two of the companies when he first told me about them."

Barley frowned and looked distracted.

"But you knew him before, didn't you?" I asked.

"Not really. I may have met him. He was a bundler for Maggie. Over a hundred thou, if memory serves. But he's Walter's friend. I think they met when Walter was at State."

Charley jumped in while I scribbled a note. "The press is badgering me to get you to hold a news conference."

Barley turned to me again. "How do you weigh in on that?"

"It's as good a time as any. Your numbers are up and the focus will be on the Metro bombing."

"Ok, set it up," he said to Charley. "For next week. Check with Janice." (Janice Rogers had been on Barley's Senate staff. Now she kept his calendar, among other duties.)

He looked at his watch. "That does it for me, unless you guys have something more."

I said I did. I gave Charley a look, and he stood up and left the room.

"I was sorry to hear about your medical issues the

other night," I began.

"It was an overreaction. I'm fine."

"I think we ought to start planning for your presidency."

"I thought that's what we've been doing."

"No, sir. I mean, *your* presidency. According to her neurosurgeon, Maggie isn't coming back."

"She's made tremendous strides."

"Yes sir, she has, no question. But with the possibility of a repeat or a regression..." I felt the sentence didn't need to be completed.

"Dawson told you that?"

I nodded.

"I don't like it."

"Yes sir, I know. No one likes it. But the country needs a president with all the trimmings, not a wounded president. Or, for that matter, an acting one."

Barley sighed. "So what do you propose?"

I told him I had a friend in Speaker Claymore's office. I said I thought I should get in touch with him, get the lay of the land, and see what our options were. And the politics.

"That's a dangerous area. Do what you have to do, but be discreet."

++

MAN IN THE NEWS: MORGAN WALKER
by Barry Jagoda
Cleveland Plain-Dealer

WASHINGTON, D.C. -- The man credited with keeping passengers calm and leading them to safety after a bomb exploded on the Metro Blue Line, killing 32 passengers, is no lover of the trappings of power, including limousines (and, for that matter, even taxicabs), which is why Defense Secretary designate Morgan Walker was riding a Blue Line train when the explosion occurred.

Walker had ducked out of a State Department briefing in order to get to the Pentagon for another meeting.

In an interview, Secretary-designate Morgan said he had just taken a draft of the proposed 2018 Pentagon budget out of his briefcase and the train had just pulled out of the Rosslyn, Virginia station when he was rocked by an explosion. "Fortunately, I got my right hand in front of my face, which kept my head from hitting the back of the seat in front of me," he said.

Passengers said that as soon as the train came to a screeching stop, Mr. Walker was on his feet, urging calm in a voice that more than one passenger described as "reassuring." Several passengers credited him with preventing panic and saving lives, a notion the secretary-designate dismisses.

"I didn't do anything special," he said, "I just suggested we'd all be better off if we stayed calm."

Walker grew up the oldest of three boys and one girl on a dairy farm outside Racine, Wisconsin, which, he said, "provided more than the bare necessities for a family of six." But the Walkers did not take vacations. They owned a single 21-inch black and white television set that they kept well into the era of color TV. (To this day, their modest 3 bedroom farmhouse makes do with an outdoor antenna.)

Walker said his family also owned a succession of Plymouth automobiles, all of which were purchased used. As a teenager, Walker said, he loved to tinker with the cars and was "pretty good with carburetors. As I recall," he said, "we never got rid of any car with less than 150,000 miles on it."

At Racine Central High School, Morgan made the Second Honor Role with a B+ average (As in civics and social studies, Bs in English and math, Cs in Spanish) and was captain of the debate team. Too small for football and, in his words, "too uncoordinated for baseball" (though he played shortstop on the junior varsity team), he excelled at wrestling and, in his senior year, went to the state championships in Madison, where he was defeated in the 120 lb. division semi-final.

"That hurt," he said.

But by the time of that defeat, he had accepted an appointment by his congressman, Ben McGeahy of Wisconsin's First Congressional District, to the United States Military Academy at West Point, on which he had set his sights in his sophomore year: "Right after I learned it was free," he said with a smile.

He was the first person in his immediate family to attend college. At West Point, he graduated with the rank of cadet captain in the top fifth of his class.

As a first lieutenant in Vietnam in 1972, Walker was assigned as an advisor to the 5th Division of the Army of the Republic of Vietnam (ARVN). At the battle of An Loc, a rare, decisive victory for South Vietnamese forces that was credited with delaying the North Vietnamese advance toward Saigon, Walker was riding in a helicopter strafing North Vietnamese forces. When the retreating North Vietnamese fired into the helicopter's cockpit, Walker was hit by shrapnel in the legs and abdomen. "It looked worse than it turned out to be," he said. He received a Purple Heart for his injuries.

The incident marked the end of Walker's combat experience. He was evacuated to the Army's 3d Field Hospital in Saigon for three-weeks of recuperation, after which he was rotated back to Virginia's Ft. Belvoir. At Ft. Belvoir, he was given command of an administrative platoon dealing with soldiers who suffered health or family issues, had gone AWOL or otherwise violated the Uniform Code of Military Justice. Four months later, in April 1973, Walker was honorably discharged.

Returning to Racine, he hung up his uniform and helped his father on the family farm for several weeks before accepting a management training position with InSinkErator, a manufacturer of garbage disposals and one of Racine's major employers.

After a week's indoctrination at InSinkErator, Morgan was assigned to the factory floor, charged with overseeing 34 men and 27 women—one of whom, Elizabeth Lukens, had been three years behind him at Racine Central High and who he would later marry.

Although he said he liked working at InSinkErator, he left after less than a year when Congressman Ben McGeahy urged him to run for the House seat he was leaving to run for the U.S. Senate (unsuccessfully as it turned out).

Walker said that until Representative McGeahy approached him, he had not given much thought to politics and had not contemplated a political career. Thanks, he said, to his war record and McGeahy's endorsement—the Congressman even campaigned for his protégé—Morgan won commandingly, defeating a Democratic hotelier from neighboring Twin Lakes.

Reached by telephone at a retirement community northwest of Orlando, Florida, Mr. McGeahy called Walker a natural politician, whose low-key delivery on the stump was as responsible for his victory as his war record.

"I was very proud of him," McGeahy said. "In fact I'm as proud of persuading Morgan Walker to run for the House of Representatives as I am of anything I ever did while serving there myself."

In 1980, six years and three terms later, Walker stole a page from McGeahey's playbook and ran for the U.S. Senate. There he became known as a hard working, middle-of-the-road Republican in the Nelson Rockefeller mold.

"He was always willing to work across the aisle, even in the most polarized of Congresses," said Senator Scott Bailey (D. Rhode Island). "We did some good things together, including tax reform, though sadly, nothing came of it."

When Republicans took control of the upper body in 2002, Walker realized a long-standing ambition by becoming chairman of the Senate Armed Services Committee, on which he had served for two of his three terms.

Walker said he first met Maggie Mathews at a dinner party at Ben Bradlee and Sally Quinn's Georgetown townhouse in the early 90s. Despite being from opposing parties, he said, they became fast friends. It was to Walker that Maggie quietly (and secretly) turned to advise her on military matters when she first began thinking about running for the Democratic nomination for president.

Walker's confirmation hearings have yet to be scheduled. But considering his 12 years as chairman of Armed Services Committee, he is not expected to encounter much difficulty.

"He's a slam dunk for confirmation," said Senator Bailey.

Closing the door to my office, I dialed the White House operator and asked her to put me through to McClandish Murphy, legislative aide to the speaker of the house. Five minutes later, she told me that Mr. Murphy was on line two.

"Mac?"

"Hey, Skeeter. Long time."

"And a long way from Indianapolis." We'd first met during the '08 Indiana primary, when I was working for Obama and he for Romney. Four years later, I was his boss during Romney's second campaign.

"What've you been up to?"

Of course I knew he was yanking my chain; at least I hoped he was. "Slinging hash for minimum wage," I replied. "Just like you."

Mac laughed. "Ain't that the truth. Except you get more press than I do."

"And you sell more pork. Speaking of which, how's it working out with Claymore?"

"He's an asshole, but hey, there's no shortage of them around here. On both sides of the aisle."

"At least he's an *influential* asshole."

"If you say so." He lowered his voice. "You wouldn't believe some of the shit that goes on around here. Let's have a drink sometime and I'll tell you about it." He turned the volume back up. "So what can I do you for?"

"I need to bounce some ideas around."

"Bounce away."

"I have to pledge you to secrecy first."

"What's up with that? You'd think we worked for the government."

I laughed. "It's about Maggie."

"I saw her on TV not long ago. She looked good."

"Yes, she did. Everyone says so. She's a remarkable woman." I let that sink in. Now I lowered *my* voice. "But I'll level with you, Mac. She looked good and sounded good, but she's not *that* good."

"I hear you, Skeeter."

"So what happens if she's never a hundred percent again?"

"Funny you should ask. That's exactly what the speaker wants to know: the answer to the question that's on all our minds."

"So what *is* the answer?"

"I don't know."

"C'mon, Mac."

"I'm not being a smartass. Nobody knows. We've never had a vice president in charge without a sitting president. You might say it's, er, unpresidented."

I groaned. The worse puns were, the more Mac liked them. That one was low even by his standards.

"We're making it up as we go along," Mac continued. Kinda like Chinese food: one from column a, one from column b."

"In that case, pass the flied lice."

Mac chuckled. "From the 20th amendment on succession," he said, sounding like he was reading. "Congress may, quote, 'provide for the case wherein neither a President-elect nor a Vice President-elect shall have qualified.' Close quote."

"Yeah, we know that much. Not terribly helpful," I said.

"But the relevant part is that it *falls to Congress*."

"Which is you guys, and the reason for my call."

"Hold your horses. The 25th says when there's a vacancy in the vice presidency, quote, 'the President shall nominate a Vice President who shall take office upon confirmation by a majority vote of *both houses of Congress.*' Close another quote."

"It's not exactly the situation we're in now, but I see where you're going with this."

"I'm drafting a bill for Claymore that says, basically, that the VP elect, or, in Barley's case, the *actual* VP, must be confirmed as president by a majority of both Houses. The new president then nominates his own VP, who in turn must be confirmed by both Houses."

"Oh, boy," I said. "Can you do that with just a bill? You don't need a Constitutional amendment?"

"Maybe, maybe not. But a bill would be a lot easier and faster. In any case, that's Claymore's problem. All I have to do is draft the damn thing."

"It could also be *my* problem."

"True. Amendments take time and money. I assume Barley wants the job. Did he put you up to this call?"

"Not at all; it's my job to think ahead for him. As for his wanting it—it's not about Barley. The country needs an *actual* president, not an *acting* one."

Mac said he agreed. "But would Maggie go along with Barley taking her presidency?"

"I don't know," I said. "I think so, but I'm less sure about Walter."

"How so?"

"I can't put my finger on it, but something's always sideways with him."

"Does it have to do with pulling back from state?"

"I don't know that either. Dare I ask about the confirmation process?"

"You may. Morgan's a shoe-in, but I've heard no scuttlebutt about anyone else."

"We'd very much like to have our own team to work with. Under the circumstances, I'm sure you can understand."

"Claymore gets that." Again he went sotto voce. "He may be a jerk, but he's not an impossible jerk."

"How about that drink, Mac? Can we make it sooner rather than later."

"Now *there's* a request that doesn't require an act of Congress. I'm busy tonight. Tomorrow?"

"I'm not exactly in a nine to five around here."

"Nor here. I'll meet you at the Willard at seven tomorrow, unless I hear from you."

"You're on."

∽ ∽ ∽

I had just gotten back to my office after lunch when Walter appeared at my door, looking pleased with himself and out of uniform. Wearing a double-breasted blazer with shiny brass buttons, he could have come off one of the fancy *bateaus* tied up at the Capital Yacht Club on the Potomac. He wore a Vineyard Vines necktie and he'd traded his wing tips for a pair of black, Gucci loafers.

"Afternoon, Skeeter," he said in a jaunty voice.

"Walter," I said, failing to match his bonhomie. "Good to see you. Maggie looked terrific on TV. 'Free at last!' Nice touch."

Walter beamed. "Yeah, she's doing great."

"So what can I do for you?"

"A reporter named Barry Jagoda called me. He wants to talk to me about my nomination—why I pulled it, my role here, etcetera. And about Maggie, of course."

"I'm sure you're getting a lot of interview requests."

"Too many. But Jagoda said you'd vouch for him."

"He's a good reporter. When does he want to do it?"

"Tomorrow, after Barley's press conference. Speaking of whom, any chance I could steal a minute with him?"

"Not today, I'm afraid. He's fully booked."

"That's odd. I'd heard he'd canceled several appointments. Since you're his gatekeeper, I thought you might slide me in."

"I'd be happy to deliver a message for you."

He stood in the doorway drumming his fingers against the frame. "That's ok, it can wait."

"By the way," I said, "what can you tell me about Klaus Hunt?"

"Who?"

"Klaus Hunt. The oil man. Barley said you and he were

pals."

"Klaus Hunt, huh? What else did Barley say?"

"That he's a six-figure bundler for Maggie."

"Oh, yeah I remember now: the Texan. He was very helpful during the campaign."

"Is he a straight-shooter?"

"As far as I know. Why?"

"He's advising us on climate issues."

I thought I saw a look of worry cross Walter's eyes before he shrugged, and turned to go. Then he turned back.

"Is there anything I shouldn't talk to Jagoda about?"

"Such as?"

"I don't know. I think he wants to talk about Maggie's return to the political orbit. That's his word, not mine."

I felt my guts twist. "Well, only you can answer that. Or Maggie."

Walter nodded, waved and walked away.

∾ ∾ ∾

Just up from a nap, Barley looked ragged when we met in his Blair House apartment at 2:30.

"Are you ok, sir?"

"Not much energy. The doc's got me on a beta-blocker, a statin and a blood thinner."

"This won't take long. I thought we might go over tomorrow's schedule and a couple other things. You know about the presser at 10:30? I expect a lot of questions about the Metro incident. As you heard from Conover this morning, new information is coming in."

"I need details at my fingertips, typed up on three-by-five cards. Along with any other questions I might get. I'd like to keep this brief, under half an hour. Blame it on scheduling conflicts. "

"Of course. I'll have the notes for you by the end of the day."

"What else?"

"Claymore's looking into the process of getting your

presidency validated. How long it will take is uncertain, but I'm trying to get them to expedite things."

"Why?"

"As I've said before, I believe it's important that your administration is fully appointed."

"But what's the hurry? We're only ten days in and look at all that's happened. Give the poor bastards on the Hill some time."

"I'll be blunt, sir."

"When have you not been?"

"It's part of the job description."

Barley smiled.

"Your health is one concern."

"In case I croak?"

"In case of whatever. Politically we need a smooth transition. No more stumbling blocks."

Barley stifled a yawn. "Yes, I know, you want a vice president: my replacement, in the event I check out."

"Among other things."

"Have you got someone in mind?"

"No, sir."

"Then draw up a short list. Candidates who meet your criteria."

"And yours."

"Have I ever not taken your advice?"

"I'm taking that as a rhetorical question."

"Take it however you want, but we're in this together."

"And we'll get out of it together."

"By the way, any thoughts about the task force on cyber terrorism?"

"It's a great idea. My guess is it'll sail through Congress without a hitch once it gets there. At least through committees. The libertarians might balk, but I'd be surprised if you don't get bipartisan support, sir."

"Any ideas on who might lead it?"

"Someone at Justice—"

"Let me guess. Angela Mercado."

"She'd be good, but her plate is pretty full."

"I want to move on this. Want your veep candidates along with the task force names."

I made more notes. "There's something else to think about."

"What's that?"

"Muslims."

"Yes, I'll say that's indeed something to think about."

"It's inspired by a conversation I had with Angela on Saturday."

Barley smiled. "Pillow talk?"

I ignored that. "She's smart and she's given a lot of thought to this. Her ideas track with Morgan Walker's. I think they'll work well together."

"So what's her angle?"

I told him about Angela's idea of an Arab spokesperson who could talk meaningfully about Islam in a way that unites religious viewpoints. "A Ghandi type," I added.

"And where do we find this knight in shining armor? Someone palatable to the various factions."

"That's the problem. The Muslims are so divided, politically and geographically, they're hard to package."

"So where do we begin?"

"Secret shuttle diplomacy by someone knowledgeable and respected in the region."

"And what about Israel and Palestine, do we leave them out?"

"For now, yes."

"There's no centrality and no consensus," Barley said. "I don't see it happening."

"I agree it's grim and a long shot. Plus the past doesn't offer much hope for the future. But if all of our options are bad, it might be worth trying something different."

Barley stood up and stretched. "Point taken. Get me a one page report with suggestions for proceeding."

"Will do." I stood also.

"And one more thing. That therapist who worked with me at the Watergate."

"Robert Bork."

"How could I forget? See if we can get him back, a couple times a week at least."

I jotted another note. "Just so you know. Walter was here earlier. He wanted to see you."

"About?"

"He wouldn't say. We talked about a couple of things. Klaus Hunt came up. He acted like he didn't know him until I reminded him Hunt was a Maggie bundler."

"Walter." Barley shook his head.

"You should also know that Barry Jagoda is doing a piece on him. The interview's scheduled for tomorrow after the presser."

Barley looked at me as if for guidance.

"I'll check with Barry," I said.

Barley stared at me. "Do that," he said.

A polite but personal email from Angela arrived, thanking me for the note I'd left, saying she'd enjoyed the evening and hoping I was restored. Try as I did to read between the lines, there was nothing to interpret.

The phone rang while I was working on a reply, something along the lines of *Looking forward to doing it again sometime on a little more sleep and a little less wine.* The operator said Barry Jagoda was on line one.

"I'm in a meeting. Tell him I'll call him back in half an hour."

I thought I knew what he wanted but needed time to figure out how to put him off, yet again, from trying to blow up Barley's presidency.

I spent an hour on a draft proposal for implementing a meeting with Islamic leaders around the shuttle diplomacy idea, then another getting the next day's potential questions in order, together with answers. Then I began making notes on potential veep candidates. I put Angela Mercado at the top of the list, pointing out that she was a woman, a daughter of immigrants, and politically astute. Whether she had any interest and what sense it would make to take her away from Justice, I had no idea. And Walter? He might angle for it if Maggie were out of the equation. But, could he even be considered after withdrawing his nomination for State? I'd have to advise against it.

It was five o'clock when I thought of Maggie. Looking in my Rolodex, I found the private number Dr. Dawson had given me what seemed like ages ago, then listened as his phone rang four, then five times.

"Hello, Skeeter. What can I do for you?"

"I'd like to see Maggie."

"Sure. When?"

"As soon as possible at a time when you're around but Walter isn't."

If that gave him pause, he hid it. "I start patient rounds at five-thirty. Can you be here by six? I often see Walter in the morning, but I've never seen him during evening rounds."

"I'll be there before six."

"I'll let security know."

❧   ❧   ❧

Maggie was awake, watching an old movie. Although not as fluffed up as when she made her TV appearance, she was still wearing the beret and seemed alert. It was almost two weeks since we'd last seen each other.

Finding an empty vase to house the bouquet of pink lilies I'd brought, I said I thought I'd find her keeping up with the day's news.

"The news!" Although strained and deliberate, her speech was intelligible. "All bad."

"Yes, we've had a rough few days." I pulled up a chair beside her bed.

She reached out to me. "Skeeter, I have to say, it's nice to see you."

"And you." We held hands; her flesh was soft and pliable.

"You're chief of staff?"

Remembering Walter's comment that I wouldn't have been *her* choice had Maggie assumed power, I could only nod.

"How is it?"

"The hours are long and the pay's more than I deserve."

Her smile broadened. "I don't think so."

The door opened and Dawson entered. "She's looking good," I said as we shook hands.

"And doing well—right, Maggie?" Dawson said.

"If you say so."

She flashed another smile when I asked her if she was walking. "Baby steps."

"With assistance," Dawson added. "Fifteen, twenty minutes a day."

"Any physical therapy?"

"Besides walking, only what she can do from bed, squeezing a ball, that sort of thing."

I signaled to Dawson to step outside the room.

"We'll be right back," I said to Maggie, then joined him in the corridor. "I have to talk to her about some political matters. She seems perfectly coherent."

"Absolutely, but she tires quickly. She also struggles with vocabulary, the result of the partial paralysis she suffered. I hope that will be temporary, but it'll take time. What I can say now is that her cognitive function is beyond anything I could have wished for. She's perfectly lucid."

"Will you witness our conversation?"

"I don't see why not. But if it's a legal matter, we might want to bring someone else in."

"It may require Maggie to make what could be a legal decision. She may not want to, but that would be ok. I'm not here to put pressure on her, and I need a witness to the fact that I didn't. But she and I have to have this conversation. And so that you understand why I didn't want Walter here, I want Maggie to answer my questions without him influencing her."

"Would he object?"

"He might." I paused. "Yes, probably he would."

"In that case, I think we should have the hospital administrator as an independent observer."

"Whatever you feel is appropriate, but I want to be sure that Maggie is fully rational and capable of making decisions."

"As her doctor, I can say that she is."

An hour later, I had a signed statement from Maggie Mathews addressed to the speaker of the House and the Senate majority leader, stating that she was incapable of assuming the responsibilities of the presidency and wished to withdraw.

There seemed absolutely no doubt in her mind. She had no interest in resuming her political career.

As I left the hospital, however, I knew I was walking into a shit storm named Walter Mathews. How much destruction it would cause I had no way of knowing.

-- 18 --

When I returned Barry's call the following morning, he sounded annoyed. Apologizing for the delay, I explained that something had come up that I'd had to deal with personally.

"You and doctors," he barked. "You think your time is more valuable than anyone else's."

"I think you'll agree it was worth the wait."

"What is it, the Pulitzer you've been promising?" At least the edge had left his voice.

"Not that big, but it's the story *du jour* and you could be the first to run with it."

"The president?"

"It concerns Barley, yes."

"But before you pass it along, you want something in return. You always do."

"And it's the same as always."

"Nothing about Barley's indiscretion."

"Right."

The silence was deafening. Finally he said he didn't want to play that game anymore. "Look, Skeeter, every time you want to plant a blind story—'According to a highly placed administration official, blah, blah, blah...'—you put me in a tight spot."

"For a guy in a tight spot, you're doing ok."

"Maybe, but it's not the way I want to operate. I'll tell *you* something now. The *Washington Post* has been in touch. If they were to find out how you use me..."

"Congratulations. How are they going to feel when you hand them thirty-year-old gossip you can't substantiate?"

Another long silence. "All right, Skeeter. I'll sit on Barley's student rape for now. But I'm also not saying never or forever."

"I'll take it as a point of honor you'll let me know before you publish."

"Yeah, yeah. So what have you got today?"

"Maggie's withdrawing all claims on the presidency."

Barry whistled. "And you can back that up?"

"With letters she's written to Claymore and Thorne."

"You *have* the letters?"

"I have copies."

"Have they been sent?"

"They'll be hand-delivered tomorrow. If you can keep it under wraps 'til then, you'll have the exclusive. I haven't given this to anyone else."

"I need to quote you."

"Stick with blah, blah, blah."

"No way. I can't get away with an anonymous source on this one."

"Fine," I said after a pause. There were witnesses to Maggie's statement. My name would come out anyway.

"What about Walter?"

"What about him?"

"Is he ok with this?"

"You're interviewing him today. Ask him."

Despite having studied the 3 x 5 cards (which I'd delivered to him the night before, later than promised), Barley was getting more and more nervous as the press conference approached. I wanted to tell him about Maggie's letters and how I'd obtained them. But I worried it might throw him off his game right before his first interrogation by the press. So I kept my mouth shut. I figured there'd be plenty of time to release that information. I should have known better. Live and learn.

A little after 9:00 a.m., Charley and I escorted Barley into the hideaway room off the Oval and pitched him every question we thought he might get asked. After a few good answers and a bit of coaching, he calmed down somewhat, and I felt he was as ready as he'd ever be.

The opening statement Charley had drafted—an update on Maggie's condition that was guardedly upbeat while avoiding specifics—could be read as it was written. Looking it over, Barley made a single notation, then nodded to Charley, meaning put it on the Teleprompters. We were good to go.

Charley and I headed for the East Room to our places behind and stage left of the podium. While the 160 credentialed reporters, some standing and some seated on chairs set up for them, gossiped and chatted, the place buzzed like a high school lunchroom. To the amusement of some, two cable network correspondents were doing stand-ups to camera, predicting, with sonorous certainty, what Barley would say.

"Ladies and gentlemen, the President of the United States." As the announcement over unseen speakers quieted the room, the two TV reporters wrapped up their spiels. Barley approached the podium, and the assembled press stood to their feet as one.

"Good morning, everyone. Please be seated." I began to breathe more normally when he started reading the opening statement. By the time he'd finished, he seemed more relaxed.

"All right," he said, "I'm happy to take questions."

He'd already memorized a good share of the correspondents' names and faces, and Charley had had one of his minions sketch a seating chart with the reporters' pictures on it.

"Abby," Barley smiled directly at a slight, dark-haired young woman in the front row. Abby Fraser, the White House correspondent for the Associated Press, traditionally asked the first question. As everyone expected, it was about Aashif Abaan and his four co-conspirators, or *alleged* co-conspirators. Somehow Barley managed to sound both forthright and resolute even as he fell back on the old saw that he couldn't provide more specifics because the matter would come before a court.

"I think it's pretty clear that this government can and will act swiftly to apprehend those who wish us ill," he said. "And I commend the various agencies—police, FBI, Homeland Security and others—for their quick, professional work identifying and capturing the four alleged terrorists. But now that they've been apprehended, this is a matter for the Justice Department, and I won't comment further."

To the next four questioners, he answered that 1., he was forming a bipartisan commission to protect against cyberterrorism, 2., considering legislation to criminalize access to extremist propaganda on the Internet and, 3., hoping that all of President-elect Mathews' cabinet appointments would be confirmed quickly and 4., he had no plans to move into the White House.

"Amanda and I are very comfortable in Blair House. And the commute"— a walk of a few hundred yards —"is tolerable." That earned a few chuckles.

When the *Huffington Post's* Martha Blaine asked what plans he had to deal with global warming, Barley said he preferred the term climate change, "especially after some of the winters we've seen lately." More laughter.

"But by any name, climate change is real and there's no longer any doubt that it's caused by man." Pausing for effect, he then prompted snickers by adding "and *women*."

"I don't have all the answers, by any means, but I do know there's no one single solution. Obviously, we must encourage alternative energy sources—wind, solar, geothermal, biofuels, etcetera—and cut back on carbon-based emissions wherever possible. We're looking into new ways to do both. Finally, we think creative technology and entrepreneurship can make a big difference by reducing carbon dioxide in the atmosphere, the primary cause of climate change."

Better than at the run-through, I thought. In fact, nicely done.

"You know," Barley said, "there's some interesting stuff going on by small, innovative companies that are attacking this problem in some very exciting ways."

He responded to the raised hand of Robbie McFarland of the Knight-Ridder group.

"Mr. Vice President, you mentioned innovative companies. Can you give any examples?"

"As a matter fact I can." Barley consulted a legal pad on the podium. "Companies like Carbonaide, which is liquefying millions of tons of carbon to be stored underground, where it can't be absorbed in the atmosphere. Then there's"—he looked down again—"And/Ore, which is dumping iron ore in the oceans to promote the growth of algae, which absorbs carbon dioxide in the water. There's also Dew Drop Inc., which is spraying the atmosphere with droplets of water to reduce solar heat. The ultimate solution to climate change may well lie in the approaches companies like those are making."

Charley mouthed *last question* to Abby Fraser, who nodded. It went to Bill Robertson, of the *Philadelphia Inquirer*.

"Sir, I think everyone would appreciate hearing how you're fitting into your job. Are you enjoying it?"

Barley looked at the chart Charley had prepared for him.

"Well, Bill, I don't think 'enjoyment' is quite the word I'd use, certainly not with last week's terrible events. But I will say I'm finding my way around and finding the challenges to be of a grown-up nature—work worth doing. Serving the American people, doing what I can to make their lives safer and I hope a little better is a satisfying way to spend one's days. And I'm pleased and proud to do it until President-elect Mathews takes the oath of office, and I can re-assume my rightful role as stand-by equipment."

During the laughter, Charley signaled Amy Fraser.

"Thank-you Mr. Vice President," she said, ending the press conference.

I kicked myself for not forestalling Barley's endorsement of Maggie as president only hours before the world was to hear she'd already renounced the office, but that's what sometimes happens when you take a calculated risk. I thought of calling Barry and telling him to hold his story for a day, but I didn't. The letters were dated the day before. I couldn't sit on such momentous news much longer. Barley looked relieved when I caught up with him en route to the West Wing.

"Well done, sir."

"Wasn't so bad, was it? I think they went easy on me, considering it was my first East Room outing and the situation with Maggie."

"That could be. But by the next one you'll have a better lay of the land and feel more confident."

"We'll see." I remembered that's what my mother used to say to me when what she really meant was: "Don't bet on it."

"Sir," I said after taking a deep breath. "We need to talk."

"Uh oh. Whenever I hear that tone of voice, I'm sure trouble is coming. Let's go to the Oval."

I gave Barley the news about the letters.

"She signed them willingly?"

"Yes, sir, quite willingly."

He took in the news, then thanked me for doing something he said he didn't think he could have done himself. Apologizing for not telling him before the press conference, I said I hadn't wanted to complicate things.

Turning grave, he asked about Walter. I told him I hadn't heard from him yet and would let him know the moment I did. I added I was expecting Jagoda to break the news about Maggie in the next day's paper.

"There goes the press conference."

"No, sir. He has it exclusively. The others will go with the presser."

"Won't I look out of the loop when they find out you knew about this before I did?"

"*If* they find out. The timing may get lost in the news."

"Good luck with that."

"Let me think about it. If I don't come up with anything, you can blame it on me."

"I may have to," Barely said sharply. He was clearly

annoyed.

There was nothing else to say. When I left him, Barley was staring out the window at the South Lawn, which was covered by a thin layer of fresh snow.

Walking back to my office, I decided to call Mac Murphy to confirm the time and place for our after-hours drink rather than dwell on the rapid cascade of events. We agreed on 6:30 at the Round Robin Bar in the Willard Hotel, my favorite watering hole. No sooner had I hung up than the phone rang. Just as I feared, it was Walter, who wasted no time on niceties.

"I don't know what your game is, Jamison, but I'm not taking this lying down." I couldn't remember the last time he called me by my last name.

"Walter, you know it's for the best for Maggie *and* for the country,"

"Fuck the country."

"I'm sure you don't mean that."

"We're not done here." He hung up.

Now it was my cell that was ringing. Only a privileged few had that number. Once again, there were no niceties.

"You've been played," said a voice I couldn't place.

"Who's this?"

"Never mind that, you've been *had*."

"What are you talking about?"

"Those climate change companies."

"What about them?"

"I read in the papers that a Texas oil man named Klaus Hunt was summoned to the White House to talk about climate change."

"Which is a matter of public record. What about it?"

"Klaus Hunt just happens to be Carbonaide's single biggest investor, the majority stockholder. And it wouldn't surprise me if he's heavily invested in the other two the president mentioned. While you're at it, you might want to check Walter Mathew's involvement too. "

The caller hung up.

I immediately put in a call to the White House technology director, Mark Clifford. Three minutes later he was in my office. I explained about the anonymous call and showed him the number on my phone,

"Can you trace it?" I asked him.

"Trace it? No," Mark said. "We can do that only when it's actually engaged. But we should be able to find out who has that number, unless it's encrypted. You want us to try?"

I said that indeed I did.

"Give me a little time, I'll see what I can do."

The Round Robin is a stately, circular bar that has been serving generous libations to the likes of Mark Twain and Walt Whitman since the Lincoln administration. For me, as well as for the 19th century supplicants who did their special interest pleading in the hotel lobby (thus the word "lobbyists"), the opulent Willard could not have been more convenient, standing as it does in the shadow of the White House.

Although I arrived early, Mac was already seated at a table against the wall, nursing a Budweiser. We shook hands.

"You look older and wiser, Skeeter. Power must agree with you.

"Older anyway, let's leave it at that." It had been a long day and I felt awful. I ordered a whiskey sour on the rocks.

"What's new with you, Mac?"

"That legislation I was working on is pretty much finished."

"Congratulations. Turn out the way you outlined it to me?"

"Yeah, pretty much."

"So how do we bring it to the floor?"

"Are you sure you want that? Last I heard Maggie was doing better."

"She is. But there's better and then there's *well enough to run the country*."

"Still, you're going to have to convince the public she's not coming back. Either that she doesn't want to, or she *can't*."

"I'm not sure I'll be the one to do the convincing."

"Meaning?"

"I think Maggie's the one who doesn't want it." I winked and took a sip of my whiskey sour. "I think she knows she's not up to it."

"You son of a bitch," Mac said. "You got her to renounce."

I glanced around the room to make certain we weren't being overheard, then nodded and we clinked glasses.

"Congratulations, Skeeter. Now there's something you should know."

"What's that?"

"Claymore wants to be Barley's veep."

I almost choked on my drink. "Won't happen," I said when I recovered.

"You know he's next in line?"

"I do know, yes."

"I'm just the messenger. That's what he wants. I don't think he'll move on this for less, and he's capable of stalling for months."

"I'll take it to Barley, but he won't go for it, guaranteed. See if you can feel Claymore out on what he'd settle for—something realistic."

"That may be the first time 'realistic' and 'Claymore' have been used in the same sentence. And by the way, I'm sure he'd sweeten the pot for you personally if you could sell Barley on it."

Now Mac looked around the room before lowering his voice again.

"The Speaker has been known to be...*generous.*"

"I'll pretend I didn't hear that."

Mac laughed. "And I'll let Claymore know you're not for sale."

+++

MATHEWS RENOUNCES PRESIDENCY
by Barry Jagoda
Cleveland Plain-Dealer

WASHINGTON, D.C.--President-elect Margaret Mathews, who could not be sworn in as President of United States due to a ruptured aneurysm she suffered ten days before her scheduled January 20th inauguration, has written to Speaker of the House Jake Claymore and President of the Senate Pro Tem, Oscar Thorne renouncing all claims on the presidency, Bruce ("Skeeter") Jamison, Barley Thompson's chief of staff, said today.

Her action is likely to set the nation on a course into uncharted waters.

Thompson's press secretary, Charley Philbrick, released a statement in which Mr. Thompson, Ms. Mathews' running mate who is serving as acting president, called Ms. Mathews' action "heartbreakingly courageous."

"I'm saddened to learn of her decision," he said in the statement. "But I respect it and I will do everything in my power to ensure that she never regrets making it." The statement made no reference to the acting president's plans or political future.

The president-elect remains a patient at Sibley Hospital in the District of Columbia and was unavailable for comment. Her husband, former Secretary of State Walter Mathews, confirmed that his wife had signed the letters but said she did not write them herself. "Obviously, someone else prepared them for her signature." He declined to elaborate.

Asked about the origin of the letters, Chief-of-staff Jamison said only that "they reflected the president-elect's wishes." He added that he expected "the letters would be delivered to Speaker Claymore and to Senate President Thorne within a day or two in accordance with the 25th Amendment to the Constitution."

Speaker Claymore and Senator Thorne both said they would await receipt of the letters before making any comment about them. But Speaker Claymore added, "I have nothing but respect and good wishes for President-elect Mathews."

The current situation is unprecedented in American history; not since George Washington was inaugurated in 1789 has the nation been without a serving president for longer than a few hours. And no amendment to the Constitution, including the 25th, which deals with succession to the presidency, directly addresses the nation's present circumstances: a vice president serving as acting president in the absence of a president.

The 25th amendment, ratified in 1967, refers only to a president, not to a president-elect. But it was in its spirit, if not the amendment's specific wording, that Thompson became acting president. The amendment states that if "the president is unable to discharge the powers and duties of his office...Congress shall decide the issue."

Winston Upham, a former Solicitor General of the United States who currently teaches constitutional law at Georgetown Law School, said, "We could find ourselves in a very muddy situation indeed if the president-elect has in fact chosen to renounce her claims on the presidency. Both houses of Congress will likely have to resolve the matter through the legislative process, but just how they would do that, nobody knows for certain."

In an interview conducted shortly before Chief of Staff Jamison revealed the existence of the president-elect's letters, former Secretary of State Walter Thompson, said he was happy to report that his wife is improving daily "and is looking forward to jumping back into the political fray in the near future."

Asked about the letters after their existence became known, Secretary Thompson said that he would have no comment "for at least a day or two to make certain there are no irregularities." He again declined to elaborate.

"I just want to make sure that everything is copacetic," he said. "I will support my wife, the president-elect, no matter what."

Secretary Mathews surprised many observers when he withdrew his nomination for State in Thompson's administration.

"I want to devote myself completely to my wife's recovery," the Secretary said at the time.

PART THREE

-- 19 --

Two days after Jagoda's interview with Walter appeared, he called a news conference to say that his wife's letters had been coerced, called my action "outrageous" and called for my immediate resignation.

He had whisked Maggie away from Dawson and out of Sibley to a private facility, where she was secluded and out of the public eye. As flagrant and open as he'd been in reintroducing her via CNN, Walter now clammed up about her condition, state of mind and, most especially, whereabouts. As for Maggie, she was observing radio silence.

Walter then hired Washington's legal counsel of choice for the political elite, Bill Mules, to represent him. For my part, I was being subjected to repeated questioning by various White House lawyers, at times with Barley present, but more often on my own.

For the most part, Barley, suffering from hypertension and sequestered in Blair House, stayed out of the fray. Officially, he was supporting me, but how long that would last was anyone's guess. Reading the tea leaves, I figured my days were numbered.

"Tell me again," Roger Kostmayer, a deputy White House counsel asked, "When did you inform the president you'd persuaded Maggie to sign letters to the speaker and the senator pro tem?"

"I object to the characterization," I replied. "I didn't *persuade* Maggie to do anything. I asked her what she wanted."

"In regard to signing those letters?"

"In regard to whether she wanted the presidency," I said. "When she told me she didn't feel up to being president, I asked her if she would sign letters required by the Constitution to remove herself from any rightful claim to it."

"And she agreed? With witnesses present?"

"Yes, her neurosurgeon, Dr. Dawson, and a hospital administrator."

"Was the hospital rep a lawyer?"

"I'm not sure."

"And when did you actually take possession of the letters?"

"That same evening."

"The evening you spoke to Mrs. Mathews about the matter?"

"Yes. They were typed up at the hospital on Sibley letterhead and brought to her to sign. After reading them, she did so."

"And what did you do with the letters?"

"I brought them with me to the White House."

"That evening?"

"Yes, I locked them in a file in my office."

"And did you see the president then, or talk to him?"

"No."

"Why not?"

"He had a lot on his plate and I didn't want to add to it just then."

"Something so momentous and yet you didn't let the president know about the letters?"

"I knew he had a press conference the following morning. I knew he was worried about it. *Very* worried. I thought it likely he'd be asked about Maggie. Given the potential furor an answer about her disavowal would cause, I thought it better for the president not to get bogged down in questions about her decision."

"Why furor?"

"I expected Walter to object. Which he did, but not before the press conference, and not publicly."

"He objected?"

"Yes, as you well know."

"To his wife signing the letters, or to the fact that you didn't inform him that you planned to *ask* her to sign them?"

"My guess is that it was both."

"And why *didn't* you inform him?"

"Because I was sure he would object."

Kostmayer shook his head. "You didn't think it important to tell either the president or Mrs. Mathews' husband what you intended to do, or to seek their permission to do it?"

"In the case of Walter Mathews, I was pretty sure he wouldn't have allowed me to see Maggie alone."

"Even though you were friends?"

"I worked on Maggie's campaign. Friends? I'd like to think so, but I don't know. I'm certainly closer to Maggie than to Walter. I spent a lot more time with her."

"And the reason you think Mr. Mathews wouldn't have wanted you to be alone with his wife was the very reason you wanted to get—sorry, to *ask*—if she would sign the letters necessary to relinquish her claim to the presidency."

"It was an important matter. I acted on behalf of the acting president. And, if I may say so, in the interest of the country."

"Without the president's knowledge."

"Yes. I think limbo is a dangerous state. I thought it important that this administration have a president and a vice president. I thought—I still *think*—there's a need to stabilize the continuity of the process in these difficult times. If Maggie had indicated she felt capable and intended to fulfill her election responsibilities, I would have acted entirely differently."

Kostmayer put down his yellow pad. "Do you think, Mr. Jamison, that you did anything wrong?"

"Criminally?"

"Or ethically."

I bowed my head and thought about it, not for the first time, but I always returned to the same answer. "I did what I thought was right."

"Would you do it again?"

"I honestly don't know."

⤜ ⤜ ⤜

Walking back to the White House, I could see a crowd gathered in Lafayette Park, some holding placards that I couldn't read. The media was filled with debate over my actions, some in support, others uncertain, while others—those who'd expected to see Maggie president and who'd had their hopes dashed— were certain I'd overstepped. Outraged, in some cases.

Having been asked by various radio and TV talking heads—everyone from Bill O'Reilly to Rachel Maddow—to appear on their shows, I'd declined. What was the point? It made no sense to me to argue my case in a public forum, just to be praised—or vilified.

So I hunkered down, basically a prisoner of the White House, not unlike the man who was holed up at Blair House. I'd heard that a revolving stable of newshounds were lying in wait for me in front of my apartment building. Before their anticipated encampment, I'd brought changes of clothing and toiletries to work, and I slept on the couch in my office. If I had to venture out, a car and driver were at my disposal, and I hid behind tinted windows.

As soon as Walter called for my head on a platter, I'd offered Barley my resignation. I'd undergone the first of what I thought of as my interrogations. They only added to my sense of captivity.

"I won't hear of it," Barley said after I offered to resign. "Don't mention it again."

We were in his living quarters at Blair House, overlooking Pennsylvania Avenue.

"How are you and Amanda holding up?" I asked.

I knew she had fled to Cleveland to escape the ruckus.

Barley stood at the window, his shoulders slumped in a posture of defeat, unlike the aura that had surrounded him when he'd first found his footing shortly after the inauguration. Was that only three weeks earlier? Now his eyes were as bloodshot as mine, and pallor clung to him like a thin fog, casting a shroud of gloom over everything around him.

"Amanda isn't cut out for this," he said.

"Who is?"

"I suppose, if you live here long enough, you get used to it. I imagine there are those who thrive on it. She doesn't, and I don't either. How about you?"

Seated on the couch, I stared at Barley's back. "I'm a chameleon. Throw me in the pea soup and I'll turn green."

"I'd say you're more survivor than chameleon."

"That's not much of a distinction. We're all survivors. Until we aren't."

"But that's what worries me—survival."

"Yours or mine?"

"Both. You know I was never prepared for this, never meant to be here. I think of myself as a caretaker president."

"But as such, you've done damn well. Your poll numbers shine."

Barley turned from the window. "Polls. What do they mean at this point? Next week, six months from now, they'll be in the tank. What price is anyone willing to pay for this office?"

It was a question I couldn't answer. Some had paid the ultimate price—Lincoln, McKinley and Kennedy, to name a few. For others, the cost was perhaps less dear but not much. LBJ came to mind, as did Nixon.

"It's me who should think of resigning," Barley said. "Not you."

"Mr. President, we're in the midst of a constitutional crises. Take a look at the protesters in Lafayette Park. If you were to resign now, this could turn ugly fast. We need leadership. We need clear succession. Without you, this ship would be rudderless. I don't want to sound alarmist, but the possibility for anarchy is out there, maybe all across the nation."

Barley came and sat next to me on the couch. "Skeeter, not even a month has gone by since we were together in the Watergate apartment. I was a broken man. You brought me through it."

"Please, sir."

"No, let me finish. You know my past; you know my secrets. It would have been easy for you, a Maggie man, to walk away. I've survived because of your loyalty and determination."

"I could never have walked away. No more than either one of us can walk away now. You survived because of something in yourself, some strength that you probably didn't even know you had. And now I'm a Barley Thompson man. You said it the other day: We're in this together."

A bit of light came into his eyes, and when he smiled the gloom lifted for a moment.

"Are you religious?" he asked.

"No sir."

"One of those liberal heathens?"

"I just didn't grow up with it."

"I did. I had a strict Catholic upbringing. Altar boy, communion, all of it."

"You don't go to church."

"There's hardly been time, and I'll confess to you—as if I haven't confessed enough—I'm a lapsed Catholic."

"Well, I can't absolve you."

"No, but perhaps you would pray with me."

"Pray?" Even though it wasn't an unheard of request—Nixon had asked Kissinger to pray with him shortly before he resigned—when Barley got to his knees and asked me to join him, I felt a palpable discomfort. Especially after he took my hand. I dropped to my knees and offered up a silent prayer that this would be brief.

Back at the White House an array of messages were in my tray: most were from reporters, including two from Barry Jagoda. There was also a note from Angela, as well as a message to call Mark Clifford in regard to that message on my cellphone.

But when I reached him, Mark told me he couldn't be all that much help. The call had been placed from a pay phone in a BART station—the Bay Area Rapid Transit in San Francisco.

"A public phone?" I asked.

"Yes. Hard to believe they still exist. But if you want anonymity, it's still a pretty safe way to communicate. Your call was placed from the Embarcadero Station at 2:14 PST. A train had just come in, and a lot of people were in the terminal. A camera picked up a grainy photo of a man making a call at that hour. Wearing a hat, a windbreaker, and a scarf, he was partially hidden from view. I'll send it up to you, just don't expect much. We might get someone in to try and track voice recognition, but, in my view, it's a long shot. If you want to pursue it, I'd suggest taking it to the FBI."

"Thanks, Mark. Not the end of the world."

"No, I guess you've got bigger issues right now. But we're here if you need us."

Mark's suggestion that I ask the FBI for help made me think of Angela. She might have contacts at the agency that could expedite a search if I decided to go forward. But it was also an excuse to get in touch with her. When her voice message kicked in immediately, I did as I was told: left a message.

Barry Jagoda answered his cellphone on the first ring.

"Quite a mess you've got over there," he said. "Walter on the warpath, Congress up in arms, the Supreme Court standing by. Any comment?"

"Nothing on the record, but I think you might look into Walter's financial involvement with those climate change companies the president mentioned at his press conference."

"I've already done a little background on them. They're privately held and aren't required to identify their investors."

"It's quite possible that Klaus Hunt is a significant investor in at least one and possibly all three companies. He was the first person to tell us about them, though he didn't mention his involvement. And Walter recommended Hunt to the president. That should set off alarms."

"It would set off a lot more if Walter hadn't withdrawn his nomination."

"I'd say it's still worth investigating."

"You would because you've got an ox to gore."

185

"Could be. But maybe you could benefit from a well placed spear."

"Why do I get the feeling I'm being played again?"

"You're the fourth estate. So make a contribution."

❧   ❧   ❧

"I thought you might need bucking up," Angela said when she called back.

"I'm feeling beleaguered, that's for sure."

"How about lunch?"

"If I can sneak you inside the stockade."

"That bad?"

"It's no picnic in the park."

"Not even in Lafayette Park?"

"The tension's mounting everywhere."

"I can be there in about forty-five minutes; twelve fifteen okay?"

"Something to look forward to. I'll let the honor guard know you're coming."

At twelve twenty-five, an aide ushered Angela into my office. After taking off her coat, she hugged me; the last several hours seemed to vanish.

"You were right about the guard. Secret Service and uniformed police are swarming. How's Barley coping?"

"He hasn't been out of Blair House since yesterday. He's praying."

"Praying?"

"Before I left him this morning we were on our knees together. He's rediscovered his Catholicism."

"Not a good sign."

"True believers might disagree, but I don't."

"Is he having a breakdown?"

"I don't think it's come to that. But high blood pressure for sure."

"What's your plan?"

I laughed. "I wish I had one, at least a master plan. For now I'd like to get the inner circle together, and try to come up with one."

"Who would that include?"

"You, obviously. Morgan Walker, someone from Intelligence, and someone from Congress. The question is who? The old cabinet, or our nominees?"

"If you're looking for procedural and tactical advice, go with the people you trust. When it comes to Congress, I'd look for someone who's been around, won't be polarizing and has a powerful constituency."

"I was thinking of Kris Gilman."

"Good choice. She's smart and in my view has a bright future." Angela looked around the office, taking in the mess.

"Something else has come up," I said. I picked up my cell, scrolled through to find the anonymous message and played it for her.

"Interesting. You don't know who it is?"

I shook my head. "Our I.T. guys located the call, but if I want to take it any further, they suggested the FBI."

"Do you want to do that?"

"I wondered if you might know someone who could handle it discreetly."

"Maybe. Career techies, some who may have worked their way up since I was last there. I can ask. Is this all you've got, a message and a number?"

"And a blurry photo from a BART station in San Francisco—the phone booth where the call was made."

"That's a start. Send it to me, and I'll see what I can do. It's a long shot. Is it because Walter is mentioned?"

"That's part of it."

"He's slippery."

"So you once said, or words to that effect."

"There were rumors when I was at Justice and he was at State."

"Anything you want to share, now would be the time."

"I'm going out on a limb. Can I trust you?"

Our eyes locked. "I'd like it if you would."

Angela nodded. "The gossip was that Walter had a love affair before Maggie, one he never really got over. They say there was a child."

"I'll be damned."

"Purely rumor. I don't know any more than that."

"And it's nothing lurid."

"No, not by D.C. standards, but maybe worth knowing."

"Thanks. I appreciate your confidence. Now would you like to share a ham and cheese sandwich?"

Angela laughed. "Are you really living here?"

"More avoiding the press than living."

"I think I should be direct."

"Please."

"You can't hide here much longer. It'll look as if no one's in charge. The president has to show himself. Speak to the nation."

"I'm not sure he's up for it."

"You primed him once. You're going to have to do it again."

"One more for the Gipper?"

Angela rolled her eyes before breaking into a fetching grin.

-- 20 --

"Good evening."

The vice president spoke from behind the Oval Office's ceremonial desk, salvaged from the HMS Resolute and used by several presidents dating back to FDR. Except for a sheaf of papers and a pen and inkwell set, the desk was bare. The American flag and the presidential colors flanked either side of the backlit bay windows overlooking the Rose Garden. Television lights flooded Barley, diminishing him, with too much blush on his cheeks.

From the back of the room, I watched the monitor and said, "Cut".

The lights went off, and the cameraman stepped away from his collapsible dolly. Barley stood up. Dabbing at his sweat-flecked hairline with a white handkerchief, he walked to the front of the desk, and perched on one corner, where he seemed to relax for a moment. "Sorry," he said. "It's just too—*regal.*"

I agreed. With the exception of Reagan, no modern president had managed to appear both comfortable and in charge when speaking to the nation from behind that desk. Dubois couldn't manage it, and Bush the Younger called Howdy Doody to mind. "Let's move to another room and put you behind a lectern in front of Lincoln's portrait?"

"I'd prefer to go to the Lincoln bedroom and lie down."

"One more rehearsal. After your address tonight you can sleep in any bedroom you want."

Having written Barley's speech, his first to the nation, I'd handed it off to Charley and his team for a polish. Since I felt responsible for the crisis my intervention with Maggie had created, I thought the least I could do was draft something to start our rebuilding effort.

But after an hour of setting up video equipment and lights and pushing Barley through two more run-throughs, we were both feeling out of sorts. Barley announced he was going back to Blair House for a nap. We agreed to meet again at 8:30, half an hour before the cameras would go live.

In my office I returned Barry Jagoda's call.

"Hey, must be a slow day over there." Jagoda quipped.

"When we get a slow day, I'll invite you to lunch."

"I'll be buffing my nails in anticipation."

"What's up?"

"Nothing so far on Walter and those climate stocks. I did talk to the PR people at all three companies and struck out each time. But I haven't given up. I just have to find someone willing to talk."

"Good. Keep at it. Is that why you called?"

"Not exactly. But it is about Walter. I have a source in the State Department. Good source. He's been there a long time, going back to Bush 41. There was nothing anyone could pin directly on Walter, but according to my guy, everybody who worked with him—*everybody*—felt there was something off."

"Off?"

"He had his own agenda. People thought he was up to something. At the very least he was out for himself and playing it close to the line."

"I need specifics."

"My guy claimed they could never prove anything, but there was a feeling that some of Walter's overtures—his diplomatic initiatives as secretary—were more in *his* best interests than the country's. Especially when it came to the 'Stans."

"The *stans*?"

"The former Soviet republics that got their independence after the Soviet Union dissolved in the early '90s: Kazakhstan, Uzbekistan, Turkmenistan and Kyrgyzstan. They're all rich in petroleum and natural gas, most of it untapped. Apparently Walter paid more attention to them than he needed to. For one thing, he spent as much time in Central Asia as he did in Europe."

"Are we talking money, financial gain, what?"

"Dunno yet, but something ain't kosher."

"You saying Walter's bent?"

"Your word. But yeah, he could be."

"Does your source have any hard information, any evidence?"

"I'm pursuing it. That's all I've got right now."

"But you'll keep me posted?"

"Yeah, sure." Jagoda cleared his throat. "Skeeter, is your job safe? There's talk..."

"The only talk you need to listen to is the president's. Nine o'clock tonight."

∾   ∾   ∾

I went to the men's room and washed my hands. In the mirror, I looked even worse than I felt. My face was the color of wet cement. I dried my hands and headed to the White House Mess for coffee, the worst in the world. It tasted like "sock juice," as a French friend used to call American coffee. That was before the gourmet grinders came along and raised the taste level of our national drink. But not at the White House where it tasted like something from the Truman administration. Maybe that's when it was brewed.

But bad as it was, the coffee wasn't the worst of it. Overnight I'd become an invisible man. There were no "Hey Skeeter, howzit going?" greetings. No cheesy smiles or friendly waves, or kowtowing to my place just beneath Barley in the executive branch pecking order. Someone I knew slightly from the economic section gave me a grim-faced nod, and I got a shy smile from a young woman I'd recommended for a job answering letters. But most avoided my eyes or pretended to be occupied with their smart phones. I tried to put my own spin on it: They were embarrassed for me.

After adding extra sugar to my Styrofoam cup—no china was to leave the Mess—I headed back to my office. Curiously, the trip to the Mess—and my demotion to non-person—energized me. It gave me just the shot of adrenalin I needed for what I had to do next. Before the feeling faded, I asked an operator to get Klaus Hunt for me. Five minutes later he was on the line.

"Mr. Hunt, it's Skeeter Jamison."

"Skeeter, it sounds like you stirred up a hornets nest out there. You ok?"

I was in no mood for empathy, least of all his, or small talk either. "I'm calling because your name has come up in connection with Walter Mathews."

"What about him?" His tone had changed to wariness.

"When did the two of you first meet?"

"I think you know I was a bundler for Maggie."

"I do know that. But it's my understanding that you and Walter go back before that." I was bluffing. I knew nothing of the sort.

"I may have met him when he was at State."

"Were you friends?"

"What's this about, Skeeter?"

I ignored the question.

"As I understand it, you and Walter were more than friends. You did business together?"

"Business? What you're driving at?"

Apparently, I'd touched a nerve. I took a chance. "Yes, the oil and gas business in the 'Stans."

"Now look, I don't know what this is about or where you got your information, but you'd better be damn careful with your insinuations." His voice was tinged with anger—or fear. "I hear Walter's suing you. I'm sure he'd be quite willing to add slander to his list of grievances."

I started to tell him his reaction seemed a bit overheated, but I didn't get the chance.

Klaus Hunt had hung up.

∽ᕲ   ∽ᕲ   ∽ᕲ

I needed air. Taking off my suit jacket and tie, I got a baseball cap and sunglasses from my office closet and put on a scruffy tan windbreaker that bore evidence of more than one take-out Chinese dinner. Pulling the cap down low I headed past the East Wing and out the East Appointment Gate. Once onto East Executive Avenue, I took off the White House ID I wore around my neck like a talisman, put it in my inside jacket pocket and slipped unnoticed onto Pennsylvania Avenue, which I then crossed to enter Lafayette Park.

At 5:30, it was jammed. The protestors I'd seen the other day had been supplemented by pale-faced area office workers smoking cigarettes or blinking in the winter sun like prairie dogs emerging from underground tunnels. I could smell the sweet aroma of marijuana. A TV crew was setting up for a reporter's stand-up that would no doubt include protest placards as well as the White House. A middle-aged woman carried one I hoped would not make the nightly news. "Shoot Skeet" it read. Not a good sign, in more ways than one.

A burly man in an olive drab car-coat was bellowing into a megaphone. "The scriptures tell us the end time is preceded by tribulation. Oh my, do we have tribulation. What we don't have are leaders. We have no president. We have no Cabinet. Our only Congress is a sexual congress, and we the people are the ones who are getting...fornicated. These are the end times, my friends, these are the last days, these are the final..."

I moved on through a sea of more signs. "Impeach Thompson." And: "Give me Liberty or Give me Maggie." Another: "Barley Belongs in Beer, not the White House." One appeared to be recycled from the fall campaign. It read, simply: "Maggie/Barley." It seemed as out of date as "Tippecanoe and Tyler Too." It took me a few seconds to decipher the one that read "Leave it to the Supremes." I admired the wordplay on the top court even as I hoped it wouldn't come to that.

A homeless man wearing a tattered, navy blue overcoat sat alone on a park bench. The tips of his fingers poked through dirty woolen gloves. Next to him a supermarket cart was filled with his possessions. I remembered a poem from college, "The Old Cumberland Beggar" by Wordsworth. I remembered it because it occasioned one of the few times I ever spoke up in class. As the beggar goes around his village, people give him things: food, money, and clothing.

"Why do they respond to him that way?" the professor had asked.

I surprised myself by saying, "Isn't it 'There but for the grace of God, go I?'" Though I'd sat for months in his class, the professor looked at me as if for the first time.

"There..." he said in a voice just above a whisper, "go...*I*."

The homeless man accepted the five-dollar bill I gave him without looking at me, as half a dozen choristers began to sing "We shall overcome."

Further away a brass band was playing "The Battle Hymn of the Republic."

I wiped my eyes before retracing my steps toward the People's House.

Back at the gate a Secret Service guard checked my ID, and after looking me up and down, waved me through. When I got to my office, I called Barry Jagoda on my cellphone, leaving a message on his.

I told him his old-timer at State was on to something. Walter and Klaus Hunt were connected in that period, and it almost certainly had to do with petroleum and natural gas in the 'Stans. "Keep at it," I said.

"The President of the United States."

Sitting in the media room, in front of the bank of TVs, I watched as the camera panned to Barley standing at a lectern in the East Room.

"Good evening. I know that many of you are concerned about the events of the last few days. I share your concern, and tonight I want to talk to you about what we can do together to alleviate it.

"As most of you are aware, three days ago, my chief of staff, Bruce Jamison, visited President-elect Mathews in Sibley hospital. He was relieved to find her alert and looking healthier than he'd seen her since she was admitted on January 10th.

"The president-elect told Mr. Jamison that she did not feel capable of assuming the presidency and she felt it was unfair to put the country through protracted uncertainty. She therefore wished to renounce any claim to the office she'd been elected to hold.

"When asked if she was certain about her intentions, Mrs. Mathews answered that she'd never been more certain about anything in her life.

"A hospital administrator, along with Dr. Dawson, witnessed her signing the letters that would be given to the speaker of the House of Representatives and the president pro tem of the Senate, relinquishing her claim on the presidency. Those letters have been made public.

"Much has been made of the fact that Mr. Jamison did not inform me at once of Mrs. Mathews' decision, instead waiting until after my Friday morning press conference to tell me.

"In discussing those events, he believed that had I known about her decision, I would have been obliged to reveal it at that press conference. As a result, other important issues would have gone unaddressed. While my chief of staff acted in what he thought were the country's best interests, he made an error in judgment, as he admits. He agrees that he should have informed me at once about Mrs. Mathews' decision.

"He has admitted he was wrong, but I believe—I *sincerely* believe—his motives were honorable.

"So where does that leave us? There have been calls for Mr. Jamison's resignation. I have urged him to stay. Congress —both the House and the Senate—is looking into the matter of Mrs. Mathew's decision and the question of presidential succession. In due time, they will recommend a course of action in accordance with the Constitution."

I left the room before Barley finished speaking. He had done just fine, more than fine; it was a warm and heartfelt performance. I couldn't have asked for anything more. I was proud of him, even if I did write the speech myself.

-- 21 --

At 9:30 the following morning, the "inner circle" I'd cobbled together met for breakfast at Blair House. It was our first assembly: Morgan Walker, Angela Mercado, Patricia Washington and Jason Merriweather, who continued to aid in the transition. The junior Senator from New York, Kris Gilman, who Barley knew slightly from his days in the Senate, was his pick as our congressional liaison; she arrived ten minutes late. Gilman's talent for getting legislation onto the floor, even as a freshman senator, had impressed Barley. I seated her next to me at the dining room's oval table.

The headwaiter took our breakfast orders from a printout of choices: eggs, granola and yoghurt with fruit, even a Belgian waffle, Barley's favorite. Another waiter poured coffee. To my surprise the Blair House brew was almost acceptable. Would wonders never cease? Or did we have Amanda to thank?

At 9:50, the chief usher came in with a note from Barley saying he was delayed and we should start without him, asking that I lead the discussion.

"Is he ok?" Morgan Walker asked, turning to me. "He looked a bit unsteady last night."

"A lot of stress these past few days. I haven't talked to him this morning, but I think he's fine. I haven't heard otherwise."

"I thought the address went well," Angela said. "He hit all the right notes. Congratulations to whoever wrote his speech."

I felt my face flush. The last thing I wanted was to

acknowledge any part in that.

"Charley and his people," I said.

"Too early for polls," Jason Merriweather said, "but let's hope it gives him a bounce."

"We're still under 50%, but the free-fall has stopped," I said. "Barley's unconcerned. 'One day you're up, the next you're down,' he told me the other day. We can't play to polls."

"Better up than down though," Patricia Washington added.

"True. And with that mind I'd like to focus today on domestic issues. I know the agenda lists some other items, but it was drawn up before the fan spattered us with some unpleasant effluence."

Mild laughter loosened things up. "As you know from his address last night, Barley has rejected my offer to resign. But as far as I'm concerned, the offer remains on the table, and if I feel I'm a drag on the team, or the team considers me a drag, I'll leave. So before we begin, I'd like to know if I have your support. You're free to voice your opinions. Anybody?"

"I don't see any reason for you to leave," Gilman said. "There was no malice in what you did, only poor judgment in the way you went about it. As we all know, there's no shortage of that in this town. Unless the effluence gets too deep, I think you should hang in there."

"I'll second that," Angela said. "You're key to how this administration functions. Beyond that, to leave would spell defeat and weakness. It would make things worse than they already are."

"The Tea Party and the Libertarians in the House would have a field day," Walker added. "They're just itching to see you fall on your sword. But as long as you have the president's confidence, I think you'll weather the storm."

"I agree," Merriweather added. "Stay."

"Ms. Washington?"

"Hang in there."

"Thank you everybody. I appreciate your confidence."

From the kitchen two waiters came into the room, handed out plates and poured coffee refills.

"This coffee is good," I said. "Would anyone object to a bill that mandated a similar upgrade across the street?"

"Full bipartisan support on that," Gilman said. "Except perhaps from the senator from Massachusetts, who prefers tea."

"Which one?" Morgan asked.

"I couldn't possibly comment," Gilman replied, echoing a trope in the British version of the TV series "House of Cards."

"The first agenda item is Mrs. Mathew's letters," I said. "Senator, can you tell us where things stand in Congress?"

"The letters are in limbo, and I suspect that's where they'll stay until there's a resolution on Walter's lawsuits, at least on their legal standing. Neither Claymore nor Thorne have even acknowledged receipt."

"Any way of knowing if any of this will go to the Supreme Court?" I asked.

"It could, if Mathews gets legal standing, but that's a big if. I expect a lower court will decide within the next few weeks."

I nodded. "How about the confirmation process for our nominees?"

Gilman shook her head. "Also in limbo. The majority leader won't move on confirmation until he gets his legislative agenda passed, or some of it anyway. He's holding everything up because of Dubois's leftover EPA bill that taxes carbon emissions. The Republicans have attached an anti-abortion rider, which Democrats can't accept. There are also concerns about those companies the president mentioned in his press conference. One of the committees I'm on, Environment and Public Works, is looking into them, but if it comes to a filibuster, we don't have enough votes for cloture. On almost anything."

"Jesus, what's wrong with these people?" I asked. "Will they ever understand they were elected to actually get things done around there?"

"One of the problems is the president is considered weakened, and Congress views him more and more as a caretaker," Gilman said. "They smell blood in the water, and they'd like to find a way to call for a new election."

"That might play in Peoria," Angela said, "but I don't think it will get traction in the rest of the country."

"Probably not," the senator said, "but it'll keep the news cycle churning until something is done to relieve the stalemate we've got now."

"If we can get to a point where Barley could be confirmed as president," I said, "we need to put some thought into who his VP might be. Right now Jake Claymore is wangling for the job. More than wangling. He's threatening to throw a monkey wrench into the whole shebang unless he gets the nod."

"He'd be a disaster," Gilman said. "And even if it were offered to him, the Senate won't move on Barley until Maggie's letters have been decided."

"For the record," I said, "I'd like each of you to give me a list of your three top VP picks. Senator, I'd also like to know your take on who could get confirmed. That may be a separate list."

I mentioned the story I'd recently come across about Nixon's attempt to replace Spiro Agnew as his veep after Agnew had resigned in disgrace in 1973 for accepting bribes when he was governor of Maryland. Of the four names Nixon proposed—Nelson Rockefeller, Ronald Reagan, John Connolly and Gerald Ford—Ford was his last choice; but he was the only one acceptable to Democrats in Congress. Nixon was therefore obliged to pick a "Ford," as the vice president was later to say, "not a Lincoln".

It would be better to get the lay of the land, I offered, even if we had to wait before making our selection.

As we ate, I turned to Jason Merriweather and Patricia Washington. "What's the level of terrorist chatter these days?"

"Ratcheted up," Jason said. "They also smell blood in the water."

"You think we should go back to issuing George Bush-era color alerts?"

"I don't recommend it," Morgan jumped in. "I was in Congress back then, and those damn colors did nothing but aggravate the country's already high level of anxiety, exactly what Al Qaeda wanted."

"Yes, but it also affected the news cycle," Patricia said. "Isn't that how the Bush crowd used it, Cheney in particular? When they wanted to distract the public from something unsavory in their own downward drift."

"It was a cheap tactic," I replied. "Do we really want to go back to that?"

"I suppose the answer is, only if we have to," Angela said.

A titter of laughter.

"All right, then, back to the logjam we're in with Barley and Congress," I said. "Any ideas on how we break it?"

After polling everyone, I heard the same two words repeated: "Margaret Mathews."

"But does anyone have access to her?" I asked.

Nobody spoke up.

"Doesn't Walter have her under twenty-four hour security?" Patricia asked.

I nodded.

"I think if anyone could get in, it would be Barley," Walker said.

Just then the chief usher entered the dining room and handed me a note. After reading it, I excused myself and followed him to Barley's bedroom, where he lay in bed, looking like a ghost. A doctor stood over him, a stethoscope pressed to Barley's chest.

❦ ❦ ❦

Ten minutes later, back with the inner circle, I gave them the news. "Barley has atrial fibrillation, also known as A-fib. He's got a pulse rate of 210."

"Jesus," Walker said. "Is he in the hospital?"

"Not yet, but a doctor's with him, and an ambulance is on the way."

"Is he conscious?" Walker asked.

"Yes, but once they get him to Walter Reed, they'll

defibrillate and shock his heart back into a normal rhythm."

"They'll have to give him an anesthetic for that," Walker said, which reminded me that Morgan had trained as a medic when he was in the service. "As I understand it, A-fib can be controlled, but the risk of stroke is greater in people who have it."

"Barley is already on a blood thinner to help lessen that risk," I added.

Morgan looked around the room. "There's another problem."

I met his eyes. "I know. For the time Barley's unconscious, we won't have a president in charge."

"I assume we have to announce it," Patricia said.

"Absolutely," I said. "Word will get out the moment Barley arrives at Walter Reed."

"Any idea how long he'll be out?" Angela asked.

"It's impossible to predict," Morgan said. "It might be only ten or fifteen minutes, but we can't take any chances."

"Meaning?" Patricia asked.

I answered for Morgan. "I have to inform Jake Claymore. He's next in line of succession."

-- 22 --

Jake Claymore was away from his office. I left word with his secretary to have him call me a.s.a.p., then dug out Mac's business card and called his cell. After a single ring, a voice message said: "*You've reached me. Now do the right thing.*"

I left my name and number, then followed it with a text: "*POTUS alert.*"

Two minutes later my phone rang, and Mac said, "You know how to get a guy's attention."

"Where's Claymore?"

"Caucusing with freshmen. Geeze, Skeeter, share the gloom."

"You need to get him out of caucus and on the phone to me. Pronto."

"Tell me this isn't what I think it is."

"It isn't what you think it is. But *get* him."

"Ok, Skeeter, sit tight."

Ten minutes later, Mac got back to me. "Skeeter, I'm putting Speaker Claymore on."

"Jake Claymore here." His booming voice was full of self-importance. "What is it, Jamison?"

"Mr. Speaker, the president has been taken to Walter Reed. He's been diagnosed with atrial fibrillation, and they're going to have to defibrillate. That means Barley will be undergoing anesthesia. The 25th amendment..."

"I know the 25th," Claymore interrupted. "When's this all going to happen?"

"He was taken to the hospital twenty minutes ago."

"You're at the White House?"

"Blair House, but I'm on my way there."

"So am I. I'll be right over."

"With all due respect, sir, I don't think that's necessary."

"Forget 'due respect'. I'm speaker of the United States House of Representatives. And I'll decide what's necessary."

Whoa, I thought, but before I could say anything, Claymore had hung up. It would take me almost as long to walk from Blair House, as it would for Claymore to get to the White House in a limo.

After calling the switchboard there, I spoke to the chief of protocol, told him what was happening and asked him to alert the Secret Service. They would need to provide protection for Claymore. Then I called my assistant to see if she knew where Morgan Walker was. More and more, I had been thinking of him as one cool dude, someone who inspired confidence whenever he was around. Jane, Barley's assistant, said Walker had gone with Barley to Walter Reed. What am I, the last to know? I left Blair House and ran to the sweatshop.

The bitterly cold air felt good. When I got to the West Wing, I went to the men's room to pee, before hustling over to the East Portico to await yet another acting president.

A crowd of 30 or so people had gathered on the South Lawn. Walking toward them, I soon saw they were all members of the press, all, that is, but the man they'd formed a semi-circle around: Jake Claymore.

Edging closer, I got within spitting distance and heard Claymore's voice all too loud and clear.

"I've been assured he's going to be fine," he was saying, "at least physically. But until he is one hundred and ten percent, I'm pleased and proud to stand-in. I just want to say to the American people, there is no need to worry, you're in very good hands."

What the hell? The last thing the American people needed was to be told not to worry. And very good hands? Give me a break.

Reuters' Bill Rappaport asked the very question most on my mind.

"Mr. Speaker," he said, "what brings you to the White

House?"

"What brought me to the White House? A brand new Cadillac Seville." He provided his own laugh track. "But seriously, as acting president to the acting president, I figured this is where I ought to be. Give you folks a chance to look me over and me to answer any questions you might have."

And to get your sorry, sallow face on the evening news and tomorrow's front pages, I thought.

Jocelyn Green of Knight-Ridder was recognized next. "Sir, you've said nothing in the last few days about the letter Maggie Mathews wrote to you and Senator Thorne. Did you get the letter, and what are you planning to do about it?"

"Well now, ma'am, let me answer that. Haven't read it myself, so I can't comment on what it says, but my staff is studying that letter and the Constitution to see what it has to say about the present circumstances. I'm sure we'll have more to add in a few days."

Unable to take any more of his embarrassing grandstanding, I turned and headed back toward the portico entrance. A Secret Service agent was just inside. I'd never spoken harshly to anyone in the agency, but this was unacceptable.

"Speaker Claymore is out there"—I pointed to the media scrum—"surrounded by the press. He has no security, no protection. He's effectively the acting president at this moment. Get your ass out there and do your job. And get some back-up!"

The agent gave me a dirty look as he headed out the door. But at least he moved.

Heading toward my office in the West Wing, I ran into Charley Millbank, Barley's press secretary.

"What's going on?" he asked. I swallowed hard. I'd forgotten all about him.

"Shit, Charley, I'm sorry." I didn't say why. I didn't have to. Inexcusably, I'd left him, of all people, out of the loop. "It's been one of those days. I should have told you what you surely know by now."

Charley nodded. "It's ok, Skeeter. You've got a lot on

your plate. Anyway, I've seen CNN; Barley's at Walter Reed for some sort of procedure having to do with atrial fibrillation. He's going under anesthesia, which puts Jake Claymore, God help us, in charge. Hopefully just for an hour or so, 'til Barley's out of recovery."

"That's about it. I telephoned Claymore as a courtesy, and the asshole showed up here a few minutes ago. He's out there now pulling an Al Haig."

Charley looked at me blankly.

"When Reagan was shot in 1981, Haig was secretary of state. He came here immediately and said he was 'in control here at the White House'. At that point he was fourth in line of succession. He never lived it down."

"Holy shit." I didn't think Charley was talking about Al Haig.

"That about sums it up."

"What do you want me to do?"

"Not much you *can* do. When the great man"—I jerked my thumb in the direction of Claymore—"finishes his inaugural address, you should get over to the pressroom and do some damage control. Issue a statement: routine treatment for A-fib; nothing to worry about. Could be discharged tonight."

Wait a second, I thought. First things first.

"Hold that," I said, "you better go listen to Claymore. Make sure he doesn't declare war on Canada just because he can. Or worse."

"I'm on it." As he was leaving he turned to me. "You see that piece in today's *Plain Dealer*?"

Jesus, with everything going on, I had only had time to glance at the *Post's* front page.

"What'd it say?"

"Walter's being investigated by State. Seems as Secretary he got a bit too cozy with Turkmenistan and Uzbekistan. He may have been up to something not quite kosher."

"No shit."

"Talk later?" Charley said from the doorway.

"You bet. And thanks for the heads up re Walter. Maybe

there is a God."

I hurried to my office to read Jagoda's piece. When I'd finished it, my head was spinning. I had to hand it to Barry; with very few facts and even less hard evidence, he'd suggested that Walter had played fast and loose in the former Soviet Republics. And if Barry was right, the former president, "Slick Sammie" Sutton, was even slicker than I'd thought. How could somebody so smart, so talented and so skilled, be such a scumbag when it came to women and money?

But I had no time to muse on the follies of my fellow man. I had to focus on the future. What would Claymore do next? What was Walter's move? And how could I find out where Walter had stashed Maggie? It was like a three-dimensional chess game.

Jagoda, I thought. Come to papa. I put in a call.

"Nice piece," I said when he picked up.

"I thought you might like it."

"Can we meet?"

"I've got to file my Barley story tonight, but I could meet at 6:00 for 20 minutes, half hour at the most."

"You know the Hirschorn?"

"The doughnut on the Mall? Yeah, sure."

"Does that work for you?"

"Fine. Six o'clock. Where at the Hirschorn?"

"Gift shop."

"You paying my entrance fee?"

"The Hirschorn's free, art lover."

"I knew that."

The Hirschorn Museum and Sculpture Garden is one of the 21 (or 22, depending on who's counting what) of the museums and facilities that make up the Smithsonian Institution. It displays mostly modern art. The building itself is an object lesson in why architects shouldn't get too trendy. Opened in 1974, the circular edifice, which has been likened to everything from Barry's descriptive cement "doughnut" to a parked spaceship, screams the '70s. "Timeless" or "classic" it most definitely is not.

I got there early and was thumbing through a coffee

table book about Willem de Kooning when Barry walked in.

"I didn't know you were such a Renaissance man," he said, eyeing the book.

"I'm not, and I'm more interested in the art of the steal than I am in abstract expressionism. Let's go up to the second floor. There're some videos playing up there that'll cover anything we have to say."

Barry knew that Barley had been taken to Walter Reed, but when we got upstairs I added a couple of tidbits about his high blood pressure and his meds that would give the reporter an edge and keep him on the reservation. Careful not to say anything about Claymore that could come back to bite me, I filled him in on the impromptu press conference on the South Lawn, which he'd missed.

Barry flipped his reporter's notebook closed and gave me a look.

"So," I said. "Walter. What's going on? Is it as bad as I think it is?"

"If it's all true, it's pretty bad. Some of the things my State Department buddy was telling me I couldn't even allege, much less prove."

"Such as?"

"Padded expense accounts, personal expenses charged to State, including, I'm told, a chandelier for the dining room in his house. He supposedly even had his swimming pool resurfaced at government expense."

"A prince," I said. "Where was Maggie in all this?"

"He's cagey. Kept her away from State and in the dark as much as possible. Can't be sure, but I don't think she had a clue."

I couldn't imagine the Maggie I knew tolerating any of that.

"Since my piece about him went live last night, other stuff has started coming in over the transom, mostly anonymous and some of it obviously bullshit, but there are certainly people out there who have it in for him. Looks like your Walter has been a naughty boy."

"What else?"

"Like taking payoffs from Niyazov and Karimov."

"Say again. Who and who?"

Opening the notebook, Barry leafed through it. "Sapamurat Niyazov and Islam Karimov," he said. "They were the presidents of Turkmenistan and Uzbekistan back when Walter was at State. For all I know, he could have a fortune stashed away in the Caymans or a Swiss bank account. I wouldn't be surprised if he also got money from Klaus Hunt for greasing the skids for oil and gas deals Hunt made in the two 'stans."

"You think there's anything indictable?" I asked.

"Possibly. Tax evasion, maybe even fraud. Oh, and those climate change companies? That guy who told me Walter and Hunt are both heavy investors in them is still unwilling to go public, but I think he's coming around. My piece seems to have loosened a few tongues."

"You hear anything about...?" I stopped myself. Barry had no need to know anything about Walter's personal life.

"Hear about what?"

"Nothing important. Senior moment."

"Yeah, but you're only 40."

"Aging fast."

"Ok, so what's in *your* pipeline?"

"God only knows. It's crazy around here, and it's getting crazier by the hour. The one person who might be able to straighten things out is Maggie, but Walter has stashed her in a private facility somewhere."

"What needs straightening out?"

Once again I had to improvise. "She reins Walter in. And if she's anywhere close to her old self, she has great political instincts. She'd know the best way to deal with Claymore." I paused for effect, then added: "I just wish I knew where the hell she is."

"You want me to find out?"

"How would you do that?"

"Well, I'd probably..."

"Never mind. I don't want to know. But if you were able to track her down, I'd owe you big time."

"You already owe me big time, but I'll see what I can do. Right now though I've got a story to file."

"I'm going right by your office. I can drop you."

"That'd be great. Where're you headed?"

"Walter Reed."

+++

STATE DEPARTMENT INVESTIGATES FORMER SECRETARY OF STATE
by Barry Jagoda
Cleveland Plain-Dealer

WASHINGTON, D.C. -- Former Secretary of State Walter Mathews, husband of President-elect Margaret Mathews, is the subject of an internal investigation by the State Department for "possible irregularities" in the performance of his duties, Elaine Caldwell, a spokesperson for the department said today. She declined to elaborate on the investigation beyond affirming that the inquiry stemmed from a reporter's request for information under the Freedom of Information Act (FOIA).

In a telephone interview, Secretary Mathews said the inquiry was "politically motivated" and he was confident "my reputation for probity and integrity will not be tarnished" by the inquiry.

Following the revelation that the president-elect had written to Congress renouncing all claims on the presidency, Secretary Mathews threatened lawsuits against Sibley Hospital, where his wife was taken after suffering a ruptured aneurysm on January 10; Dr. Carlton Dawson, her neurosurgeon; and Bruce "Skeeter" Jamison, President Barley Thompson's chief of staff and the person to whom Mrs. Mathews entrusted the letters. She has since been transferred to an undisclosed location. Asked if he thought the inquiry was related to the lawsuits, Secretary Mathews said, "What do you think?"

Before she was taken ill, President-elect Mathews had proposed her husband to be her secretary of state, but Secretary Mathews withdrew his name, citing his responsibilities to care for his wife during her recovery.

According to a State Department source, Secretary Mathews, who served as President Sutton's Secretary of State, is being investigated in relation to official State Department trips he made to former Soviet republics in Central Asia during his tenure. The source, who asked to remain anonymous due to the sensitivity of the investigation, said that as secretary, Mr. Mathews came under suspicion among his colleagues and subordinates for his many trips to the oil and gas rich nations of Turkmenistan and Uzbekistan.

"We could never figure out what he found so compelling about those two 'Stans,' " the official said. "America's interests in the region are not insignificant, but I can't think of anyone here who thought these countries warranted a dozen or more visits in so short a time."

According to the source, State Department officials were also puzzled by the Secretary's seeming lack of interest in Kazakhstan, the world's largest landlocked country, which boasts the most robust economy in Central Asia.

"We wondered," the source said, "whether the boss told him to stay out of Kazakhstan. We thought maybe he wanted it all to himself." Asked who he meant by "the boss," the source said "Jim Sutton."

Four years after he left office, President Sutton supported Kazakhstan's leader, Nursultan A. Nazarbayev, to head an international agency that monitors elections. Critics said at the time that Mr. Sutton's support ignored the country's poor human rights record and undercut official U.S. foreign policy. That same year Mr. Sutton accompanied a Canadian businessman, Frank Guistra, to Kazakhstan. Within days Mr. Guistra was able to gain rights to three Kazakhstan uranium projects worth tens of millions of dollars. Months after the deal was finalized, the William J. Sutton foundation accepted a $31.3 million donation from Mr. Giustra. According to news reports, Mr. Giusta pledged an additional $100 million to the foundation.

State Department records show that Secretary Mathews visited Turkmenistan 14 times and Uzbekistan 12 times during his three years as Secretary of State. In the same period, Secretary Mathews visited England five times and France three. He did not visit Kazakhstan once.

In an email response to a question, Meret Orazov, the Turkman ambassador to the United States said that "Walter Thompson has been a friend to Turkmenistan for many years." Bakhtiyar Gulyamov, the Uzbekistan Ambassador to the United States, did not reply to an email asking about Secretary Mathews' relations with his country.

During the secretary's State Department tenure, Turkmenistan was ruled by President for Life Sapamurat Niyazov. Mr. Mathews attended Niyazov's funeral as a private citizen. He also attended the inauguration of his successor Gurbanguly Berdimuhamedow a year later.

On both trips, Secretary Mathews was accompanied by Klaus Hunt, president of Hunter Gatherer Gas and Oil Company of Midland, Texas. According to its website, Hunter Gatherer "is an exploration and production company with operations in Texas, Oklahoma, the Arab Emirates, Turkmenistan and Uzbekistan." Also according to the website, Walter Mathews is a member of the Hunter Gatherer board of directors.

According to Uzbekistan's official website, "the largest corporations involved in the nation's energy sector are the China National Petroleum Corporation (CNPC), the Korea National Oil Corporation, Lukoil and the Hunter Gatherer Corporation of the United States."

A White House official who asked for anonymity due to the sensitivity of the issue said that it was Mr. Hunt who provided Barley Thompson with the names of three companies, Carbonaide, And/Ore and Dew Drop Inc., all of which the vice president praised at his first press conference in January. "The ultimate solution to climate change may well lie in the approaches companies like these are making," the acting president said at the time.

Reached by telephone, Mr. Hunt said, "Secretary Mathews and I are old friends. I'm honored that a man of his stature accepted my invitation to join our board." He said that he had travelled with Secretary Mathews "on many occasions to many destinations, including Turkmenistan and Uzbekistan. We went as tourists." Asked about his company's dealings in Central Asia, Mr. Hunt said, "As president of a private company, I do not discuss its operations."

Mr. Hunt was also asked if he was an investor in the three companies he recommended to Vice President Thompson. "I invest in lots of companies," Mr. Hunt said. "Frankly, I'm not sure about the ones you mentioned." He said that he provided the names to the acting president "only because I heard they were innovators in the area of climate change. They're doing good things."

According to Reuters, Turkmenistan's Galkynysh gas field is the second largest in the world, with reserves estimated at more than 20 trillion cubic meters. Gas production is the most promising sector of the nation's economy.

According to Human Rights Watch, "Turkmenistan remains one of the world's most repressive countries. The country is virtually closed to independent scrutiny, media and religious freedoms are subject to draconian restrictions, and human rights defenders and other activists face the constant threat of government reprisal."

The International Helsinki Federation for Human Rights describes Uzbekistan as "an authoritarian state with limited civil rights" that practices "wide scale violation of virtually all basic human rights."

Ms. Caldwell, the State Department spokesperson, said she had "no idea" when the investigation of Secretary Mathews might be concluded.

-- 23 --

Twenty-four hours after being admitted to Walter Reed, the president was released. Flanked by Amanda, his doctor, and Morgan Walker, Barley made a brief statement to reporters from the hospital grounds.

He beamed and flashed the victory sign.

"According to my doctors, A-fib is a popular disease," Barley said. "Why the electrical circuitry goes haywire in so many people, I don't know. Maybe the heart needs to get with solar power. Anyway, it could be worse; I could have plumbing problems."

Amidst laughter the press pool began shouting questions.

"Not now." Barley held up his hands. "There are no sick days on this job, and I need to get back to work. I'm sure my doctor will answer any medical questions you might have."

Barley started to walk away when a reporter shouted, "Mr. President, won't you at least comment on how Jake Claymore handled your job?"

Smiling, Barley turned back. "From what I saw on television, I'd say he overtaxed himself, and I know that's a hard thing for a Republican to do. Speaking of Republicans, I'd like to thank my good friend Morgan Walker, who's been by my side through all of this and who truly knows how to cross the aisle."

Muted laughter followed Barley as he walked down the path, Amanda and Morgan on either side of him, toward "The Beast." In the background his doctor was explaining the defibrillation process and the Holter Monitor, a device that would provide Barley's medical team with a continuous EKG of his heart, which the president would be wearing for the next couple of weeks.

I'd watched the entire episode on a TV screen mounted inside the presidential limo. When Amanda and Morgan Walker had settled in, I congratulated Barley.

"You give good shtick, Mr. President. Colbert will be calling to book you on Late Night."

Barley sighed and settled back. With two black SUVs in front and two more behind, the "Beast" headed into bumper to bumper traffic, lights flashing and fender flags flapping.

∾ ∾ ∾

Once the first couple were settled back into Blair House, I asked Morgan to walk with me to the White House. The winter sun provided little warmth, but the cloudless blue sky made the cold seem less abrasive than in the past few relentlessly overcast days.

I saw that the Lafayette Park vigils continued, as they would, come winter freeze or summer fever.

"Who wrote the president's quips?" I asked. "They sounded pretty good to me."

Morgan grinned. "Well, the doctors provided plenty of material on electrical versus plumbing, so that didn't require much work. It seemed pretty obvious he'd get a question on Claymore. I suggested the overtaxed Republicans line."

"Nice. So what's your take on Barley's overall condition?"

"That's a tough one. The next couple of weeks are crucial. He's on a stronger dose of meds, and I think the doctors feel confident he'll manage. But I think Amanda is quite worried."

When we reached the White House, we paused under shelter of the South Portico and I faced Morgan. "You seem to have established a bond with Barley."

"Two Midwest boys, but yes, I'd say we have a mutual understanding."

"Are you aware that Barley is a reluctant president?"

"From conversations with him, I've suspected as much. Sometimes I think we'd be better off with more reluctant and fewer ambitious ones."

"What if Barley were to offer you the vice presidency?"

"Well, not to be too flip about it, but the last time I looked, Barley was the vice president."

"That's going to change."

"Not from what I've heard, if Claymore has anything to say about it, unless of course he gets tapped himself."

"As you must know, Jake's a buffoon. After his performance yesterday, I doubt he could get a membership in the local Elk's Club back in whatever Dixiecrat backwater he climbed out of. He knows it, too; Jake doesn't have skin in the game anymore. Trust me, Barley will be president, sooner or later, one way or the other. And he'll pick his own veep. I think it should be you."

"And why is that?"

"Because you're a respected Republican, and Barley believes the only hope for unifying the country is with a Republican partner. And because you could be confirmed without a brawl."

"Am I your choice or Barley's?"

"Mine initially. But the president likes you and trusts me. From what I've seen of the two of you together, I'm pretty sure he'd go for it."

Morgan laughed. "Maybe, but what about Defense?"

"We can fill that. You might even have some suggestions."

"And you want an answer now?"

"No, but I'd like you to be thinking about it. Of course, I'd also like to think this conversation won't go further than the two of us."

"You have my word, on both counts."

"Another couple of Midwest boys," I said with a smile.

Morgan nodded. We shook hands. Then I went inside to find what bedlam had been unloosed in the asylum.

What I found was about the last thing I expected: a text

message from Walter suggesting lunch. Like a wounded bear, he must have been aroused by all the noise surrounding him and was growling and prowling. In the message, he proposed an out of the way French bistro, Le Chat Noir—the black cat—on Wisconsin in Tenleytown, where we could talk without drawing attention. So, he was willing to sit down with me. Was the diplomat finally showing diplomacy, or was this merely a ruse?

Chat Noir, one o'clock, I texted back. *No guns.*

An hour later, as I was getting ready to leave to meet Walter, Amanda poked her head into my office.

"Barley's ok?" I asked, fearing a setback.

"He's having a light workout and massage with Robert Bork."

"That's positive."

Amanda ignored my response and asked if I had a minute?

I said I did and pulled out a chair for her.

Shedding her car coat, I saw she'd changed from the gray tweed suit she'd worn to the hospital into dark slacks and a charcoal cashmere sweater. Widow's weeds came to mind. I'd never thought of Amanda as an attractive woman, in the conventional and no doubt male-centric sense of the term, but she did her best with what she had. Sitting across from me at what I called my powwow table, she now struck me as anguished.

"I'm curious," she said to me. "How do you see Barley's future?"

The question caught me off guard, and I attempted to diffuse it. "I'm hardly a fortune teller," I said.

"No, I'm serious. Because I think you are something of a fortune teller. It's what politics is. Polling, collecting data, assessing it, and afterwards making predictions that will lead to a course of action—both in human and policy terms. Who's up, who's down. What bills will pass, what you decide to shelve."

"Putting it that way I suppose brings the game closer to science. But I still believe there's more art than science."

"Interesting word choice, *game*."

"Of course. It's competitive and it's a contest. At times a board game—chess, Monopoly—other times, something closer to tag—in the playground."

"Is that why you've been able to play both sides?" Amanda asked with a smile. It was hard to tell if she was being devious or lighthearted, and I was beginning to think I had underestimated Amanda Thompson.

"In a debate you sometimes have to argue both the pro and the con," I said. "Seeing both sides of an issue makes it easier to stay objective."

"In other words, you don't take yourself too seriously."

"Well, I try not to."

"But even when you're seeing both sides, you still have core beliefs, don't you?"

"Amanda, is this why you came to see me, to ask about my convictions?"

"In a way, yes. Because I'm not sure Barley has any."

"Convictions?"

Amanda nodded.

"Well, even if I agreed with you, and I might have when I was first getting to know him, I don't believe now is the time for this discussion."

"It makes you uncomfortable?"

"In a word, yes."

"I wonder if that's true of men in general. Barley feels the same way."

"Is that why you'd like me to weigh in on his future?"

"Like everyone who's been married as long as we have, we've been through all the ups and downs."

I snuck a look at my watch, hoping I wasn't going to get a recitation of her marriage woes.

"Don't worry," she said, reading my mind. "I'm not going to give you chapter and verse. Anyway, domestic strife is all the same, right? In everyone's life."

"I thought it was happy marriages that were all alike."

"*Anna Karenina*." So she was also well read. "I'm not sure Tolstoi got that right," Amanda continued. *All* marriages, even happy ones, are complicated. In Barley's case, there's a complication in particular I want to talk to you about that happened before Barley and I got together."

"Amanda, I...."

"Barley told me about it a long time ago. I'm not naive. Was I supposed to be shocked? Had he told me he was born the wrong gender and was in the process of transitioning—now that might have shaken me up. But a single gay sex act. Please."

"Amanda, Barley isn't just anyone..."

"I know. I know. He's the acting president, the commander-in-chief, and a world leader. But he's still a man." Dabbing her eyes with a handkerchief she'd been gripping, Amanda added, "He's also not the strongest man in the world. And I'm not talking just about physical strength."

"Amanda, he's been in office little more than a month. For a man who wasn't prepared for this, I think he's shown courage and decisiveness."

"Thanks to you. Without you, he'd have folded."

"I think you underestimate him."

Amanda shook her head. "Barley told me you saved the day."

"I'm just an advisor, one of many. Every president relies on others for support. But even if what you say is true, men change; more than one president has grown into the job. I don't think anyone's ever entirely prepared for this."

Amanda's gaze fixed on my eyes. "Barley will resign," she stated.

I couldn't speak. I was stunned. And at that moment I think I understood, maybe for the first time, the nature of their relationship. Amanda was the strong one, the person behind the throne. For a time I had usurped her position. But now she was reclaiming it.

I started to speak, to ask why, to try to persuade her to talk Barley out of it. But she cut me off.

"Don't," she said, "it's been decided."

"Give me forty eight hours."

Standing, Amanda nodded. "Thank you, Skeeter. For everything you've done." With that the first lady walked away.

❧   ❧   ❧

From the back of the limo taking me to meet Walter at Le Chat Noir, I checked my iPhone for messages. Two of the ten got my attention. The first was a text from Barry: *Got her.*

I hit the call button for Jagoda. "Tell me you didn't break any laws," I said when he answered.

"Courtesy of the *Plain Dealer,* I put a 24-hour tail on Walter. If he was suspicious, he didn't act it. Anyway, she's at the Sunset Arms in Cleveland Park. It's an assisted living facility. Walter's retained a private specialist in neurological disorders, with nursing staff around the clock. Plus a security detail."

"I'm on my way to have lunch with Walter."

"If you need backup, I'm on standby."

"I'll call with any breaking news."

Another message was from Angela. I pressed the call button. She answered and gave me the news that the FBI had identified the blurry figure in San Francisco who'd called me from the BART station.

"Tell me more."

"He works for Carbonaide in Palo Alto. He's got an axe to grind."

"Whistleblower?"

"Possibly, but more important he's friends with someone named Andrew Walter Korbut."

"Who is he?"

"His father is Walter Mathews."

❧   ❧   ❧

Although I was fifteen minutes late, Walter showed up ten minutes later. I suspect he'd waited to make sure I was alone. He strode up to the table in the back of the *Chat* and sat down without a word. Even dressed to the nines, he looked disheveled.

"I'm sorry, Walter."

"Are you? I'd say I'm sorrier. I'm sorry Maggie ever brought you on board."

"What's done is done. We can't hit rewind and start over."

A waiter took our orders. The special was filet of sole—flounder—and that seemed appropriate for what I would be doing. Walter asked for skirt steak with *frites*, also appropriate—medium rare, and a half bottle of St. Emilion, 2001, obviously not meant to be shared; I settled for a glass of Chardonnay.

"How's Maggie?" I asked, once the waiter had disappeared.

"How should I interpret that question? As a sincere inquiry about her health or as a prompt for further dirty tricks on your part?"

Sitting back in my chair, I studied Walter. This wasn't going to be easy. I owed him nothing. But Maggie was a creditor I needed to pay back, no matter how difficult.

"We get nowhere by trading insults. I was a loyal member of Maggie's team."

"That's hard to believe."

"What happened to her wasn't my fault. I wish it hadn't. I wish she were president, but wishing doesn't make it happen. In politics, there's no standing still. Like a boxer, you have to keep moving. Stand still and you'll get knocked on your ass."

"I'd forgotten you were a jock."

"I don't need to remind you what else you seem to have forgotten, Walter. The newspapers are doing that."

"You think you've ruined me?"

"It doesn't matter what I think. What matters is what you can sell to the public."

Walter brushed a hand across his face as though he were swiping at a fly, but there were no flies in the dead of winter, only the annoyance of his own flighty miscalculations. "All this will blow over," he said. "It blew over for Sutton, it'll blow over for me."

"I wouldn't bet on it. But even if it does, you've got other worries."

The waiter returned with his half bottle of Bordeaux.

After pulling the cork, he handed it to Walter to examine before poring a trifle of wine into his stemmed glass. Walter swirled, sniffed and finally tasted, and then gave his nod of approval. As the ruby liquid gushed into the goblet, I thought about all he'd be missing, even in the country-club, white-collar prison where he'd likely be sent if he were convicted of bribery or fraud.

Without fanfare the waiter brought my Chardonnay, setting it on the table as though it were water, and left.

Closing his eyes, Walter stuck his nose into his glass again and inhaled the fumes of the fermented grape. Coming up for air, he said, "Maggie's doing fine."

"Given what she's been through, she may be doing fine. But we both know she wasn't up to handling the presidency. You've accepted that much, haven't you?"

"If you want a pardon, Skeeter, I'm not the one to give it to you."

"I'm not looking for a pardon. But it would help if you acknowledged reality."

"Your reality, not mine."

I shook my head. "No. Not mine, or yours. Maggie's."

Walter tilted his head back. "No."

"No what?"

"She won't be president." Walter leaned forward, looking at me.

When lunch arrived, my sole was white on a white plate, with boiled potatoes; Walter's steak leaked pink around its edges. I watched as he cut into it, making it bleed even brighter when he took a bite and then followed it with wine.

From his expression, I saw the pleasure he took in eating and drinking well. I was about to ruin that for him. I touched the flounder with my fork, but ate nothing.

"Walter, I know about your son. I even know where he is," I said.

-- 24 --

As we headed out Connecticut Avenue toward the Sunset Arms, I led the way in my Forester in what may have been one of the oddest convoys in American history. Up front with me was Eleanor Booth of the Associated Press. White House staff photographer Peter Lawrence shared the back seat with Barry Jagoda.

Some might call it favoritism, but I felt Barry had earned this ride-along. And not just because he'd come up with Maggie's hiding place, which, when it came down to it, I'm not sure we even needed; by the time I'd sprung my knowledge about his son on Walter, the fight had gone out of him. I think he knew the game was up. Maybe it wasn't the proverbial last straw, but letting him also know I knew where he'd stashed Maggie had sealed the deal.

Then too, Barry no longer reported for an out-of-town paper hardly read in the nation's capital. The *Washington Post* came through with a job offer and, as fate would have it, this would be his first story for his new employer; not the worst way to begin.

Walter, driving his personal Lexus—no black SUVs today—followed close behind us. The Secret Service had objected to the use of a private vehicle to transport the president, but Barley had insisted with such uncharacteristic vehemence that, however disapproving, they were finally forced to yield. One Secret Service agent sat in the passenger seat, and two others in back flanked Barley, wearing a hat and sunglasses in a half-hearted attempt at disguise.

The third car held a freelance production crew we'd

engaged for the occasion, with two cameras and hi-rez, broadcast quality, HD video.

When I'd telephoned Supreme Court Chief Justice Johnson Wilkes to invite him to the Sunset facility, he'd asked to know the reason why. Even though I said it was urgent and involved national security, he'd declined unless I could be more specific. I couldn't. Next I called Ann Holstrom Schapiro, Maggie's favorite justice and her choice to conduct the ceremony. (I felt I'd done my duty in reaching out to the Chief Justice first.) Schapiro not only said yes immediately, she even knew the Sunset Arms and agreed to meet us there at 3:00 p.m. One of her law clerks would drive her.

Walter had already scoped out the Sunset's underground garage. The plan was to park, and then make our way to Maggie's private suite by way of a seldom-used emergency staircase. There were no guarantees we wouldn't be spotted, but that was a risk we'd have to take.

Pulling in a few minutes before three, Walter led us through the mercifully deserted garage, and silent as burglars we crept up the stairs to the second floor. Responding to Walter's gentle knock, Maggie opened the door to her room. Seven of us filed inside, while two Secret Service agents remained in the corridor.

Maggie was hard to read. Dressed in a red wool suit, she seemed even more alert and with it than the last time I'd seen her at Sibley. There remained a faint droop in one corner of her mouth and her right arm hung limply by her side. She still wore a beret to cover her short hair and surgical scars.

She greeted each of us with a nod, but barely glanced at Walter. I assumed she'd seen the television coverage of the inquiry into his Central Asian escapades. Was it possible that she'd known about them all along? Stranger things had happened in political marriages, but the chill between them now suggested his activities in the 'Stans had come as an unwelcome surprise. I'd also heard she hadn't been happy about having to move from Sibley, where she'd made friends among the medical staff.

When she came up to me and kissed my cheek she told

me she had wanted to call me. Her speech was halting, but clear, and she sounded sincere. "I never expected you to take such a beating over those letters."

Thank you was all I could say.

Although Walter had already outlined the reason for our being there, Maggie wanted to hear more about the approach we were taking and the reasoning behind it.

Barley gave me a nod.

We think this is cleaner, I told her. Congress was so dysfunctional and Speaker Claymore so intransigent that taking the Congressional route could have meant months of uncertainty. Possibly even court challenges, since neither the 20th nor the 25th Amendments strictly applied. "Besides," I added, "this way you get to be president."

"Can I declare war on Congress?" Maggie asked.

There was polite laughter.

From my pocket I took a single sheet of paper and handed it to her. "No war declarations, but here are a couple of executive orders I thought you might want to implement."

Just then, the intercom buzzed and Walter answered it. Turning to us he announced that Justice Schapiro and her law clerk were on their way up.

"Ten seconds, Mr. President."

The TV cameraman had omitted "Vice" as a courtesy, but I knew it as a fact: Barley had indeed been sworn in as President of the United States two hours and thirty minutes earlier.

"Five seconds, four, three, two, cue him." The assistant director pointed at Barley.

"My fellow Americans," President Thompson began.

From my perch on an Oval Office sofa, he looked surprisingly calm, relaxed even, in a solid blue suit and a blue paisley tie.

"At 3:26 this afternoon, Margaret Mathews took the oath of office as President of the United States. I'm happy to report that she spoke in a strong voice that reflected the great distance she has travelled in the weeks since suffering the ruptured aneurysm that prevented her inauguration.

"President Mathews was sworn in at a health care facility in Northwest Washington by Supreme Court Chief Justice Ann Holstrom Shapiro. Secretary Walter Thompson and I, along with my chief of staff, Bruce Jamison, witnessed the ceremony.

"She immediately issued two executive orders. The first changes the name of Chicago's O'Hare airport to Barack Obama Airport. The second grants American citizenship to undocumented immigrants who came to this country before the age of two.

"I will now read a letter from President Mathews to the American people:

" 'My dear friends and fellow Americans. I am so proud and grateful to you for electing me your president. I would so love to carry out the duties of that office and to try to earn, through actions taken on your behalf, the faith you have placed in me. But, I'm sorry to say, that will not be possible. Despite the unstinting efforts of the wonderful doctors, nurses and staff at Sibley Hospital, my health will not permit it. Not today and, I'm told, perhaps not for years to come.

" 'You deserve nothing less than a healthy president. So tonight I am placing the leadership of our great nation in the capable hands of Vice President Barley Thompson, who has done such a remarkable job as acting president. I want to thank him, and I also want to thank all of you who have kept me in your prayers. Many of you have written me warm, caring letters, which have buoyed my spirits beyond words. I am *so* grateful. I want each and every one of you to know that my heart is overflowing with love for you and for the country we all cherish. God bless you and God bless America.'

"President Mathews then handed a letter to Justice Schapiro. I will read it in its entirety: 'I hereby resign the office of President of the United States, effective immediately.'"

The assistant TV director turned and looked at me with surprise. Giving him a quick, reassuring nod, I wondered how many Americans were simultaneously reflecting the assistant director's confusion.

"At 4:03 p.m.," Barley continued, "Justice Shapiro asked me to raise my right hand. I then took the oath of office."

Barley picked up a glass and took a sip of water. Then he turned to face a second camera.

"Tomorrow I will submit to Congress my choice for vice president, a man whose name is synonymous with integrity and good judgment. In the interest of bipartisanship at this unsettled time, I have asked Senator Morgan Walker, a Republican, to serve in that capacity. I am more than confident he will do us all proud.

"These are critical times. There will be more challenges ahead, but I am confident we will face them together and be stronger for having done so. America is a great and good nation. America is strong and will become stronger still. God bless you all, and God bless the United States of America."

The cameraman turned off the TV lights. Barley took out a handkerchief and mopped his brow. Standing, he looked in my direction.

"Excellent, Mr. President. We'll just have to wait and see how it plays. You've given the folks quite a lot to digest."

Barley shrugged, said goodnight, and shook hands with everyone present before returning to Blair House in the center of a phalanx of four Secret Service agents.

∻   ∻   ∻

Jesus, it had been a crazy couple of days; and the preceding ones hadn't exactly been a walk through the National Zoo, although 'zoo' wasn't far off the mark.

When I'd told Walter at lunch that I knew where his son was, he'd nearly choked on his steak. When he regained his composure, he asked how I'd found out about him.

"Someone who worked with him at Carbonaide."

Staring at me, the anger in his eyes was gone, replaced by a mixture of defeat and relief. "I had nothing to do with Klaus Hunt's gambit with those companies," he said. "And that's the truth."

"But you *did* invest in them?"

"I did. But that's all I did. Klaus told me they were solid ventures. Bright people were behind them. He didn't tell me he had any plans to help them along."

For once, I believed Walter. He had no reason to lie about that any longer. We sat in silence for what seemed like several minutes. Finally, I asked him if he wanted to talk about his son.

It's a long story, he'd said.

"I've got time."

Walter pushed his plate away. Half his steak remained uneaten. It wasn't an original story. "Jerry Ford was president," he said. "I'd just joined the Foreign Service, assigned to the Africa desk. During lunch hours, I'd often visit the National Gallery of Art. Which is where, among the Titians and Fra Lippo Lippis, I met an assistant curator who specialized in the Italian Renaissance."

Nancy Collins, the assistant curator, had grown up in Denver and had gone to Bennington College in Vermont to study art history. When Walter asked her to join him for a quick lunch in the cafeteria, she accepted, and a few nights later they met for dinner at *Le Chanticleer*, in Georgetown. They clicked immediately. After a few months, she moved into his one-bedroom apartment on M Street, which they shared for almost a year.

Walter couldn't remember a happier time in his life.

When the State Department offered him Nairobi, Kenya —something of a plum for a first foreign posting, he knew he'd gotten it in part because he was single. In the late-70s, junior officers did not take dependents to Kenya.

Nancy did not want to leave Washington, at least not as a single woman.

Walter could have turned down the assignment. "I was young, you know how it is, and ambitious. And I thought we had all the time in the world."

They'd written to each other and made plans for Nancy to come to Kenya for a visit. When the two years were up, they would get married.

Nancy didn't tell him that she was pregnant. Uncertain how he really felt about her—after all, he *hadn't* turned down Nairobi—she didn't want him to feel obligated or bound to her by an unplanned child.

I asked Walter why she hadn't terminated the pregnancy.

"I wondered about that, but I never asked. She was Catholic, so I assumed that was the reason. She had regularly attended mass. And I must say I'm very glad she didn't terminate."

I nodded.

"I loved Nairobi. I was busy, challenged. I liked the people I worked with, and I liked the Kenyans. I really did miss Nancy, but it was a very special time there."

When the baby was born, the letters stopped.

After his two years in Kenya, Walter returned to Washington. Nancy was nowhere to be found. The M street apartment was occupied by strangers. They had not known the previous tenant. At the National Gallery, he was told that Nancy had given notice some eight months earlier. No, she hadn't left a forwarding address. No, she didn't give a reason. One afternoon, Walter thought he saw her through the window of a Japanese restaurant on Wisconsin Avenue. But when he went inside, it turned out to be someone else.

Three years later, after a stint in Vienna, Walter was back in Washington working on the Europe desk when he was introduced to Maggie at a cocktail party in embassy-rich Kalorama, one of Washington's toniest neighborhood. She was a rookie member of Congress from Pennsylvania. They talked policy and discovered they agreed about most issues. It was different from his time with Nancy. They were both ambitious, and Maggie was more focused on her career than Nancy had been on hers. They saw themselves as a power couple, a good team, with a real future in the political arena.

Eighteen months later they were married. It was a worthy match.

"It must have been about 2000, the turn of the century.

Andy was 15 at the time. Out of the blue one day, I got a phone call at the office. It was Andy calling to tell me I was his father. I couldn't believe it. But the more he told me about his life, when and where he was born, his mother's name, the more plausible it seemed. Andy admitted that he'd discovered a photo album Nancy had hidden. He had pestered her so relentlessly about the man in several of the photographs that she finally broke down and told him the truth.

Walter had asked Andy to ask his mother to call him. After several days, a week perhaps, she did. "The long and short of it is that she admitted Andy was my son—*our* son." Nancy had married an attorney and moved to Shepherdstown, West Virginia. They had two children together. In the beginning, life had been difficult, but they had a good marriage."

"How did you take it—finding out about Andy?"

"It was a shock. I was upset. Maggie and I had tried to have children. We couldn't. I was fine with that. Maggie had resigned herself to it. She was making her way in Congress, thinking about running for governor. It was a heady time.

"But you know, the more I thought about it—the more I got *used* to the idea of being a father—the more I liked it. *My son.*"

Walter explained that Nancy had arranged for him to see Andy from time to time—although not as often as he would have liked. He went to Shepherdstown a couple of times a year. Andy played lacrosse. And the boy would come to Washington for a day, sometimes two, every so often, and father and son would get together for a meal or a visit to a museum. It took time, but they developed a relationship.

"Does Maggie know?"

Walter shook his head. "I never told her. The moment never felt right. Then the secret became a burden, but even though I felt guilty I justified it by telling myself it might wreck something in our marriage."

Walter said he had supported his son financially, sending a $200 check every month to a Shepherdstown post office box, doubling the amount when Andy went off to

Gettysburg College on a scholarship.

"That's enough of this," Walter said suddenly. "I don't want to talk about it any more. That's my story. So where do we go from here?"

"Meaning?"

"Maggie, to start with. The lawsuits. That reporter you put onto me. Klaus. Barley." He looked as if he'd aged in the last hour.

I still wasn't sure I could trust him, but I had little choice.

I told him I knew where he'd hidden Maggie. And about the plan I'd discussed with Morgan Walker and Barley. When I'd finished, Walter picked at a crumb on the tablecloth. When he looked up, he nodded.

"I'll drop the lawsuits," he said at last.

"My heart is heavy but my conscience is clear." Barley looked directly into a single TV camera in the East Room. He had been president for one day shy of a month. Less than a week after he took the oath of office, following only perfunctory debate, the House of Representatives unanimously confirmed Morgan Walker as Vice President. The following morning the Senate followed suit, and Senate President pro tem, Oscar Thorne, swore Walker in at noon. Barley told me that he slept more soundly that night than at any time since Maggie's collapse.

From the East Room, Barley continued his address:

"On the advice of my medical team at Walter Reed and my personal physician, and with the support of my wife, Amanda, and our daughters, Blake and Rebecca, I have regrettably concluded that I must resign the presidency, effective noon tomorrow. Vice President Morgan Walker will be sworn in as President of the United States at that time."

I'd written the speech and knew it pretty much by heart. Barley would thank the American people for the privilege of serving them; he would ask for their understanding, he would say that he believed his action was in the best interest of the country and that Morgan Walker would be an outstanding president.

It was all true. Barley wasn't in good health. He had A-fib and angina. The stress of the presidency would likely make both heart conditions worse.

But it was also true that Barley, for all his good intentions, was not cut out to be president. Hopefully, Morgan Walker was. In a way, it was just that simple.

There was also the matter of Barry Jagoda. The *Washington Post* had struggled for both readership and advertising since the glory days of Ben Bradlee, Bob Woodward, Carl Bernstein and Watergate. The paper was desperately trying to regain some of its lost luster. The current editor, Martin Barron, wanted a big story—the bigger the better—and in hiring Barry Jagoda, he thought he might have found one. He had dispatched Barry to San Francisco to talk to Rob Craig. To his credit, Barry had kept his end of our bargain by giving me a heads up about the trip. I'd felt honor bound to let Barley know the story was still alive.

"What happens if I'm no longer president," Barley asked me.

"I can't make any promises, but it becomes much less of a story. And unlike Dennis Hastert, there's no violation of banking laws and no lying to the FBI."

Barley nodded. "You know Amanda's thoughts. She thinks the job will kill me. Do you agree?"

"I won't be drawn into that debate. The decision has to be between you and Amanda. Besides, the last time I looked, I didn't have a medical degree."

The next day he called me into the Oval and told me what I'd already learned from Amanda, that he had decided to resign. He didn't ask my opinion and he didn't offer any further explanation. Nor did I ask him for one.

≈ ≈ ≈

When Barley finished his East Room address he walked over and gave me a bear hug. Then he took me aside.

"I've got two favors to ask. First, I want you to promise that you won't write about me as long as I'm alive."

That was an easy one. I had no interest in writing about him. I waited for the second favor.

"And promise me that when I do die, assuming I predecease you, you'll write the book."

"The *book*?"

"Everything. No holds barred. You're the only one who

knows the whole story. I want it told."

I felt I owed him that much. I said I'd try.

"That's good enough for me," he said. He thanked me, we shook hands, and I wished him well. Then, with a little wave, he turned and headed for the Portico and what would be his final night at Blair House.

It was the last I would ever see of him.

EPILOGUE

Arlington National Cemetery, five years later.

With Memorial Day a week away, the cemetery was in abundant finery. The American flag flew at half-staff, and, according to protocol for the funeral of a president, a 21-gun salute greeted the small cortege as it entered the grounds at 11:15 a.m. Row upon row of identical tombstones layered over the checkered patchwork of freshly mown grass were adorned with simple floral displays of remembrance. Magnolia trees were in bloom. The eternal flame marking JFK's gravesite, visible in the distance, provided the touchstone for ceremonial sorrow.

Out of deference to the family, Barley Thompson's burial had been designated a private affair. In order to avoid the chaos a presidential attendance would command, Morgan Walker opted to remain in the White House. He had sent his condolences.

Both Amanda's daughters were there: Blake with her own, curly-haired daughter, Heather, age three, and Rebecca with her partner Miranda. (Blake's husband, unable or unwilling to leave work, had remained in Columbus.) I stood between Angela Mercado and Maggie Mathews, holding each of their hands.

A priest read a homily Amanda had selected from Romans 5.

"Therefore, since we are justified by faith, we have peace with God through our Lord Jesus Christ. Through him we have

obtained access to this grace in which we stand, and we rejoice in our hope of sharing the glory of God. More than that, we rejoice in our sufferings, knowing that suffering produces endurance, and endurance produces character, and character produces hope, and hope does not disappoint us, because God's love has been poured into our hearts through the Holy Spirit which has been given to us."

A small detachment of the Marine Corps band—known as "The President's Own"—played a dirge-like *Hail to the Chief*, as members of all four branches of the military folded the flag that had adorned Barley's brushed metal casket. Amanda wiped away tears.

Whether Barley would have been proud, embarrassed, or amused, I had no way of knowing. But these rituals were more for the living than the dead. As Barley's coffin was lowered into the ground, the honor guard brought rifles to "Present Arms." Standing in the distance among tombstones, a lone bugler played "Taps".

Once the honor guard had marched off and we were alone, each of us stepped forward and tossed a white rose onto the coffin in the open ground. Then, after a moment of silence, feeling the cool whisper of a spring breeze through the trees that filled the air with the scent of magnolias and lilacs, we hugged one another and started back toward two waiting black Mercedes Benzes.

Barley Thompson had been laid to rest, five years after serving one day less than one month as President of the United States. I hoped history would be kind to the reluctant president.

Looking back on those frenetic days, I can't help but think my greatest achievement was persuading Barley to choose Morgan Walker as his vice president. Not that I could claim any credit for Walker's accomplishments, but I did take some small measure of pride in them, particularly the creation of the Palestinian state in Gaza and the West Bank, a fulfillment that had eluded so many earlier presidents.

There were other triumphs, to be sure, but the establishment of the physical state of Palestine had to be the most significant. Over time Walker's foreign policy had led to the neutralizing of ISIS by a coalition of regional forces. Not that the area is without remaining problems, but I think most people would agree that the Middle East is less volatile than it was prior to Walker. Even Iran, the inspectors assure us, is living up to the nuclear agreement signed in Obama's waning days as president and strengthened under Walker.

Domestically, I'd say Morgan's great achievement has been a more harmonious Congress. While partisanship will always be with us, some important bills have been passed into law: the Restoration of the Bridges and Highways Act, Obama's renamed and repositioned jobs bill and improvements to Obamacare, to name just a few. Nobody's singing Kumbaya yet, but neither is anyone threatening to shut down the government every few months.

As for me, even though President Walker asked me to stay on, I decided it was time for a change. So shortly after Barley resigned and returned to Ohio, I handed in my White House credentials and took a few months off. That first spring, I'd joined a group biking through France's Loire Valley and Burgundy, followed by three weeks walking from Merano, Italy, south to Lake Garda with an agreeable group of about 20 mostly hardy souls. From there I spent time relaxing in and around the Veneto locale. While in Verona, after visiting the Casa di Giulietta on the Via Cappella, I sent a postcard with the bronze, naked statue of Juliet to Angela Mercado, Morgan Walker's Attorney General—signing it, Romeo.

By late summer I was back in Washington, ready for the fall semester to begin at George Washington University, where I'd accepted a political science professorship.

∽ ∽ ∽

The next few years passed in the flick of an eyelid. Now, standing at a remove from us as we approached our cars, Barry

Jagoda waved, beckoning me. I walked with Amanda and her daughters and their families to one of the limos and with Angela and Maggie to ours, then excused myself to greet Barry.

He had distinguished himself at the *Washington Post* and had been appointed White House correspondent just as Morgan Walker's first term was coming to a close.

But Jagoda had never forgotten who'd brought him to the table. Every Christmas I received a case of decent wine, with a card asking when I was going to get back into the game.

"Sorry about Barley," Jagoda said. "The guy could never catch a break. I know he had cancer, but I'm hearing it was assisted suicide that took him out. Any comment?"

"None."

"The other thing I'm hearing is that Angela's considering a run for president."

"Sorry, Barry."

"Come on, Skeeter. For old time's sake?"

"What I can tell you, off the record of course, is that Angela, Maggie and I are flying down to Havana tomorrow to lie on Veradero beach."

"Putting together Angela's exploratory committee?"

"You don't give up, do you?"

Jagoda smiled. "It's what I'm paid for. By the way, I hear Walter's out in Sonoma buying vineyards."

"I've heard that too. Ironic for a guy who disdained California wine."

"And Maggie's moved on?"

"She has. She's doing great."

"Well, for the record, if Angela did decide to run, and won, how would you feel in your role as first man? Or would you prefer first dude?"

Lifting my thumb, I smiled and walked back to my wife and Maggie waiting in the car.

Just at that moment, noon, a fifty-gun salute, one for each state, boomed from below the Tomb of the Unknowns. The sound of the big howitzers pealed across Arlington, echoing through the hallowed grounds as respect was paid to the   former   president,   Barley   Thompson.

ACKNOWLEDGEMENTS

The authors would like to thank R.E. for answering many legal and presidential succession questions and Robert Poole for explaining the funeral and burial protocols at Arlington National Cemetery. Any remaining errors are solely the fault of the authors. We would also like to thank George Feifer for editing an early draft, Marilyn Shames for her tech support, and Fred Klein who opened new doors. Finally, we would like to acknowledge the staff at Azur restaurant in Key West for abetting many a delicious story conference.

ABOUT THE AUTHORS

John Leslie lived for many years in Europe and the Middle East. As a freelancer, he wrote for newspapers and magazines in Key West, where he has lived for 40 years and where his many mystery novels are set. He now divides his time between there and northern California with his partner, Marguerite Whitney.

Carey Winfrey's half-century as a journalist included stints at *Time*, *People*, WNET/13, *The New York Times* and CBS Magazines. He was editor-in-chief of *Cuisine*, *Memories*, *American Health* and *Smithsonian*, from which he retired in 2011. He and his wife Jane divide their time between Key West and Amenia, New York.

Other books by JOHN LESLIE

Border Crossing (2013)

The Gideon Lowry Mysteries
Killing Me Softly
Night and Day
Love for Sale
Blue Moon

The Florida Mysteries
Sucker Fish
Bounty Hunter Blues
Killer in Paradise
Damaged Goods
Havana Hustle

Other books by CAREY WINFREY

Starts and Finishes: Coming of Age in the Fifties

Made in the USA
Charleston, SC
03 February 2017